Under the Tulip Tree

UNDER THE TULIP TREE

a novel

MICHELLE SHOCKLEE

Tyndale House Publishers
Carol Stream, Illinois

Visit Tyndale online at tyndale.com.

Visit Michelle Shocklee's website at michelleshocklee.com.

TYNDALE and Tyndale's quill logo are registered trademarks of Tyndale House Ministries.

Under the Tulip Tree

Designed by Eva M. Winters

Edited by Erin E. Smith

Published in association with the literary agency of The Steve Laube Agency.

Scripture quotations are taken from the *Holy Bible*, King James Version.

Under the Tulip Tree is a work of fiction. Where real people, events, establishments, organizations, or locales appear, they are used fictitiously. All other elements of the novel are drawn from the author's imagination.

For information about special discounts for bulk purchases, please contact Tyndale House Publishers at csresponse@tyndale.com, or call 1-800-323-9400.

ISBN 978-1-4964-4607-7

Printed in the United States of America

26 25 24 23 22
 7   6   5   4   3

In loving memory of my parents,
Albert and Annabelle Chaparro.
Thank you, Daddy and Mom. For everything.
Revelation 21:4

"I feel now that the time is come when even a woman or a child who can speak a word for freedom and humanity is bound to speak. . . . I hope every woman who can write will not be silent."

HARRIET BEECHER STOWE, 1851

Prologue

———

"Pandemonium has broken out in the streets of New York City. Angry crowds have gathered throughout the day, demanding answers from those inside the New York Stock Exchange. Down the street, National City Bank closed their doors early, setting off a riot. Police guarding the bank are heavily armed, prepared for the worst.

"The stock exchange is now closed. We should have the final numbers momentarily. In the meantime, there are reports that riots have begun at banks and savings and loans throughout the country. Customers want their money, and I cannot find fault in their wishes. It seems—what is that? Gunshots? We are hearing gunshots along Wall Street.

"My fellow Americans, I fear our day of reckoning is upon us. Despite President Hoover's declaration last Friday assuring us the fundamental business of the country is on a sound and prosperous basis, today's events say otherwise. We've watched too many men in powerful positions build empires without a proper financial foundation, relying too heavily upon credit and loans instead of solid investment. Greed and a lust for more weakened the economy irreversibly and brought us to this sad day. We can only pray the market will rally tomorrow, as it did Thursday, but the numbers will tell the tale.

"I've just been handed the official report.

"It is worse than we feared. While the tickers are still running, trying to catch up to the record-setting activity, I can now tell you over sixteen million shares traded today. The Dow Jones Industrial Average closed at 230 dollars, down 23 percent from the opening bell.

"My fellow Americans, it is my grievous duty to inform you . . . the stock market has crashed."

CHAPTER

ONE

NASHVILLE, TENNESSEE
TUESDAY, OCTOBER 29, 1929
EIGHT HOURS EARLIER

I was convinced a more perfect day could not be found.

As I snuggled in my favorite chair on the front porch, the pink-and-purple sunrise unfurling in the Tennessee sky had me mesmerized. With a hint of woodsmoke in the crisp morning air and the trill of birds from high atop almost-bare trees, it was as though nature itself fancied to join in the celebration of my special day.

Sixteen!

I scrawled the word at the top of a blank page in the leather-bound diary Grandma Lorena gave me last Christmas.

The perfect gift for an aspiring writer, she'd declared. She was right, as usual. My last entry, a long diatribe bemoaning the loss of the election for class secretary to Sally Wortham, was barely legible, with teenage fury showing in every word. Who knew bribing voters with homemade taffy could be so successful?

With a neater hand, I continued my birthday musings.

I finally made it to that magical age—at least it seemed magical when Mary and her friends turned sixteen. Suddenly they were treated like adults and allowed pleasures I, two years younger, was not granted. Yet today I balance on the cusp of a new and far more interesting life than the one I've led thus far. The debutante ball next month will officially usher me into Nashville society, and though I care little for the art of gossip and those who participate in it, I plan to take my place among the city's finest and enjoy every benefit the position offers.

I reread the entry and grinned.

So much happiness calls for a squeal of delight. Maybe even two.

I closed the small book with a satisfied thump, thinking of the day ahead. There would be no school for me. Mama let me skip so I could help her and Mary decorate the hall we'd rented for my party later this evening. A hundred or so guests were invited to celebrate my momentous achievement. With Daddy's bank being one of the largest in the state, most of the people on the guest list were his loyal customers. Their wives were Mama's friends, women who kept themselves occupied with clubs and charitable organizations that, to me, revolved around social standing rather than altruistic issues.

I stretched and padded into the house. Mama bustled about the kitchen cooking breakfast, hair perfectly coiffed, pearl necklace peeking out from the collar of her two-piece day outfit. A frilly polka-dot apron tied around her middle accentuated a slightly pudgy waistline, but I would never point that out to her.

"Where's Dovie? She always makes her special pancakes on my birthday." While it wasn't unusual for Mama to get our breakfast on the weekends, Dovie, our housekeeper and cook, would normally be at the stove on a Tuesday morning, especially on this day.

A bowl of freshly washed blackberries sat on the counter. I popped one into my mouth before opening the new General Electric refrigerator that arrived last week. GE's sales slogan, *"It's always summertime in your kitchen,"* had struck fear in Mama regarding the safety of our food and resulted in a win for the advertising team as well as the Sears, Roebuck and Co. catalog. True to their word, the glass container of orange juice was nice and cold and free of bacteria caused by the warmth of the kitchen.

Mama didn't answer.

I turned to see if she'd heard my question and found a strange look on her face. "Mama? Where's Dovie?"

She offered a tight smile. "I gave her the day off. I knew the house would be in a frenzy, what with your party and all the preparations. It seemed best not to have her underfoot."

My mouth fell open.

Dovie had been our housekeeper since before I was born. She knew every inch of the house and handled Mama's fetishes—a word I'd recently discovered and enjoyed using whenever I could—without blinking an eye. On a day as busy as this day promised to be, Dovie's help couldn't be more needed.

"When has she ever been underfoot? Besides, you know she and Gus need the money. I hope you're at least paying her."

Mama's lips pinched, a sure sign I'd pushed the boundary. "Lorena Ann, just because you're sixteen now does not mean you can tell your mother how to manage the servants."

I gave a small shrug in apology. It didn't make any difference to me if Dovie worked or not. A catering company was scheduled to provide food for the party and clean up the hall afterward. Tables and chairs were being set up this morning, and Mama, Mary, and I would go over after lunch to decorate with pink and white streamers, roses, carnations, and even balloons.

A glance out the window revealed an empty driveway where Daddy's "money-green" 1929 Cadillac Town Sedan usually sat.

"Daddy was supposed to stay home today. We're having

lunch at the Maxwell House Hotel." The childish petulance in my voice was a bad habit I'd need to abandon now that I was sixteen, but Daddy had promised to spend the day with the family.

"He had some pressing business to take care of. I'm sure he'll have time to meet us later."

She didn't sound too convincing. We'd learned long ago the bank came first. Daddy would apologize and buy Mama or Mary and me presents to make up for disappointing us, but sometimes we just wanted him, not presents.

I popped another blackberry into my mouth, grimacing at its tartness. I imagined my face mirrored how I felt about Daddy's absence at my birthday breakfast. I hoped whatever was so important at the bank wouldn't spoil the plans we had for the rest of the day. He hadn't come home yesterday until long after supper, and he'd immediately disappeared into the study. Mama said he was tired from a busy day and not to worry, but I couldn't help it. Ever since we heard President Hoover on the radio last week, talking about something regarding the New York Stock Exchange, Daddy seemed agitated and distracted.

Mary entered the kitchen, yawning. "Morning. Happy birthday, Lulu."

I chuckled. "Thanks, Sis."

"Your sister is a young lady now, Mary," Mama said, her mouth drawn in disapproval. "You named her Lulu when she was born because you couldn't pronounce Lorena Ann. Perhaps it's time to put away the childish nickname."

Mary rolled her eyes once Mama turned her back. I covered my mouth to keep from laughing and carried my juice to the breakfast table. Had Mama forgotten most people, including herself, call me Rena? Especially when her mother, Grandma Lorena, and I were in the same room.

"What time are we going to the hall?" Mary poured herself a cup of coffee and joined me at the table. "Roy said he'd help with the decorations."

It was my turn to roll my eyes. Roy Staton, son of Daddy's most important business client, was as dull as they come in my opinion. With Mary in her first year at Ward-Belmont College, she had endless opportunities ahead of her. Why she'd agreed to date dull Roy was beyond me.

"We should be there by two." Mama glanced at the wall clock. "We'll need to finish with plenty of time to come home to bathe and dress. The guests arrive at seven."

She set a bowl of lumpy-looking oatmeal and a plate of slightly burnt toast on the table. When she returned to the kitchen, I crinkled my nose. My taste buds were set for Dovie's famous blueberry pancakes and crisp bacon, a tradition on my birthday as far back as I can remember.

Mama stopped to look out the window above the sink. She seemed preoccupied. Worried even. Which was unusual, because Mama rarely allowed herself the luxury of showing her true emotions. Sometimes I wondered what she really thought, like when Daddy embarrassed her after church last Sunday. A group of parishioners had gathered in the noon sunshine, discussing the building project that would provide more room for the growing congregation. Daddy bragged about how much money he'd donated in order to have the new education wing named Leland Hall. Mama's face turned beet red, but she'd put on a smile and made a joke about Daddy buying his way into heaven.

"Roy said his friend Homer wants to call on you after the debutante ball." Mary glanced at me for a response.

Mama brought over a platter of scrambled eggs that seemed the most edible out of all her efforts, then joined us at the table. "Homer? What's his last name? Do I know his parents?"

I groaned. "It doesn't matter. He could be a Rockefeller for all I care. I still wouldn't go on a date with him."

"You're such a snob, Lulu."

"What's wrong with the boy?" Mama wanted to know.

"Nothing." Mary and I spoke at the same time.

Mama's brows rose in question as her blue eyes pinned me to the chair.

I lifted one shoulder. "I simply can't see myself married to someone named Homer, so there's no point giving him encouragement."

Mary shook her head in disgust and dug into her meal. Mama studied me with more concentration than I felt I deserved, considering the topic of conversation. I was years away from settling down with a husband and family, so she should be relieved I wasn't boy crazy like my sister.

"If I wasn't dating Roy, I'd set my cap for Homer," Mary said right on cue, as though Mama or I cared about her latest infatuation. "He's handsome, smart, and comes from a very fine Memphis family. Roy says Homer's mother is from old money."

I gasped in mock interest. "Maybe they found buried treasure on the banks of the Mississippi left over from pirate days."

Mary shot me a narrowed scowl and opened her mouth to retort, but Mama'd had enough.

"Girls," she said in that stern way she used when she was put out with us. "It's no joking matter to find a husband who comes from a good family. You're both old enough to consider possible marriage prospects." She focused her gaze on me. "I expect you to make a fine showing at the ball, and you—" she turned to Mary—"shouldn't lead Roy into believing you care more for him than you apparently do."

Her seriousness had the opposite effect, and I felt a giggle lodge in my throat. I couldn't look at Mary. I knew I'd burst into laughter if I did.

We finished breakfast, with Mama shooing me away from helping with the dishes since it was my birthday. Mary stuck her tongue out at me as she picked up a dish towel, but then followed it with a wink. I went upstairs to my room. The gown Mama's favorite seamstress designed for the ball hung on a dress form near the window. I had to admit I loved the silky white material and lace overlay on the skirt. Mama insisted the hem fall at my ankles rather than the shorter style that was popular, but I didn't mind. At my last fitting, I couldn't believe how sophisticated and grown-up I looked.

A glance in the bureau mirror to my messy hair and fuzzy pink bathrobe brought me back to reality.

I'd always considered Mary prettier than me. With her blue eyes and blonde curls, she was Mama's daughter through and through. I, on the other hand, had Daddy's boring brown hair and eyes, which although striking in the right light, didn't catch boys' attention the way Mary's did. Maybe that's why I never cared too much about catching their attention. The man I married someday would like me just the way I was.

A single sheet of printed paper lay on my desk. I snatched it up and stretched out on the bed, grinning. Seeing my byline in the school newspaper never ceased to please me. Mr. Snyder, my English teacher and editor of the paper, said I had a gift for storytelling. He'd encouraged me to join the small group of *reporters* during my sophomore year and promoted me to assistant editor this year. I dreamed of writing for *Life*, *Collier's*, or one of the other major magazines in New York City after college, but for now my article on who stole the school's stuffed eagle mascot would have to suffice.

Much to my disappointment, Daddy did not come home for lunch. Mama didn't want to drive into the city, so we ate bologna sandwiches instead of shrimp and lobster at the Maxwell House Hotel. True to Mary's prediction, Roy met us at the hall. He was so preoccupied with greeting her that he completely neglected to wish me a happy birthday.

Decorating went well. We were almost finished when the catering truck arrived. Mama waylaid the rotund man—I forgot his name—and issued directives to his two helpers on where to place the platters of food, the punch bowl, and a lovely five-tiered cake decorated with fresh flowers. At one point, however, I looked across the room and found Mama in an intense, whispered conversation with the man, which seemed odd. Mama wasn't one to flirt with strange men, and although I wouldn't necessarily call their secret conversation flirting, it made me uncomfortable.

I walked outside and noticed the two helpers having whispered conversations of their own. When they found me watching, they went back to work, but my skin crawled, as though I should be aware of something but wasn't.

Mama fell quiet on the ride home. Even Mary, who wasn't always mindful of other people's feelings, gave me a questioning look. I indicated I didn't know what was wrong and left it at that. At home, I bathed and dressed for the evening. I certainly could have used Dovie's help with the tiny pearl buttons on the back of my peach-colored party dress and breathed a sigh of thanks when Mary appeared in the doorway wearing a green silk gown that made her skin look like cream.

"Roy told me something in confidence," she whispered, coming up behind me to fasten the buttons.

"That usually means the other person doesn't want you to divulge what's being said."

She pinched my arm, and I squealed in pain. "I know that, but I need to tell someone. I can't tell Mama."

Now she had me interested. "Go on."

Finished with the buttons, she sat on the edge of the bed, looking more serious than I'd ever seen her.

I frowned. "Did Roy propose to you?" I'd be rather put out if he had, being that today was *my* birthday. I didn't want anyone or anything stealing the thunder I was only allowed once a year.

She shook her head, golden curls bouncing. "He told me something frightening."

I waited, my imagination already spinning a web. She rose and partially closed the door.

"Roy's father told his mother that Daddy's bank is in trouble. Something about the stock market in New York." She shrugged slim shoulders. "He said his father is very upset."

"What kind of trouble?" Yet even as I asked, I knew it was a silly question. Neither of us understood much about the world of finance where our father lived and breathed.

"Roy says Daddy could lose everything." Mary's whisper and rounded eyes sent a chill racing up my spine. Was this what the radio announcer meant last Thursday when he spoke of a recession? "And because Roy's father is so heavily invested in Daddy's bank, his family might be in trouble too."

I stood rooted to my bedroom floor and stared at Mary's pale face. "That's not possible." I tried to recall anything I'd ever heard in economics class about the stock market, but nothing surfaced. "Daddy's banks are here, in Tennessee. They don't have anything to do with what's going on in New York."

"Then why would Roy's daddy be worried?"

I didn't have an answer for that.

The telephone rang downstairs a short time later. I looked at the clock on my bureau. It was half past three.

I held my breath and listened as Mama hurried to answer. Her words were indistinct, yet I couldn't bring myself to tiptoe to the door and eavesdrop. I prayed the caller was Grandma Lorena asking for a ride to the party or Dovie wishing me a happy birthday.

The piercing scream that rent the air a moment later told me it was neither.

CHAPTER
TWO

NASHVILLE, TENNESSEE
SEPTEMBER 14, 1936

The old diary lay open to the page I'd never finished.

No one came to my sixteenth birthday party.
It's a selfish thing to be concerned with, considering
all that is happening to so many people, my family
included. Yet I can't help but wonder if my very
existence became invalidated when the world shifted
that day. As though my presence on the planet no longer
matters in light of such terrific loss and misery. To know
that money, status, and privilege supplanted the place
I'd held in my family for sixteen years set an ache in me
I fear will never heal. How could it, when the evidence
faces me every waking moment?

"Are you going to see Mr. Armistead today?"

Mama's voice startled me. From my place on the back porch steps, I turned and found her inside the house, speaking through the screen door. The frown on her thin face made me wonder how long she'd been there, watching me. I could hide the diary I held, but what would be the point? She'd already seen it.

I shrugged. "I suppose, but I know what his answer will be."

George Armistead, editor of the *Nashville Banner*. Six months ago I called him boss. I still didn't understand why I'd been fired—"let go," as Mr. Armistead liked to put it. Despite being a faithful employee since graduating high school, starting in the mail room and ending in the news office as a city reporter, I was fired on a Monday. So every Monday for the last six months I'd made my way to his smoke-filled office to beg him to rehire me. And every Monday he'd said no.

"I don't know why you put yourself through that humiliation each week. If the man hasn't rehired you by now, he isn't going to. Something else will come along. Something that better suits you."

Her words, meant to encourage, only grated. I wished Mama would, just once, kick and scream and complain with the rest of us. I wasn't sure which was worse: my mother's continued pretense that everything was fine or my father's wallowing in a whiskey bottle.

I tucked the book under my arm and stood. "Mrs. Davis asked me to help her hang wallpaper next week. She said she'd pay me ten dollars."

Mama's eyes widened. "Sissy Davis? Oh, Rena, I hope you told her you didn't need the money."

"Why would I tell her that? I do need the money. *We* need the money. Lots of people are out of work, Mama. There's no shame in accepting help when help is offered."

My tone was far from respectful, considering to whom I was speaking, but I wouldn't amend it. I was sick of ignoring the fact that our family was broke and broken. Mama thought asking Mr. Armistead for a job was humiliating. Had she forgotten the humiliation of learning my own father severely mismanaged thousands of dollars belonging to his customers? When he didn't come home at his usual time the day of the stock market crash, we'd feared the worst. It was the only time I could recall Mama letting herself sink down into the pit of despair. He eventually banged on the front door at three o'clock in the morning. Mama, Mary, and I silently watched him stumble inside without a word of explanation about the crash, the bank's fate, or his whereabouts all evening—although the smell of alcohol and cigarette smoke gave us the answer to that question. He locked himself in the study with a bottle of bourbon, and that's where he'd spent most of the past seven years.

"Sissy Davis is one of my dearest friends. I won't have my daughter performing manual labor for her."

So many words flew to my lips. I stopped them all from escaping. I'd come to the recent conclusion that Mama's sanity was tied to her determination to act as though all was well in the Leland household. Of course, most of Nashville knew it wasn't. People who'd once been considered friends turned away and whispered when we ventured beyond the house. To make ends meet, Mama took a job at a sewing shop in a neighborhood where she was certain her friends wouldn't see her. That was, if one could still call the women she used to associate with friends. Most of their husbands had lost money in my father's bank failure, and although they didn't blame Mama, they weren't completely forgiving either.

"Mrs. Davis simply needs help, Mama. She enjoys decorating her home herself." I stomped up the steps and faced her through the screen. "I'm not too keen on manual labor myself, but I don't have much choice, do I?"

After a moment, she conceded. "I suppose it wouldn't hurt for you to help a friend with her decorating. Sissy does have excellent taste. You can learn about the latest trends in decorating while you're there."

Leave it to Mama to put a positive turn on hanging wallpaper.

I joined her inside. A glance toward the study revealed a closed door. I hadn't seen Dad in three days. Mama took food to him when she got home from work in the evenings, but despite being home nearly all day together, he and I rarely spoke. Not because I didn't have plenty to say to him, but because I realized shortly after my sixteenth birthday that he somehow linked me to the stock market crash. As though the date on my birth certificate served as a painful reminder of the day he lost everything. He retreated from my world and barred me from his, with a whiskey bottle between us.

"I'll stop at the library after I see Mr. Armistead. Some new job listings might've been posted over the weekend." Odds were there weren't any, but I enjoyed going to the cool, quiet building to think without the scrutiny of my mother or the indifference of my father looming over me.

Mama opened a high cabinet and took down a soup can. She turned it over and removed the false bottom. A wadded-up handkerchief was stuffed inside, and she unwrapped it to reveal dozens of coins and some dollar bills. I'd seen her do this a hundred times or more in the past seven years, yet it still struck me as one of the saddest things I'd ever witnessed. A banker's wife hiding money from her husband in a soup can.

She handed me two nickels for the streetcar. "I won't be home until late. Mrs. Watkins needs me to help with inventory."

I nodded, if only to cover the awkwardness that always stood between us when she mentioned her job. I still found it difficult to accept my mother working in a sewing shop. Before the crash—that was how I measured time: before and after the crash—I'd never seen Mama sew anything, not even a loose button. How she'd managed to find this job, I didn't know, but she'd been there over four years now. Her meager wages kept food on the table, although she had to hide the money so Dad wouldn't take it and buy liquor. Somehow, he managed to get his hands on alcohol anyway. Even during Prohibition, he was rarely without bootleg bottles.

The morning was sunshiny and cool, which made the three-block walk to catch the streetcar pleasant. Gone were the days when my parents drove the latest cars. An old 1925 Ford sat in the garage behind the house, covered with dust, its tires flat. Fuel cost too much, as did repairs and upkeep. I wasn't certain the thing even ran anymore. Grandma Lorena owned a car and used it from time to time, but I didn't like to trouble her if I could take the streetcar.

The *Banner*'s offices were located in Printers Alley, a street teeming with publishers and the city's two largest newspapers. I missed coming downtown each day, feeling a part of the city's lifeblood and flow. Nashville's business district hummed with activity, although I noticed men's suits were more threadbare and fewer vehicles clogged streets in desperate need of repair. Our city, like the rest of the country, was feeling the effects of the depressed economy, yet folks valiantly met each day head-on with the determination to *get back to normal.*

Every time I heard that phrase, I silently asked myself if we'd ever see normal again. What was normal anyway? It had only been seven years since the crash, but the life I'd lived then seemed to belong to someone else.

Mr. Armistead's office sat at the back of a noisy room filled with desks. Several reporters looked up from their typewriters as I entered, nodded at me, and went back to work. No doubt they'd guessed long ago what my weekly visits were about, but I trusted Mr. A. not to divulge the details of my begging sessions, which was what I'd dubbed them. He might not be the most compassionate person in town, but he was no gossip.

He saw me coming through the glass window that separated his office from the larger newsroom. His thick graying brows folded over the black rim of his glasses. "Leland." His gruff greeting never changed. Smoke swirled from an ashtray on his messy desk where a stub of cigar rested.

"Good morning, Mr. Armistead. How are you today?" I put on my brightest smile even though I knew he wasn't fooled. He might be as old as most grandfathers, but he was no pushover.

"Same as I am every Monday. Behind schedule and in need of a front-page story." He continued to shuffle papers and act busy.

I stepped into the room. "You know I'd love to help with that."

He nodded without looking up. "And you know why you can't."

My smile drooped. Yes, I knew. The crash. The failing economy. Money. Money. Money. The failures of other people had dictated my future for too long, yet what choice did I have?

After a long moment, the question I'd avoided the past six months resurfaced in my mind. I feared his answer, which was why I had yet to verbalize it, but perhaps it was time to know the truth and move on.

With a deep breath, I plunged forward. "Mr. A., if things were different and you were able to hire staff again, would you rehire me?"

His hands paused over the mess that was his desk.

My stomach clenched. Now I'd gone and done it. I'd handed him the perfect opportunity to get rid of me once and for all.

Yet when he finally looked up, it was with an expression I'd never seen on his face before. Sympathetic, I suppose, which seemed out of place on the hard-nosed newspaperman.

"I would, kid."

Three simple words, but oh, how they lightened the heaviness in my heart.

I smiled again, satisfied. "Thanks, Mr. A." I turned to leave.

"Kid, wait."

My heart skipped with hope. Had my boldness changed his mind?

He dug through piles of paper until he found the one he sought and handed it to me. "This came in the other day. Maybe you should take a look into it."

A quick glance revealed it was typed on letterhead from a government agency called the Works Progress Administration. I looked back to Mr. A. "What is it?"

He jabbed a fat finger at the paper in my hand. "Read it, Leland. It's a job. A writing job."

A writing job? My interest piqued. However, the more I read, the more confused I grew. When I reached the end of the brief missive, I met his gaze. "I don't understand."

He huffed. "The WPA is Roosevelt's baby. It's his idea of providing jobs for folks out of work. Writers, as you are well aware, are among the unemployed. Under the umbrella of the WPA, they've created something called the Federal Writers' Project. That letter states they need writers here in Nashville to do interviews. You're a reporter with experience. No reason you shouldn't get the job."

I glanced back to the typewritten words. "But it says something about former slaves."

"Yeah, that's who's being interviewed. To preserve their stories or something of that nature."

I was sure my expression revealed too much because Mr. Armistead sat back in his chair and narrowed his gaze on me. "I never thought of you as the type to care about the color of a person's skin, Leland."

"I don't." Dovie had been one of the dearest people in my world before it all fell apart.

"So why not do this?" He indicated the letter again. "They'll pay twenty dollars a week. All you have to do is spend an hour or two with each interviewee, type up your notes, and turn them in to the WPA office. Sounds like easy money to me."

It did sound like easy money, and yet . . .

"I'll think about it," I finally said.

Mr. A. shrugged and returned his attention to the chaos on his desk. "Suit yourself, but this opportunity won't last long. Plenty of writers are willing to do the job if you aren't."

I left his office with the letter tucked in my purse and frustration rooted in my mind. I needed the job, but to interview former slaves? My ancestors had owned slaves. Shouldn't that disqualify me from the position?

The job posting board at the library held a small number of new handwritten cards, but they required experience I didn't possess. As restless as I felt, sitting in the quiet solitude of the big building didn't appeal today. I needed to walk. And think. I left the building and headed in the direction of home.

Questions poured from my brain. Why would the government care about preserving the stories of former slaves? Wasn't it the government who created the very laws that had kept people in bondage for over two centuries? Surely there were more important issues to write about. With so many people suffering these days, no one even thought about slavery anymore. The War between the States happened when Grandma Lorena was a small child, over seventy years ago.

But twenty dollars a week was more money than I'd made at any of the odd jobs I'd taken over the past six months. Even with occasional help from Grandma Lorena, who survived the stock market crash surprisingly well, I knew we were in terrible financial shape. Mama never verbalized how destitute we actually were, but I'd seen the bankruptcy papers she'd hidden in her bedroom bureau shortly after the crash. I hadn't meant to see them, but I was putting away laundry and there they were, plain as day.

My feet grew weary in my heeled shoes, so I sat on a bench at the next streetcar stop and waited. A minute passed before an older black man, neatly dressed, walked up. When our eyes met, he nodded politely but remained standing as he too waited for the streetcar. Although we were the only people at the stop and there was plenty of room on the bench, I knew the unspoken rule as well as he did.

A colored man could not sit next to a white woman.

An odd thought struck me as we waited for the streetcar. What would this man think about the Federal Writers' Project and its proposed interviews? Did the stories of former slaves interest him? I couldn't imagine they would, since they would bring up an unpleasant time in the history of our country. People had moved on from the issues of slavery, leaving the ugliness in the past.

The image of nine black teenage boys on the front page of a newspaper flashed across my mind.

The Scottsboro boys. Convicted of raping two white women in Alabama despite overwhelming evidence of their innocence.

When the trolley arrived, I boarded in the front of the vehicle while the man boarded in the rear. I sat beside a young white woman with a small child on her lap. The pair was too engrossed in their babbled conversation to acknowledge me.

As the streetcar jerked forward, I peeked behind me.

From his place at the back of the vehicle, the older man I'd boarded with looked right at me.

CHAPTER
THREE

"You're going to do what?"

My sister's shrill voice rose above the loud squabbles of her two oldest children. We sat at the dining room table attempting to enjoy dinner, yet not having much success thanks to an overcooked chicken and cranky kids. Mary's youngest, a chubby two-year-old boy, was curled on her lap, thumb poked in his mouth and eyes drooping despite the bedlam.

"I'm applying for a job with the Federal Writers' Project," I hollered back.

Mama sent me a disapproving look, whether for shouting at the table or for the job, I wasn't sure. Roosevelt's "New Deal" ideas to help the unemployed weren't popular with everyone.

"Holly, James. Enough." Mary thumped her eldest on the arm, only because he was closest.

"She started it," he whined, rubbing the spot.

"Did not."

Four-year-old Holly had the looks of an angel, with a head of golden curls and eyes as blue as the sky, but that's where the angelic similarities ended. Her bottom lip perpetually stuck out, as it did now, and her glare when she was mad, which was most of the time, could freeze a camel in the desert.

"Finish your supper and go outside to play, both of you."

Mary sounded exhausted. In fact, she looked awful, now that I studied her from my place across the table. Dark smudges contrasted with pale cheeks, and her hair, normally rolled and teased to perfection, lay flattened on one side. I'd been too preoccupied with my monumental decision to take notice when she first arrived, unannounced, with boisterous youngsters piling out of her old Hudson.

A wave of compassion for my sister washed over me. The crash had changed her life, too. Roy dumped her the day after our father's bank failed. Five months later, while we were still coping with the aftermath of the stock market crash, Mary, with tears in her eyes, confessed she was pregnant. Mama locked herself in her bedroom for two silent hours while I was left to console my sister, who, if I was honest, I thought was an idiot for getting herself into this mess. She wouldn't say who the father was until Mama came out of her room and demanded an explanation. When Mary finally sobbed out his name, my jaw practically hit the hardwood floor.

Homer Whitby. The very same Homer who supposedly planned to come calling on *me* before the crash.

The story wasn't pretty nor romantic. He wasn't a knight in shining armor come to rescue Mary after Roy broke things off so abruptly. They'd met accidentally on Vanderbilt's campus, where Homer and Roy continued to attend classes. Mary had to quit Belmont after we lost everything, and she'd gone to the school that day in hopes of finding Roy, intent on mending their fractured relationship. She found Homer instead. He offered a sympathetic shoulder to cry on, then invited her to dinner, which in hindsight seemed rather two-faced considering she'd been Roy's girl so recently.

What happened next was none of my business, but eight weeks after their impromptu date Mary tearfully announced she was pregnant. Dad came out of his drunken self-pity to do the right thing, which was to drive Mary to Memphis and meet with Homer's parents. A hastily planned wedding ceremony took place a week later.

"What kind of writing is it?" Mama asked once the children ran outside, letting the screen door bang behind them.

I'd known this question was forthcoming, but the answer I'd planned, which was basically a lie, lodged in my throat. I didn't like to lie to Mama, but the truth wouldn't satisfy her. She wouldn't approve of the subject of the interviews nor of the need for me to travel into the poorer areas of Nashville where I'd never stepped a toe.

I settled on a half-truth and hoped for the best.

"It's a job Mr. Armistead told me about, interviewing different people for a government project. It pays twenty dollars a week."

I knew that would interest her more than the job itself.

"Well, if Mr. Armistead thinks you should apply for it, you should. Goodness knows we need more money coming into this house."

"It's not guaranteed I'll get it," I added, not wanting either of us to raise our hopes too high. Mr. Armistead's warning about there being other out-of-work writers willing to do the job echoed in my mind. As reluctant as I'd been to consider the position when he first handed me the letter, now that I'd convinced myself it was worth my time, anxiety swirled through my stomach. What if I *didn't* get the job?

"Maybe you'll interview someone famous, like Greta Garbo." Mary's face took on a dreamy expression. "Or Clark Gable."

Though difficult, I managed to keep myself from rolling my eyes at such a ridiculous statement. I offered what I trusted was a smile and not a smirk. "I doubt the government would pay for the kind of interviews you can read in *Film Fun* magazine."

Mama gasped. "You don't read such trash, do you?"

"No, Mama," I said, which was true for the most part. Some reporters I'd worked with at the *Banner* brought in copies of the gossip magazine, boasting racy covers and tales of movie stars' lives. I'd peeked over the shoulders of my coworkers a time or two, but I wasn't about to confess that to Mama.

"So who will you interview?" she asked. "Did Mr. Armistead say?"

I wasn't prepared to defend against the disapproval I knew she'd direct my way the moment I divulged who the interviewees were, so it seemed prudent to come up with another vague answer. Mama'd convinced herself long ago she wasn't narrow-minded when it came to station or skin color, yet I'd witnessed her treatment of Dovie throughout the many years the old woman worked for our family. When Dovie was sick and missed a day, Mama took it as an affront and called her lazy. She'd dock Dovie's pay if the woman accidentally broke the smallest item, and more than once I heard Mama talk down to Dovie for no reason other than she could.

"The letter doesn't mention the names of the people who are to be interviewed." I scooted my chair away from the table, ready to escape her line of questioning, and picked up my plate with half my meal still intact. "I'll do the dishes," I said with a bright smile. "You and Mary visit and watch the kids."

Mary eyed me with a hint of suspicion, but neither of them protested as I cleared the table. While I ran hot water into the kitchen sink, I heard Mama ask Mary about Homer's new job at a manufacturing company in East Nashville. I shut off the faucet to hear her answer.

"It doesn't pay as well as his last job," she said, her voice lowered but still loud enough for me to hear from the next room. "His daddy knows the owner and made Homer take it. Papa Whitby told Homer he wouldn't help us anymore if Homer kept getting himself fired from perfectly good jobs."

I turned the water on again, drowning out whatever else she had to say about her good-for-nothing husband. What a disappointment Homer Whitby turned out to be. His handsome face and winning smile were a facade for a lazy charlatan and gambler who couldn't keep a job and who'd been linked to several women despite having a wife and three children. Homer's daddy threatened to cut him off financially after each scandal, and Homer would promise to end his wicked ways. Yet the scenario repeated itself so many times no one—not even my poor sister—believed him anymore.

With the dishes washed and put away, I could have joined Mama and Mary on the back porch, where they watched the children play under the branches of the same magnolia tree my sister and I had played beneath. I could have, but I didn't. Mama's questions about the job with the FWP weren't something I wanted to revisit, nor did I wish to pretend my sister's life wasn't a disaster.

I quietly went out the front door, making sure it closed without a sound, and hurried down the street to Grandma Lorena's, relishing the cool air on my face. September in Tennessee could be finicky, with some days as hot as midsummer and others ready to usher in autumn. This evening the weather seemed to settle somewhere in the middle, making it more than pleasant.

Grandma's cottage sat at the end of our street, tucked behind a hedge of laurel. She loved the neighborhood and hadn't wanted to move too far away after selling her larger house—the one we now lived in—to Dad after Grandpa passed away. Mama and Grandma weren't as close as I felt they should be, considering Mama was Grandma's only child, but then I reminded myself I wasn't close to Mama either. I'd never been able to talk to her the way I could with Grandma.

A light shone through the lacy living room curtains. With a soft tap on the door, I called out to let her know I was coming in. Grandma sat in her favorite armchair, a book open in her lap.

"Rena, what brings you by so late?" She glanced at the antique clock on the mantel. "I hope everything is all right at home."

I grinned. It was only a little after seven o'clock. "I have some good news. At least, I hope it's good."

"Tell me." Grandma put her book aside.

Settling on the sofa, I pulled the FWP letter from my skirt pocket and handed it to her. "Mr. Armistead gave me this today."

Grandma took the paper and silently read through it. She looked up a minute later. "What a wonderful project. And you're thinking about joining them?"

"I am." My shoulders seemed to lift on their own accord in a shrug. "I guess."

"What do you mean, you guess? Why wouldn't you? It sounds like a job right up your alley. You interviewed all types of interesting people when you worked for the newspaper. This would certainly be an answer to our prayers."

I nodded rather halfheartedly, knowing she was right, and yet the doubts piled up.

"Give me one good reason why you shouldn't take this job." She leveled a no-nonsense look at me.

I bit the inside of my lip. Hadn't I come to see her for this very purpose? To finally verbalize the answer to a question I'd never come face-to-face with in all my twenty-two years?

"Because I can't waltz into the home of a former slave and ask all kinds of personal questions. Why would they tell me about their life? Our family owned slaves. What if they figure that out? What would I say?"

There.

I'd put to words what had been bothering me from the very moment I read the letter in Mr. Armistead's office. My ancestors—Grandma's grandparents and great-grandparents—owned slaves at one time. Quite a lot, from what I understood. Surely that fact alone should exclude me from a job that involved delving into the private lives of people who had themselves once been *owned*.

Grandma's face took on a contemplative look. After a long silent moment, she nodded. "Yes, you're right. Our family did own slaves. I was quite young when the war began, barely a year old. Papa had family in Kentucky, and when Nashville fell to the Federals, he took us there for the duration of the war. But I do remember going to visit Grandma Helen on the plantation. They grew tobacco and corn in those days. I don't know how many slaves they had, but I imagine it was close to one hundred. Grandpa's family came from Ohio and never approved of slavery, but he understood it was necessary to keep the plantation going. At least, that's what Grandma's family believed to be true in those days."

"You see why I don't feel I'm suitable to interview former slaves?" I slumped against the couch.

She scowled. "No, I certainly do not. You didn't own slaves. It's been seventy-one years since the war ended. No one holds your generation responsible for slavery, dear."

That might be true, but the feeling of guilt still hovered over me. "Did you know any of your grandmother's slaves?"

A soft smile increased the wrinkles on her face. "After the war, Mama hired Cornelia to come work for us in town. She'd been what they call a mammy, the older woman who takes care of the babies while their mothers work. Cornelia lived with us until she died, probably ten years. Grandma Helen always acted a bit peeved that she didn't choose to stay on the plantation and work for wages as some of the others did, but Cornelia once told me the plantation held dark memories for her."

We sat in silence as the clock ticked off several moments, both of us lost in thoughts of the past. My great-great-grandmother's plantation had long been divided and sold, so I'd never seen the big white house Grandma remembered. It had been partially burned during the war, and she said the remodeled home wasn't nearly as grand as it had been in its early days.

"I miss Dovie," I said with a sigh, shifting my thoughts to the only black person I truly knew. The old woman had been part of my life for sixteen years. Her absence still hurt. "I wish we could've found a way to keep her on after the bank failed."

"I hear she's doing well down in Franklin with the Warrens. I saw Betty not long ago, and she had nothing but good things to say about Dovie. Gus, too, since they hired them both."

While I knew I should be happy for Dovie and Gus, it irked me that the Warrens had come through the stock market crash unscathed and snatched up our housekeeper even before the dust settled on our upturned household. Mama felt betrayed by Dovie and made a big scene the day she came to tell us goodbye, but I always felt it was more the loss of a housekeeper and the status of keeping servants rather than losing Dovie in particular that brought her tears.

"What would she think about this opportunity you have with the Federal Writers' Project?" Grandma followed her question with a bit of a smirk, as though she already knew the answer.

The image of Dovie, with hands on her hips and a tilt to her head, flashed across my mind. I grinned. "She'd say, 'Get on down there and talk to them folks. They ain't gonna bite you.'"

Grandma chuckled at my imitation of our former housekeeper's deep Southern drawl and sassy attitude. "I believe you're exactly right. And I agree."

My smile slowly faded. "Do you really think I should do it?" I whispered, the very idea tying my gut into a knot. "What if . . . what if . . . ?" I couldn't finish the sentence, mainly because I didn't know exactly what I was afraid of. All I knew was fear mounted with every breath I took.

"I think it will be good for you." Her gray-blue eyes narrowed on me. "You need to see life from a different perspective in order to move forward. I believe this job may be exactly what you need to help you find your place in the world."

The music of crickets and tree frogs filled the night as I walked home a short time later, but it was Grandma's words that echoed through my mind. Over the past seven years, I'd confessed to her more than once that I felt stuck. Stuck in time. Stuck in circumstance. Just plain ol' stuck.

How could interviewing people who'd lived in bondage decades earlier help me see my future more clearly?

There was only one way to find out.

CHAPTER
FOUR

A car horn sounded at exactly nine o'clock Thursday morning, three weeks later.

"My, he's punctual." Mama glanced out the front window to where a gray, weather-beaten Chevrolet coupe sat in our driveway. She turned to face me as I put on my sweater, her thin lips in a flat line. "A gentleman would come to the door, not sit in the car waiting for the lady."

"This isn't a date, Mama." I tucked my purse strap over my arm. "Mr. Norwood is simply giving me a ride downtown. We both work for the FWP, so we're business professionals. If he were picking up a male coworker, he wouldn't come to the door."

With more confidence than I felt, I snatched up the two steno notebooks I'd purchased per instructions from the

Nashville FWP director who'd hired me last week. A bundle of freshly sharpened pencils already occupied a place in my purse, as did the paper containing the address of my first interviewee and the folded list of questions I was to ask.

Ignoring the knot in my stomach, I turned to Mama. "Wish me luck," I said a bit too brightly.

Mama frowned. "I don't recall you ever being nervous when you interviewed people for the paper."

That was because they weren't former slaves living in Hell's Half Acre, but I couldn't tell that to Mama. "I'm just rusty, I guess. I'm sure it will all come back to me."

I stepped into the foyer. A word of encouragement from Mama would have gone a long way just then, but she simply watched me leave the house and walk down the porch steps. I hadn't made it to Mr. Norwood's car yet when I heard the door close behind me.

With a deep breath I hoped would still my quaking insides, I reached for the handle on the passenger side of the car. A young man sat in the driver's seat. His brown felt hat sat on his head at an angle, reminding me of Errol Flynn.

"Hello." He gave a small nod of greeting.

"Hello." I climbed into the vehicle, trying not to stare at several worn places on the seat as I slid over them.

He stuck out his hand but didn't smile. "Alden Norwood."

"Lorena Leland," I returned, briefly engaging his cool hand with my sweaty one. Thankfully, he didn't retrieve the handkerchief peeking out from his jacket pocket and use it as a towel.

His glance shifted to our house. He studied it a long moment before asking, "You live here?"

The odd question confused me. "Yes." Why else would I be here so early in the morning, ready to begin a new job that he himself was driving me to?

"Hmm."

That's it. That's all he said before he shoved the gearshift into reverse and backed down the driveway. With one last glance at the house, then at me, he put the car into gear and headed up the street.

I stewed over his *hmm* for a solid minute before I stole a glance at his profile.

He was far younger than I'd anticipated. For some reason I'd envisioned Alden Norwood as an older gentleman when Mr. Carlson, the director of the Nashville FWP office, told me a fellow writer would pick me up and drive me to Hell's Half Acre, a run-down neighborhood where all of my interviewees lived. Mr. Carlson had sung Mr. Norwood's praises, declaring him a true advocate for the downtrodden and a highly experienced interviewer. I was to ask Mr. Norwood any questions I might have regarding my assignment, with the assurance the gentleman would be happy to supply the answers.

Yet Mr. Norwood couldn't be much older than me. Dark hair in need of a trim poked out from beneath the Errol Flynn hat that, now as I took a closer look, I realized had seen better days. The dark-gray suit he wore might well have come from a church charity box, as threadbare as it appeared.

I couldn't help but wonder at his financial situation and how long he'd been in need of work before he discovered the FWP.

Which brought me full circle back to his *hmm*. What exactly did it mean? Was it a good *hmm* or a bad *hmm*? So intent on my ponderings, I didn't realize I was staring at him until I found questioning brown eyes returning the gaze while we waited at an intersection.

"I beg your pardon." A rush of heat rose to my face as I quickly looked away. "I was . . ." What could I say? Embarrassment jumbled my brain, preventing a logical explanation from surfacing in time to save me.

He chuckled. "You wore quite a perplexed frown as you studied me. Dare I ask the nature of such glowering?"

The car lurched forward before I could answer, and we resumed our journey. With his concentration returned to the road, my tense shoulders eased. Perhaps his humor at my poor manners boded well. I hoped so anyway.

"I simply wondered what you meant by *hmm*."

He shot me a puzzled look before returning his attention to the other vehicles on the busy street. Nashville's population had grown over the years despite the depressed economy. Sedans, delivery trucks, and streetcars clogged roads inadequate for so much traffic, yet the city had no money to alleviate the problem.

"When you inquired if I lived in my house," I said in explanation, "I informed you I did indeed. You responded with *hmm*. I wondered what you meant by that."

Understanding registered on his face. He glanced at me

before answering. "I suppose I was surprised that someone who took a job with the FWP resides in such a fine home."

His answer was not what I expected. "Why is that?"

"Because the programs under the Works Progress Administration are for people who meet certain criteria. We've all had to take the 'pauper's oath,' as it's called, proving we have no money, no property of our own, no job, and no prospect of getting any of those." He glanced at me again, this time taking in my dress, sweater, and hat. "I'll be honest, Miss Leland. You don't look like you meet the criteria."

I wasn't sure whether to take his opinion as a compliment or an insult. I'd borrowed one of Mama's old dresses she used to wear to her club meetings, hoping to appear serious and mature. The pale-blue outfit wasn't new, but it wasn't as worn-looking as most of my own things. And yet this man had the audacity to judge me and my circumstances by the house I lived in and the clothes I wore.

My blood boiled. "I wouldn't have taken the oath if it weren't true. What exactly should someone who meets the criteria look like? In your esteemed opinion, of course." I folded my arms across my belly when he chanced a glance at me.

Even with his attention returned to the road, I kept my glare on him, awaiting his response.

"The Works Progress Administration is part of the government's New Deal programs. It was formed to help the down-and-out through these hard economic times." He spoke as though explaining something to a child. I fumed as he checked for traffic before proceeding across a street. A moment later his eyes met mine. "It's easy to see your family hasn't been hit as hard by the depressed economy as the rest of us who work for the WPA. There are people—fellow writers and friends of mine—who have lost their homes and have children to take care of. They're truly suffering and could use a job with the Federal Writers' Project. Pardon me for saying so, but you aren't one of them."

I felt as though I'd been slapped. How dare this man assume we hadn't been hit as hard as anyone else. And as for not suffering?

I pictured my father, the former bank president, a man who'd dined with the governor and held positions on various boards, now holed up in a dark room day and night, bourbon bottles his constant companion. Mama tried to keep him clean and fed, but there were days when he was unrecognizable, with his unkempt hair and whiskers.

I thought of my mother, working long hours at the sewing shop in order to put food on our table, and of my sister, her life full of diapers and despair over a lazy, unfaithful husband.

No, we weren't homeless as thousands were, and thankfully we weren't starving. But this man, this stranger, had no right to judge my life based on a glimpse of our once-stately house and a hand-me-down outfit.

A lump formed in my throat, and my chin trembled. "You don't know anything about me or my family, Mr. Norwood. I'll thank you to keep your judgments to yourself."

I faced the window so he wouldn't see the unwelcome

emotion that sprang to my eyes. His misguided opinion shouldn't bother me, yet I was so weary of strangers and acquaintances alike making assumptions. No one knew what we'd been through the past seven years. No one knew the fear we lived with every single day. If it weren't for Grandma Lorena's help with bills, I didn't know how we would survive.

I dug in my purse for a handkerchief and wiped my drippy nose. With resolve, I blinked away the last bit of telling moisture, determined not to give him satisfaction in knowing he'd upset me. The opinion of Alden Norwood didn't matter in the least. He was merely my driver, and I would treat him as such.

The grand Tennessee state capitol building came into view a short time later, its gleaming white limestone walls and lantern-shaped cupola presiding over the city with dignified command. It seemed at odds with the slums that existed practically in the shadow of the stately structure where laws were created and the rights of Tennessee citizens were discussed. Did the men whose office windows must surely look down on Hell's Half Acre not notice the neighborhood whose sordid reputation of poverty, violence, and crime dated back to the 1870s? Or was it that they simply didn't care?

"What's the address of your first interview?"

Mr. Norwood's voice drew me out of my ponderings. I handed him the paper with Mrs. Frances Washington's address written on it. Upon reading the street name, he nodded. "I know where that is." Turning at the next corner, he maneuvered the car past the capitol and into an area of Nashville I'd never seen up close.

Run-down houses and overgrown lots lined every street. While some of the buildings had surely once been fine homes, time and the lack of upkeep left them with crumbling walls and sagging porches filled with what appeared to be abandoned junk. Laundry hung on lines stretched from tree to tree in the neglected yards of several homes, and my heart softened for the women attempting to keep their families in clean clothes amid the squalor of the neighborhood.

A gathering of men stood on the sidewalk dressed in shirtsleeves and hats, but they stopped their conversation to watch us drive past. Mr. Norwood nodded to them politely, but I kept my eyes averted, a tense feeling beginning to swirl through my stomach.

Had I made a terrible mistake accepting a job that forced me to spend time in this part of Nashville? Would I be safe once Mr. Norwood drove away, leaving me alone with a woman I'd never met, in a neighborhood with a reputation even I'd heard of? He might have vexed me terribly with his superior attitude and disparaging assumptions, but his presence offered a measure of safety I hadn't anticipated needing.

"Here we are."

Mr. Norwood stopped the car in front of a small house with peeling yellow paint. A low fence circled a yard no bigger than the car I sat in, yet astonishingly it held more flowers of various sizes and colors than I'd ever seen in one place. A narrow path through the foliage led to a porch with two straight-backed chairs, both worn but still solid-looking. A few pots of flowers sat between them.

I breathed a sigh of relief as I gazed out the window to the charming residence. While I didn't want people like Mr. Norwood judging me on the kind of house I lived in, I was having a hard time not doing the same for the residents of Hell's Half Acre. That Mrs. Washington took care in maintaining her little home brought a sense of calm to my whirling emotions.

"I'll meet you here at four o'clock." Mr. Norwood seemed impatient to be rid of me as he glanced at his wristwatch. "You should be able to walk to your other interviews if you get finished with this one and need to move on."

Panic rose to the surface at the thought of being left alone in a strange place among strange people. I'd hoped to ask him all sorts of questions about the interview process on our drive here, but his immediate assumptions about my family's financial status had silenced them. I regretted my sulking because I had no idea what I was doing.

It was too late now. "Thank you," I muttered, aggravated with him and myself. I gathered my belongings in one hand and opened the door with the other since it appeared Mr. Norwood had no intention of assisting me. I almost laughed, thinking about Mama and how she'd stay right where she was until the gentleman walked around the car to open her door.

Although Mr. Norwood and I hadn't gotten off to a great start, my stomach sank as I watched him drive away, leaving me in a place I never imagined I'd set foot in, let alone spend time in interviewing former slaves. When I'd gone to Mr. Armistead's office to inform him I got the job and wouldn't be visiting him for a while, he'd appeared impressed.

"I wasn't sure you had it in you, Leland. I'm glad I was wrong."

The memory of the affirming words strengthened my resolve as I made my way through the pretty flowers, their heady aroma thick and sweet, and quietly mounted the porch. Two windows flanked the door, but both had curtains drawn, so there was no peeking inside to get a hint of what awaited me. I swallowed, took a deep breath, and knocked on the door. Several long moments passed before I heard movement on the other side.

The woman who answered was not what I expected.

"Mrs. Washington?"

Sharp black eyes studied me before she answered. "Yes'm, I'm Miz Washington."

"I'm Lorena Leland, with the Works Progress Administration. I believe you're expecting me."

She continued her examination of me, perusing my face, my dress, even my shoes, before her narrowed eyes met mine again. I in turn considered her. Taller than I'd anticipated, she appeared to be in remarkably good health considering her advanced age. Her short-cropped hair was snowy white, but her cheeks were as smooth and wrinkle-free as a young woman's.

Finally she nodded. "I been expecting you. The Lord told me I couldn't go home till you come."

The strange answer caught me off guard. I stared at her, wondering if she was in her right mind. Would this be a complete waste of time? Surely the tales told by a woman whose mind bore the effects of age would not be beneficial to the FWP and their mission to preserve the oral history of former slaves.

"Let's not stand here gawking at each other. Come in, chile, come in." She turned and retreated into the small house.

With one last longing glance down the now-vacant street, I followed, letting the screen door close behind me with a bang that sounded like a gunshot. Mrs. Washington continued to an overstuffed armchair with faded floral print as though she hadn't heard it. A small shelf crammed with books stood within arm's reach should she desire to read in the evenings.

"Sit where'er you be most comfortable."

The choices were few. A low-slung couch I wasn't sure I would be able to climb out of or a stiff-looking chair near the window. I chose the latter and set my purse on the wood floor next to me. She sat silently watching while I took out a pencil, opened one of the steno notebooks, and unfolded the list of questions Mr. Carlson had given me upon signing the contract to conduct interviews for the FWP.

With a deep breath to quiet my nerves, I met her gaze. "I believe you know why I'm here."

She gave a slow nod. "Uh-hm, I know why you here. But, chile, you ain't got a clue why *you* is here."

CHAPTER

FIVE

Mr. Carlson's instructions were simple: ask the questions as they appeared on the typewritten paper he'd given me and allow the former slaves to tell their stories in their own way, talking freely of slavery and the ills suffered, without giving my own opinion on any subject discussed.

But now that the time had come, I found myself reduced to a jumble of nerves.

As Mrs. Washington looked on, I attempted to arrange the steno notebook and the list of questions, each vying for a position of prominence on my lap. My pencil slipped from my hand in the process, breaking the sharpened lead when it hit the floor.

Flashing Mrs. Washington a look of apology, I retrieved it, then took another from my purse. Somehow, after what seemed an inordinate amount of time, I was ready to begin.

With a glance at my subject, who continued to consider me with a stony face, I forced a smile. Yet before I
could get the first question out of my now-dry mouth, Mrs.
Washington stood.

"You want a cup o' tea? I find it helps quiet the jitters."

My tense shoulders eased some, knowing she was anxious
about our interview too. "That would be nice, but I want to
assure you there is nothing to be nervous about."

A deep chuckle rumbled in her chest. "I ain't nervous,
chile, but you're 'bout ready to come out of your skin. Come
on to the kitchen and we'll make you a nice cup o' chamomile tea."

Without waiting for my response, she headed through a
doorway while I remained seated, mortified that she'd read
me so well. Why was I so jumpy? Like Mama observed, I'd
never been this nervous while conducting interviews for the
Banner.

I set my things on the floor and followed her into a tiny
kitchen. A deep porcelain sink sat beneath a window that
looked out to the backside of a run-down tenement one
street over. A small icebox occupied a corner of the room
while an even smaller table and two chairs occupied the
other. Yet it was the old-fashioned wood-burning stove where
Mrs. Washington worked that brought the most surprise.
Our stove at home was fueled by gas. It never occurred to me
people still cooked over wood or coal. Was this a common
practice here in Hell's Half Acre? I wondered. Or was it Mrs.
Washington who hadn't caught up to modern times?

Seeing her at the old stove, however, forced me to consider what else might be missing from this woman's life that I had and took for granted.

"Jael—she takes care of me when she ain't studying down at the university—she likes chamomile tea, but I have to admit I prefer a strong cup o' coffee."

As she worked, I noticed one of her hands was quite disfigured. Large knots existed where knuckles should be, and it seemed at least two, maybe three, of her fingers were not lined up as they should be. It didn't slow her down though. She poured hot water from a kettle sitting on the stovetop into a plain white cup with a tea ball. Taking a pale-blue saucer from the open shelf that held short stacks of mismatched dishes, she set the cup on it and handed it to me. "You take sugar?"

I shook my head, not wanting to be any more trouble than I'd already been, especially when I realized she was not partaking. "This is wonderful, thank you."

She nodded and led the way back into the sitting room, where she eased herself into her chair. "I 'spect you ain't never been down here to the Acres." Her steady gaze held no accusation nor even curiosity. It was simply a statement.

"No, ma'am." I carefully sat down, trying not to spill my tea. There was no hope of retrieving my notebook and pencil at the moment, so I trusted she wouldn't launch into her life's story just yet.

"Well, you ain't missed much. I've lived here near 'bout sixty years. Seen all kinds of troubles. There be some good folks here in the Acres, but there also be some who want to do nothin' but cause hardship for everyone else."

I noticed she didn't refer to the neighborhood as Hell's Half Acre, as the area was known throughout Nashville. I suppose I wouldn't either if I had to live here. Why add to the discouragement of living in such conditions by labeling it after a place I hoped I never saw?

"I'll be honest, Miss Leland." She leaned back in the chair. "I was mighty surprised when I received a letter from the gov'ment wanting to hear my stories 'bout slavery times."

I smiled. "We appreciate you being willing to share about your life." Of course, I didn't know who *we* referred to, but as an employee of the federal government, I had to give appearances of being part of a larger community. The entire project was President Roosevelt's idea, so one would assume his interest in the oral histories of former slaves was the catalyst for my being in the presence of this woman.

"Fact is, I ain't never told my story to anyone since freedom come. No sense in rememberin' them days, I say." She folded her arms across her chest.

I nearly choked on the sip of tea I'd just taken. Did she mean she wouldn't share the tales of her life with me? Would my first interview for the FWP be a complete failure? Mr. Carlson would not be pleased.

A knot began to form in my stomach as it occurred to me I might not have a job by the end of the day. I set my teacup on a small table to my left, careful not to disturb the knickknacks and a framed picture of a young man, my brain whirling. Mr. Armistead taught me early on in my career as a reporter to use the power of persuasion on difficult subjects. I hoped his methods would work now.

"Mrs. Washington, I'm sure I'm not qualified to give you advice on whether or not to answer the questions I have for you, but I do believe this project is important."

In the seconds it took those words to pass over my lips, I realized they were true. I did want to hear this woman's story. I wanted to know what her life as a slave was like. Mrs. Frances Washington was a faceless name to me yesterday. Today, she was an elderly woman, living in a tiny yellow house with a yard full of flowers in a neighborhood whose reputation was as sullied as the gutters that lined its streets.

Long seconds ticked by on a clock as we regarded one another.

"Jael is the one who said I should talk to you. She's young and don't know much 'bout slavery times. Said it would be good for folks in her day to know 'bout the past."

I said a silent prayer of thanks for Jael and reached for my notebook.

"But I told her the past is best forgotten. We can't go back and change nothin' that happened, so why dredge up all those bitter memories?"

My shoulders slumped. "So you won't answer my questions?"

Her eyes narrowed on me. "I sure didn't plan to, but just this mornin' the Lord told me I couldn't go home till I talked to you."

There it was again. The same strange statement she'd greeted me with. I could only assume she referred to God, but did she truly expect me to believe the Almighty wouldn't allow her to die until I interviewed her?

Once again, I wondered if her mind was fully intact. Maybe I should pack up my notebooks and leave while I still had time to find my next interviewee. At least I'd have something to show Mr. Carlson for today's efforts.

"I'll say to you the same thing I said to him," she continued, unaware of my panicked line of thought. "I'll tell you 'bout slavery times if you want to hear it. You can ask me anything and I'll do my best to remember. It ain't a pretty story, though. You may be sorry you came askin' when I'm done tellin'."

I hesitated only a moment before nodding. I was here, seated in her home and ready to move forward, so I would attempt to conduct the interview as promised. But if at any time I felt she wasn't in her right mind and her answers proved too outlandish—such as her statement about God not allowing her to go home yet—I would move on to the next subject.

"I understand, Mrs. Washington. I appreciate your willingness to answer my questions." I lifted the typewritten list, although I'd memorized most of what was on the two pages. "We'll start with some basic information. When and where were you born?" I poised my pencil above the first page in the notebook, where I'd written her name in bold letters before leaving the house this morning.

"I was born on the Halls' plantation." A small frown settled on her face. "Don't know exactly where their place was, but it were about a day's ride to Nashville, I 'spect. Mammy always said I was born in 1835 when the leaves started changin' color."

I felt my eyes widen as I did the math.

She grinned. "Yes'm, I be 101 years old. Lord have mercy, I been around a long time."

I jotted down every word she said. The instructions from the FWP office in Washington, DC, were to write the former slaves' stories word for word, avoiding any kind of censorship of the material collected, regardless of its nature. If the subject spoke in a dialect, I was to attempt to spell the word out in such a way that a reader would understand the meaning even without proper spelling. Thankfully, Mrs. Washington's speech was quite clear, sprinkled with Southern pronunciation common in our part of the world.

When I finished recording her answer, I moved on to the next question. "What were your parents' names? Where did they come from?"

A soft smile came to her lips. "Mammy's name was Lucindia—ain't that pretty?—but I never knowed my pappy. Mammy's mama came from Africa. Her name was Frances, like mine. That's why folks started calling me Frankie when I was still a baby."

I glanced up from my notes. "I'm named after my grandmother, too. Lorena, but everyone calls me Rena."

She gave a satisfied nod. "Mammy had three other

children that I know of, but only one was older than me. A boy named Saul."

This information puzzled me. Wouldn't she know if her mother had more children? That important fact didn't seem like something one would forget despite being 101 years of age.

"I see you want to ask me somethin' that ain't on that paper of yours."

I looked up from my notes, heat rushing to my cheeks at being found curious. She was correct in guessing the most personal of questions were not included on the list provided by the government. The next question I was to ask was "What work did you do in slavery days?" Probing why this woman didn't know if her own mother bore more children than she remembered or why she didn't refer to Saul as her brother seemed far more intimate than my position as interviewer permitted.

"Go on," she said, pointing to the notebook on my lap. "I said you can ask anything and I'll do my best to answer. I'm too old these days for secrets or shame. Ain't nobody gonna judge me 'cept the Lord himself, and he already knows all about me."

I moistened my lips. Dare I? "Why . . . why don't you know if your mother had more children? They would've been your brothers and sisters."

The silence that followed my question stretched long. She closed her eyes, a pained look on her face. My shoulders fell, and I regretted voicing my curiosity, despite her insistence.

She was an elderly lady trying to remember things that happened nearly a century ago. Surely it would be difficult.

I was about to withdraw my inquiry when she looked at me again.

"You want to know why I don't know the answer to that question? It ain't because I can't remember, if that's what you're thinking." She shook her head. "The truth be far more miserable than a forgetful mind. I don't know if Mammy bore other chillens because I wasn't there. I was sold away from her when I was seven years old."

I gasped. "Sold? But you were just a child."

A hardness came to her eyes. "There is lots of things done to children during slavery times that are pure evil. Are you certain you want to hear about them?"

I was not.

Yet I also knew I couldn't leave now.

With far more courage than I possessed, I nodded. "Tell me."

———

THE HALL PLANTATION, TENNESSEE
SPRING 1842

"Frankie? Frankie!"

I heard Mammy's call, but I didn't pay no mind to it and continued chasing the little black-'n'-white kitten around the empty horse stall. I wasn't s'posed to be where I was, and I knew Mammy'd sting my legs with a switch for disobeying her if she caught me. She'd told me to leave the baby kitties be because they's too young to leave their mama yet. But I wanted to play with them, so I'd snuck into the big barn and smuggled one of the tiny creatures to the far stall where no one would find us. The little thing mewled and wouldn't chase my fingers like an older cat. When someone banged the barn door, the kitten startled and ran to hide behind a pile of hay.

I'd just captured him when I heard Mammy approach.

"Frankie! Didn't you hear me a-callin'?" She eyed the animal in my arms. "I told you not to mess with them cats, girl. Why you gotta do the opposite of what I tell you all the time?"

She stomped over and snatched the cat out of my hands. "Get on to the cabin and clean yo'self up. I got some good news to tell ya."

"Yes'm." With a last look at the cat, who hadn't been nearly as much fun to play with as I'd thought, I skipped out of the barn into afternoon sunshine, thankful Mammy'd been more concerned with the kitten and her news than doling out punishment.

The quarter where our cabin was located was just up the cart path from the barn. More slaves lived there than I could count, from cryin' babies to old men with spittle on their chins. Mammy, me, and my three siblings shared our cramped space with five other people, though two were chillens like me. My brother Saul, two years older than me, had already been sent to work in the tobacco fields, where he and dozens of other boys spent their days picking nasty worms off growing plants that had been transplanted from seed beds. If left alone, those big ol' bright-green worms would eat the whole crop in a matter of days, according to the old-timer who liked to tell tales to us chillens at night. Saul and them other boys had to search every single plant, under the leaves and along the stalks, for the critters. If they missed one and the overseer found it, they'd get a lash to their back for every worm he found. Mammy was awful proud Saul hadn't given that mean ol' white man cause to whup him yet.

When I arrived at our cabin, empty since everyone was still in the fields, I found a basin of water and a cloth laid out. Why Mammy needed me to wash in the middle of the day, I couldn't guess. But I'd already disobeyed her about the cat, so I quickly splashed water onto my face and arms, rinsing away any dirt that might have stuck to me in my romping about the plantation.

Mammy always told me I was lucky, because being only six years old, I was free to run and play as much as I desired instead of tromping out to the tobacco and corn fields early in the morning the way most other slaves on the plantation do. Mammy was lucky too, because she worked in the kitchen behind the big house, cooking and cleaning for Master and Mistress Hall. She said when I was old enough, I'd come help her, which suited me just fine.

Mammy soon arrived without the cat. She inspected me from head to toe, frowning at what she saw. "Chile, you got straw stickin' out o' your hair and dirt caked on your feet." As she set about picking hay from my braids, I looked down to my bare toes. Sure enough, they were covered in dried mud, and I remembered the puddle near the horse trough I'd splashed through on my way to fetch the kitten.

"Why I gotta be clean, Mammy? The day ain't over yet."

My childish wisdom made her grin despite her obvious frustration as she wiped my feet with the cloth. "Because you is goin' to the big house."

I stilled. "Am I comin' to cook with you?"

While the idea of being with Mammy all day was a nice one for the future, I wasn't ready to give up my freedom just yet. I had too much fun exploring the plantation and running around with the other children who stayed in the quarter with the old mammy assigned to watch over us.

She met my gaze, excitement shining in her eyes. "You ain't comin' to work in the kitchen. Miz Sadie wants you to be Miss Charlotte's companion."

I blinked, trying to make sense of the new word. Mammy seemed happy about it, so it must be something good. "What's a com-pan-ion?"

"It means you'll be Miss Charlotte's playmate. She be two years older than you, but I told Miz Sadie you's a growed-up girl for just being six. Honey, you'll get to wear a pretty dress and play with Miss Charlotte's dollies and take your meals with her in the nursery."

My ears perked up at this. "And all I gotta do is play with Miss Charlotte?"

Mammy smiled. "Yes'm, chile. I been askin' the Lord to spare you from the fields, and here he done answered my prayers."

A warm feeling started in my belly. Mammy spent many hours on her knees in the evenings talkin' to the Lord after we chillens were abed. I was pleased to know he'd listened.

"If you want me to play with Miss Charlotte, Mammy, I will."

She tugged me into her arms, and I laid my cheek against her. "You gotta be a good girl, Frankie. Miz Sadie don't take no nonsense from her slaves." She gently pushed me away so she could look me in the eye. "You obey everything they tells you, you hear me? I don't want to hear you done otherwise, or I'll take a switch to your backside."

I nodded. "Yes'm."

She grasped my hand. "Come on, now. Miz Sadie wants to look you over. If she like what she see, you'll move into the big house tomorrow."

I pulled to a stop. "I won't live here with you?"

"'Course you'll still live here, but there be times you'll need to sleep on a pallet in Miss Charlotte's room. I'll be right there in the kitchen, so I'll see you more now than when you was down here in the quarter."

Satisfied, I continued with her toward the big white house a short walk from the quarter.

As long as I'd still get to see Mammy, I was happy to become Miss Charlotte's companion.

CHAPTER
SIX

Glancing out the curtained window, I determined it was probably a little past one o'clock. Mrs. Washington had dozed off in the middle of a sentence, and I felt it best to let her sleep. Remembering her life as a slave must be wearing, but she'd insisted on continuing with her story the two times I offered to take a break.

The pages of my notebook had quickly filled up. I'd settled into a nice rhythm of writing down her story word for word, spelling out most but also using some of the shorthand I'd learned in school. I had to admit I found her tale fascinating. I could almost see young Frankie romping through the vast plantation grounds, free and unencumbered by the hardships of slavery. Admittedly, I was surprised to learn her brother had been put to work at such a young age.

After a silent stretch, I set my notebook and pencil on the

floor. The hard-backed chair emitted a loud creak as I rose, but a quick glance revealed Mrs. Washington's chin remained on her chest and her eyes closed.

I needed to relieve myself, so I quietly made my way down a narrow hallway. Two doors opened into neatly kept bedrooms with colorful quilts spread across each bed, but neither held what I sought.

Returning to the sitting room, I confirmed the only other door led to the kitchen. A little desperate now that I'd moved from my sitting position, I bit my fingernail, trying to think through the situation. Obviously Frankie and Jael had access to a bathroom, but where was it? Did it have an outside entrance?

I'd just moved to the front door when I heard a soft sound behind me. Mrs. Washington stirred before her eyes opened, momentary confusion filling them at seeing me there. Then she nodded as if remembering who I was and why I was in her home.

"Guess I went to sleep." She gave a drowsy chuckle. "Not a very good hostess, am I?"

I smiled. "We both needed a break." I gathered my courage. "Would it be possible for me to use your bathroom?"

"'Course, chile, 'course. I shoulda told you first thing how to get to the outhouse."

As she slowly got to her feet, my stomach lurched. Did she truly mean what I thought she did?

"It's out back, just past Jael's garden."

She said it so matter-of-factly, I couldn't do anything but

nod and move in the direction she pointed. A door next to the kitchen sink led to the backyard, which surprisingly held more flowers than the front yard. I'd failed to see them earlier from the window over the sink because the house sat higher than ground level, requiring a set of steep concrete steps. A well-worn dirt path wove its way through the plants to a small vegetable garden that must provide an abundance of fresh produce during the summer months. Now only a handful of green tomatoes remained on the vine, though small holes told me worms had claimed them before Jael could.

Beyond the garden and tucked into a corner of the small yard sat the wooden structure I sought. Never in all my life had I used an outhouse. Mama would be horrified to see me now, but there wasn't any choice in the matter. I couldn't wait three hours until Mr. Norwood arrived to pick me up. The ride home would surely be miserable even if I could contain myself until then.

I cautiously opened the door. The odor that met me caused me to catch and hold my breath, although I desperately wished I'd done so before filling my lungs with rancid air. With as much speed as I could manage, I took care of the deed and hastened from the shed, practically stumbling away as air swooshed from my burning lungs. I couldn't imagine using such a crude facility again, and I made a mental note not to drink anything at my interviews until I'd ascertained the bathroom conditions.

When I approached the house, I glanced up to find Frankie watching me from the kitchen window. Her gaze went from me to the outhouse, then back to me again before she turned and disappeared from my view.

Had she witnessed my desperate flight from the smelly privy? A place she and her caregiver were forced to use every day?

I entered through the back door to find Mrs. Washington seated in her chair again. Two slices of bread spread with purple jam and two hunks of cheese sat on a plate on the low coffee table.

"Thought you might be gettin' hungry." She motioned to the food.

I returned to my seat, hoping the outhouse episode would pass without mention. "Thank you. I didn't think to bring my lunch." I gave a small shrug of apology.

She helped herself to one of the bread slices. "I guessed right then. This is your first interview, ain't it?"

"Yes. And no." I took the other slice while she nibbled on hers. "I had a job at a newspaper for several years, first working in the mail room and then as a secretary, before my boss promoted me to reporter. I interviewed a number of people for news stories, including the governor." I didn't mention that Governor McAlister abruptly ended the interview when he learned who my father was. Dad, a staunch and vocal Republican, had laid blame for the stock market crash solely at the feet of the Democrats before he disappeared into his drunken exile. Although McAlister wasn't governor at the time, he didn't want anything to do with a Leland and demanded George send someone else to finish the interview.

"Well now, that's somethin' to be proud of."

We ate in silence. I noticed a glass of water on the table beside my chair. Although I could have used some to wash down my lunch, I left it where it sat. I didn't want to visit the outhouse again.

Whether or not Mrs. Washington took notice of my ignored water, she drank her fill. When she settled back against the chair, she watched me with a look that could only be described as knowing. Finally she spoke.

"I'd venture to guess you ain't never used an outdoor privy before today."

I stopped chewing the bite of cheese I'd just taken, wondering how she'd guessed. Swallowing the lump, I shook my head. There was no reason to lie. "No, ma'am."

After a moment, she chuckled. "Your face gives away too much information. I seen you come outta that outhouse like you was on fire." She chuckled again, then shrugged. "We always talked 'bout having an indoor bathing room added on, but the money seemed needed for something more important every time. After all these years it don't make any sense to worry over one now. I'll let whoever lives here after I'm gone bother with it."

I couldn't think of anything more important than the sanitary convenience of an indoor lavatory, so I simply nodded.

She grew somber. "I'd have given anything for use of an outhouse the day I went to be Miss Charlotte's companion."

That was my cue to set aside our simple repast and return to the interview. I retrieved my notebook and pencil, wondering what she meant as I began jotting down her words.

"Yes'm." She stared off into the distance as though remembering that long-ago day, massaging her deformed hand. "One trip to the outhouse woulda saved me a lifetime of pain and suffering."

———

"Hold still, Frankie."

Aunt Liza, a woman of no relation to me, gave my shoulders a firm shake to stop my fidgeting while she attempted to poke pins into the hem of one of Miss Charlotte's cast-off dresses. The smooth, soft, green material with tiny white dots felt wonderful against my skin after wearing coarse cotton all my life, but the lace around the neck and cuffs itched something fierce.

"I can't help it." I yanked again at the stiff fabric to keep it from irritating me.

Aunt Liza huffed and glared at Mammy where she sat peeling potatoes. "Lucindia." Aunt Liza's scowl landed on me again even as she spoke to Mammy. "This girl ain't got no understandin' of manners. She done talked back to me three times already, and I ain't even got this dress half finished." She brought her nose up close to mine. "You stand still or I'll take a switch to you."

Mammy sent me a look that told me she'd take a switch to me too if I didn't behave.

The kitchen was full of wonderful aromas, and my

stomach reminded us all I hadn't eaten anything since early that morning. Mammy brought me to the big house before the sun came up, since Miz Sadie had approved of me the day before. I had yet to play with Miss Charlotte, what with all the instructions I was given of things to do and not do, say and not say, and the fitting of two dresses and cotton pantalets.

House slaves came and went while I stood as still as I could. Finally Aunt Liza heaved a satisfied sigh. She lifted the dress over my head, leaving me bare from the waist up. I giggled seeing the new snowy-white pantalets against my dark skin, the funny undergarment feeling as strange as it looked.

"I'll have this hem done in no time, so don't go nowhere." The woman made her way to a chair in the corner to sew the garment while I hopped down from the stool she'd stood me on. Mammy had finished the potatoes and was now busy washing a stack of pots and pans.

"I'm hungry." I eyed two large apple pies cooling on the counter. I hoped I would get more sweets now that I was Miss Charlotte's companion. Mammy sometimes brought us treats when there was a big shindig at the plantation, but I had to share them with Saul and the little ones.

Mammy dried her hands on her apron. "You can have a slice of bread and some milk. That should keep you till you eat your supper with Miss Charlotte. She takes her meals in the nursery before we serve the grown folks. Master Burton used to, but he nearly grown now, so he joins them in the dining room."

While I looked forward to eating with Miss Charlotte, I dearly wanted a piece of pie now.

Mammy settled me at the worktable with my meal and returned to her task. I was glad she'd poured me a large mug of milk since I usually only got a small cup in the quarter. The old mammy there always gave the babies more than us older kids.

Aunt Liza finished sewing at the same time I swallowed my last gulp of milk. She hustled over and settled the dress on me, tugging here and there until she was satisfied. She fastened the row of buttons down the front, then stood back to examine me.

"Well, now, don't you look purty." Her brief smile vanished as fast as it had appeared, and she leaned toward me. "Don't you let this dress get soiled, you hear?"

Mammy came over and knelt in front of me. Her eyes were shiny, and I wondered why she'd get all teary over a dress. She fussed and fiddled with my hair, the itchy collar, and finally deemed me presentable.

"You be a good girl, Frankie." She gave me a stern look. "Do everything they tells you, even if you don't like it."

I nodded. Then I twirled, letting the skirt fly out around me. Mammy laughed, and even Aunt Liza grinned.

"Come on, chile." Liza took me by the hand and led me out of the kitchen, a separate building from the big house, through a door I'd never entered. "Miz Sadie be in the parlor."

My inspection by the mistress of the plantation yesterday had taken place in the kitchen, so my excitement nearly bubbled over as I moved through the big house, eyes wide, and my whole self full of wonderment. I vaguely remembered seeing the grand rooms and pretty furnishings at Christmastime when Mammy and us chillens were brought in to receive sweets and new clothes. Master and Mistress were good to give all their people something nice to celebrate the day the Lord was born, or so Mammy said. But today I wasn't here for only a few treasured minutes. I would be allowed to walk freely through the grand house with Miss Charlotte, playing in areas I'd only heard about from Mammy.

Aunt Liza led me into a room with pale-blue walls and soft carpet. Pretty furnishings and doodads filled the space, but I remembered not to touch anything. A large painting of an old man stared down at me from above the fireplace mantel as we came forward. I wanted to stick my tongue out at him, but I knew Aunt Liza would box my ears.

"Here she is, Miz Sadie." Aunt Liza nudged me forward to stand in front of our mistress.

Miz Sadie sat on a bright-red cushioned bench. She seemed wider than she had yesterday, but maybe that was because she was sitting down, with her voluminous skirt spread around her. Her puffy face still reminded me of a hoot owl, but I did admire her yellow hair and blue eyes, mainly because they were so different from our folks down in the quarter.

"My goodness, she looks like a different child."

"Yes'm," Aunt Liza said, a hint of pleasure in her voice.

I stood silent while they discussed the virtues of the dress, with Aunt Liza showing off the neat stitches she'd recently applied to the hem. Unfortunately, the shoes Miss Charlotte had outgrown did not fit despite her being two years older than me. Miz Sadie frowned at this information, declaring it improper for me to traipse about the house barefoot. Aunt Liza assured her they would locate a pair of shoes for me posthaste.

"Have you instructed her on proper behavior?" Miz Sadie studied me with narrowed eyes, and I felt like one of Saul's worms on a tobacco plant.

Aunt Liza commenced telling the tale of my instruction, declaring me quick to learn and obedient to all I was asked to do. It surprised me to hear her brag on me, since she'd told Mammy I was ill-mannered.

The minutes dragged on while the two women conversed. I tried to remain as still as I could, but the scratchy lace aimed to vex me something awful. Aunt Liza seemed to forget about me and changed the conversation to supper plans, wondering if Miz Sadie would prefer roasted chicken or spiced beef.

In the middle of this homey conversation, Master Hall arrived with Master Burton and Miss Charlotte. Miss Charlotte, the spitting image of her mama, wore a dress similar to the one I had on, and I wondered if she had itching issues too. She sent me a small smile when our eyes met.

"There's my darling." Miz Sadie motioned Charlotte to her while Burton remained next to his father. Although I'd seen him from time to time crossing the yard or when he went riding, viewing his lanky frame and fine clothes up close told me he was no longer a little boy. Mammy said he was four years older than Charlotte, but he looked near grown standing next to his pappy.

Miz Sadie petted Charlotte, telling her what a special girl she was and how I would help her with her clothes and her hair and play games with her.

My legs grew tired from standing so still. A raw spot where the lace met my skin began to hurt, but worst of all I had a growing need to visit the outhouse.

I tried to get Aunt Liza's attention, but she ignored me and kept her gaze on Master Hall as he spoke about the draft in the fireplace that needed attention. When I angled my head ever so slightly in order to catch her eye, she slowly moved her hand behind my back and gave me a sharp pinch between my shoulder blades.

I jerked, though I didn't make a sound.

No matter. Miz Sadie took notice. "Is something wrong, Frances?"

I couldn't tell her Aunt Liza pinched me, so I shook my head. I did wonder, however, why she called me Frances. "My name is Frankie," I offered, feeling certain she would want to address me correctly.

I heard Aunt Liza's soft intake of air, and her body went rigid beside me.

Master Hall chuckled, but Miz Sadie didn't look pleased. "You will not use that name while you're in this house, do you understand? You are Frances. Frankie is a boy's name."

I nodded, but I didn't truly understand. Frankie was my name and I was a girl. Frances was also my grandmother's name, but she died when I was a baby. I didn't want people calling me by a dead person's name.

Master Hall settled into a chair by the window. Aunt Liza moved to pour him a drink from a pretty glass bottle on a table with several other pretty bottles. She was rather stingy with whatever it was, since she only filled his glass halfway.

Seeing that golden liquid reminded me of my need to visit the outhouse.

I tried not to think about it because thinking about it made it worse.

I clamped my knees together.

When Aunt Liza returned to my side, she eyed me, shaking her head when I pointed toward the door.

Miz Sadie reminded Aunt Liza they would have guests the following evening, and the two women discussed the preparations needed.

As the conversation lengthened, so grew my need for the outhouse. It wasn't long before I felt the tiniest trickle of warmth run down my leg into my new pantalets. I pressed my thighs together tighter and held my breath.

But it was too late.

Before I could keep it from happening, my bladder released itself on the parlor carpet.

My whimper drew Aunt Liza's attention.

"Oh, lawsy!" She snatched me away from the puddle and shoved me into the corner where the carpet ended at wood flooring.

Miz Sadie shrieked, rising to her feet to jerk Charlotte away from the offensive wet stain.

I cowered in the corner, unsure what to do. I was too scared to cry, although tears sometimes worked to ease Mammy's anger when I'd misbehaved. But something told me this offense was far worse than anything I'd ever been guilty of in the past.

Aunt Liza blotted the mess with the apron she'd removed from her thick waist. I wondered if I should volunteer to help but decided it was best to remain silent.

"Come here, Frances."

Miz Sadie's hard voice broke into my racing thoughts. She'd moved to stand near the fireplace, her hoot-owl face red with anger.

Wet pantalets stuck to my legs as I slowly walked toward her. I kept my eyes downcast so she'd know how sorry I was. When I stopped a short distance from her, she reached for the poker leaning against the marble of the fireplace.

"I will teach you to never do such a dreadful thing again." She lifted the poker and brought it down on my head before I could react.

I screamed. When I saw her raise the poker again, I put my hand up as a shield. The metal slammed into my fingers. Unimaginable pain shot up my arm, and I screamed again.

"Stop this, Sadie."

Master Hall took the poker from his wife, a troubled look on his face when he glanced at me. Charlotte stared with wide, frightened eyes, but Burton, who'd moved to where he could see better, simply crossed his arms and watched.

My body began to tremble and hot tears rolled down my cheeks. I clutched my injured hand to my chest, confused. I'd never before felt such pain, such fear. I wanted to run to the kitchen and tell Mammy what Miz Sadie done, but I couldn't move.

Aunt Liza appeared at my side. "Tell Mistress Hall you sorry for all this trouble."

I stared up at her. I'd just been struck with a fireplace poker, yet she wanted *me* to apologize?

"Go on. Tell her."

My gaze shifted to Miz Sadie. Hard, cold eyes bored into me. "I sorry, Mistress Hall," I whispered, fresh tears spilling from my eyes, not from pain but from unfairness.

"See there, the girl didn't mean to do it." Master Hall patted his wife on the arm.

"Get her out of my sight. I don't want this revolting creature anywhere near Charlotte."

I didn't know what *revolting* meant, but I knew Mammy'd be disappointed I wasn't to be Miss Charlotte's companion. I was glad though. I wouldn't want to be in this house with Miz Sadie. I sniffled, ready to be away from this place and these people. My hand hurt terribly, as did my head. All I wanted was Mammy's arms around me, soothing me and telling me it wasn't my fault.

"Now, now, there's no need for it to come to that. It was

an accident. She's sorry and won't ever do it again. Isn't that right, Frances?" Master Hall looked at me.

I didn't want to be Miss Charlotte's companion, but I was afraid he might turn the poker on me if I didn't agree.

"Yes'm, Master Hall."

He gave a satisfied nod, then looked to Aunt Liza. "Tell Lucindia to take her on home, but bring her back in the morning."

Aunt Liza escorted me from the parlor. As soon as I'd cleared the threshold, I took off running toward the kitchen, my poor hand throbbing. Mammy had her fingers deep in a big ball of dough, but that didn't stop me from charging to her, crying and blubbering about the mistreatment I'd received. I wrapped my uninjured arm around her hips and clung to her as I'd never done before.

"Good gracious, chile, what be wrong?"

I felt her lift her apron above my head, most likely to wipe the dough from her hands.

"She done made water on the Halls' parlor carpet." Aunt Liza's voice thundered from the doorway behind me. "Miz Sadie smacked her with the poker for it."

"Oh, Lord," Mammy breathed, and I felt her body sag. "What you gone an' done, chile?"

I looked up through my tears. "I don't wanna ever come back here. Miz Sadie a devil woman."

Mammy gasped, as did Aunt Liza. "Hush, chile." Her worry-filled gaze searched the spacious kitchen. The other household slaves must have been busy elsewhere because we were the only three occupants in the room. "You can't never say anythin' like that 'bout Miz Sadie. She mistress of this here plantation and that be all you gotta know."

Why was Mammy angry with me instead of being angry with Miz Sadie?

I held out my pitiful, hurting hand. "Look what she done."

Blood oozed from a long split in the skin across my knuckles, and two of my fingers pointed in a different direction than the others.

Mammy stared at my hand, then met Aunt Liza's gaze. "That woman ain't got no leave to do this to a child. She only six years old."

Aunt Liza came over. She looked at my hand and some of the bluster seemed to seep out of her. She shook her head. "I'll get a rag to wrap it in." And off she went.

Mammy knelt beside me and used her apron to carefully dab at blood from the wound in my head. "I sorry she hurt you, Frankie girl. I so, so sorry." Her arms went around me, tucking me safely against her warm body.

I sniffled, appeased that Mammy understood. "She won't let me be Frankie, neither. Says I has to be Frances if I'm gonna play with Charlotte." I pulled away so I could look into Mammy's dark-brown eyes. "I don't want to play with her. I want to stay in the quarter."

Aunt Liza returned just then with a long strip of cloth for my hand. "Master Hall say she gotta come back tomorrow. Miz Sadie ain't happy 'bout it."

Mammy and Aunt Liza exchanged a look I didn't understand.

I shook my head. "I don't wanna ever come here again. I'll help Saul pick worms."

Tears sprang to Mammy's eyes. She took me by the shoulders and gave me a little shake. "You ain't got no choice, Frankie. We is slaves. If Master Hall says you gotta play with Miss Charlotte, then you has to obey. Same as me. Same as Liza. Same as Saul. Ain't none of us gets to choose. We just gotta obey so's things goes well for us." Her brow tugged as her gaze roamed over my face. "Do you understand what I's tellin' you?"

I did, but I didn't like it. "You's sayin' I gotta play with Charlotte."

"*Miss* Charlotte." Mammy's hard tone hurt my feelings.

"Miss Charlotte," I repeated, angry tears dripping from my lashes.

Aunt Liza wrapped my hand while I screamed in pain. Mammy sat watching, tears streaming down her cheeks too. She carried me back to the quarter and tucked me into the big bed I shared with her and my siblings.

Her touch on my forehead was cool as she smoothed my wild hair. "I know you don't understand all this, Frankie. All you gotta know is that Master and Mistress be our owners, and we has to do everything they tells us to do, whether we like it or not."

"Why, Mammy? Why can't we just leave here?" My hand and head throbbed, and I wanted to get as far away from the Halls as I could.

Her sad eyes met mine. "One day you'll understand, and then you'll know why I ask God ev'ry night for freedom."

I watched Mammy leave the cabin, her slim shoulders slumped. I cried until I was exhausted, angry with everyone. Why was Miz Sadie allowed to hurt me and not be the one who was wrong? Would she beat me again tomorrow when I returned to the big house? Why couldn't Mammy and us chillens leave here and find us a better mistress, a nicer one?

When I finally quieted, with my throbbing hand tucked against my heart, I felt something take hold inside me. Like a big ol' log on a cook fire, it fed my bitterness and anger. I didn't know what to call it, but the way it made me feel, I guessed it was the opposite of what Mammy taught me about love. She wouldn't be happy I had this new sensation swirling around inside me like a twister, but I couldn't help it. It was there, and I liked it.

I knew one thing for certain.

No one could take it away from me. Not even that devil woman Miz Sadie.

CHAPTER
SEVEN

Alden Norwood arrived at Frankie's house promptly at four o'clock, bringing an end to my first day as an FWP interviewer. I had more than a dozen pages filled, back and front, with Frankie's story, yet she'd barely begun telling about her life as a slave. She asked if I wanted to return the following day, and I eagerly accepted the invitation.

"How did it go?" he inquired after we'd been on the road several silent minutes.

I shifted my attention from the view of downtown traffic to him. I'd been thinking about Frankie's maimed hand and how a simple trip to the outhouse that day would have saved her from a lifetime of misery. I couldn't fathom how someone could beat a six-year-old child with a fireplace poker, crippling her for the rest of her life, because of an accident.

Yet discussing my feelings with Mr. Norwood was out of

the question. He didn't think me qualified for the job in the first place. "Fine," I simply said.

He glanced at me, then back to the road. A long minute passed before he heaved a sigh. "All right, Miss Leland. I apologize for misjudging the financial circumstances of your situation and your need to work for the FWP. You were correct in saying I don't know anything about you or your family. I'm sorry I made assumptions this morning."

Another glance, as if he was waiting for me to respond. He seemed sincere, and it pleased me that he'd seen the need for an apology. "Thank you, Mr. Norwood."

His full lips formed an easy grin. "Now that we have *that* behind us . . . how did it go today? Were you able to coax her into telling you much?"

I smiled, glad to have the morning's unpleasantness over and done. Maybe he wasn't as patronizing as he'd seemed. "I'd say so. I have thirteen pages of notes, and I told her I'd come back tomorrow to finish the interview."

"Thirteen pages? What else could she possibly tell you that she hasn't already?"

His astonishment concerned me. "How many pages do you usually end up with when you're finished with your interviews?"

"Five, maybe six. It depends on the interviewee, but most answer all the questions within a couple hours."

I worried my bottom lip. I'd been with Frankie the entire day, yet I wasn't anywhere near the end of our interview. I'd given up reading questions after the first few and let her tell her story in her own way, but maybe tomorrow I should stick with the list in order to speed things up.

"How was your day?" I asked, changing the subject. I didn't want word to get back to Mr. Carlson that my first interview wasn't keeping to the schedule. The less I said to Mr. Norwood, the better.

He told about the elderly couple he'd interviewed—a ninety-two-year-old gentleman and his eighty-eight-year-old wife who met after freedom. The man had worked in a tobacco factory since he was a young boy, but she'd been a field slave. As Mr. Norwood shared interesting details about the couple's lives, my mind drifted back to Frankie, wondering how Miz Sadie treated her the next day. Admittedly, I was anxious to get back to the little yellow house in Hell's Half Acre to hear more.

When we arrived at my house, I glanced at the home I'd lived in most of my life. In recent years, repairs to the porch and roof had been neglected, and the yard was more weeds than anything else. But it was still a grand and beautiful place, even if the family who occupied it no longer was.

"Thank you for the ride." I gathered my things into one hand so I could open the door with the other. "Same time tomorrow?"

He nodded. "But remember, you have a lot of other inter-viewees assigned to you. You'll need to finish up with Mrs. Washington and move on."

The reminder and the superior tone he used grated. So much for thinking we might become friends. "I'm sure I can manage my own schedule, Mr. Norwood. Good night." I slid from the car and slammed the door harder than I'd intended. When I glanced back, he pushed his hat back high on his forehead, a look of surprise on his face.

I'd just opened the front door when I heard his car back down the driveway and leave. Oh, the man could rile me! How would I ever put up with him for all the weeks it would take to complete the interviews?

"Rena, is that you?"

Mama came from the kitchen, wiping her hands on a dish towel. I'd hoped to sneak into the house and get to my bedroom without anyone seeing me. My head was so full, I needed time to process the day and all that had happened before Mama started with her questions.

"Hi, Mama." I put my things on the hall table and removed my hat. "You're home early."

She sighed. "Mr. Watkins is ill again, so Mrs. Watkins closed the shop at noon. As though he isn't a grown man who can do without her and get his own soup."

I nodded, but the irritation she expressed for her employer held irony. Wasn't she herself the wife of a grown man who spent his days sleeping off the previous night's drinking binge, wallowing in his pathetic life and expecting her to take care of him?

"How did your interviews go?"

"Good." I moved toward the stairs, hoping she'd take the hint and leave her questions for later. "I need to go over my notes while it's all fresh in my mind."

I'd nearly made it to the landing and out of her sight when she called, "Who did you interview? Anyone we know?"

I stood still, weighing how to proceed. I had yet to formulate an answer for that question. An answer that would prevent an argument, yelling, and who knew what else.

On one hand, it was quite ridiculous that I felt a need to hide the true nature of my job with the FWP from my mother. It wasn't that I was afraid of her reaction, nor was I ashamed of what I was doing. After hearing only one day of Frankie's heart-wrenching tales, I knew the project had merit.

Yet I also knew Mama would not approve of my going to Hell's Half Acre to spend time with former slaves. Even though she would never again be a member of Nashville's high society, holding on to small things from our past kept her sane. And maintaining a superior position over the less fortunate in the city was something I was certain she was not ready to relinquish.

"No one you'd know." I forced my voice to remain normal. "She's an elderly woman. I'm to record the stories of her life for a collection of historical writings."

I didn't wait for Mama's reply and nearly flew up the remaining stairs. At my room, I closed the door with a click loud enough for her to hear but not so loud she would grow suspicious. With my ear pressed to the wood, I was satisfied she hadn't followed me in order to gain more information.

The desk near the window held my Underwood typewriter, a gift from my parents before the crash. Ever since the

Monday Mr. Armistead summoned me into his office to tell me I was unemployed, it had sat unused.

I took a blank sheet of paper from the desk drawer and rolled it onto the cylinder, realizing how much I'd missed doing this simple task on a regular basis. Words had been such a big part of my life, I wondered how I'd survived six months without writing anything.

Two hours later Mama called up the stairs to tell me supper was ready. Now that I was working again, we would share the responsibility of getting the evening meal on the table. I did most of the cooking after I lost my job at the newspaper, so it was nice to have supper ready after a long day of work.

I stopped at the bathroom down the hall to wash my hands. Baby-blue tiles lined the walls and floor. A deep tub sat beneath the high window, and I looked forward to a long soak after supper. Glancing at the commode, I couldn't help but remember the smelly outhouse in Frankie's backyard.

As I stared at the gleaming white porcelain, a sense of guilt washed over me. Guilt for what, I wasn't sure, but I recognized the uneasiness for what it was.

What would it be like to live in such poverty you didn't have use of an indoor bathroom, something I'd taken for granted my entire life?

I looked back to my reflection in the mirror over the sink. Despite the hardships of the past seven years, I still saw what I'd always seen: a well-brought-up young woman. I didn't sport the latest hairstyles or fashions as I once had, and my dreams of college and career were gone, but my most basic needs had always been met. We remained in our comfortable home and had food on the table, which was more than thousands of people could say. I'd seen pictures of soup and bread lines in the papers and read stories of the dust bowl in the West. People were suffering, and an end to it all seemed far in the distance.

Mama was sitting at the table when I arrived in the dining room. A meat loaf with its edges burnt graced the center, flanked by a bowl of lumpy mashed potatoes and one of green peas, my least favorite vegetable. Only yesterday I might have grumbled over the imperfect meal, but after my bathroom musings, I felt a strange sense of gratitude well up from a place deep inside I didn't know existed until this very moment.

"Supper looks good." I took my seat and laid a napkin in my lap.

A look of wonder settled on Mama's face when I glanced her way. "Thank you, Rena. I hope the meat loaf isn't too done."

The evidence said it was, but I'd ruined my share of meals too.

We loaded our plates and ate in silence. I tried to think of a topic of conversation to initiate in order to avoid more questions regarding Frankie. One day soon I'd tell Mama the truth, but for now I wanted to keep the secret to myself.

"Mary said she and the children might drop by tomorrow evening." Mama forked a bite of potatoes. "Homer is working the late shift these days, so she doesn't have to get his supper."

"At least he hasn't gotten himself fired from this job." *Yet,* I added silently.

I held little faith my good-for-nothing brother-in-law would keep this job any longer than he'd kept the string of others. Mary and the kids avoided homelessness and starvation because Homer's daddy paid their bills.

Mama sighed. "I saw Peggy Denny at the market today. She couldn't wait to inform me that Roy and his new wife bought a house in Washington, DC."

Roy Staton, Mary's old beau.

Turns out Roy actually made something of himself after college. Through his family's connections he'd found a job in the governor's office and became acquainted with Senator Hull. When President Roosevelt asked Hull to be his secretary of state, Hull took Roy to Washington with him to work in his office. Not long afterward, Mrs. Denny, one of Mama's old friends and a woman who thrived on gossip, showed up at our door to see how Mama was doing with *the news.* Mama didn't know what she was talking about, and Mrs. Denny practically oozed with satisfaction when she announced—with a somber face, of course—that Roy was engaged to the daughter of a senator from Texas.

"If Roy had loved Mary, he wouldn't've broken up with her, no matter what his daddy said. There's no use wishing things had turned out differently." I shrugged. "I hope he and his wife live happily ever after, but I'm tired of hearing about him."

Truth was, I was tired of hearing about anything concerning the life we used to live. The past could not be changed, no matter how much Mama wished it so. Grandma was right. My new job with the FWP was exactly the thing I needed to help me move forward.

"When these interviews are finished, I might see if I can get more assignments with the Works Progress Administration. Mr. Carlson said the WPA has a number of projects here in Nashville." I looked at Mama. "Did you know the new post office is being built by people employed by the WPA? They're even restoring an old Civil War fort on Saint Cloud Hill. It's all part of Roosevelt's New Deal legislation."

She frowned. "I hope you won't have to work for the government for long, Rena. Doing interviews is fine until you find something else, but the New Deal programs are for the destitute. Those poor wretches we see on the streets, begging for money. I wouldn't want folks to get the wrong impression about why you're working for the government."

She sounded like Mr. Norwood. I gave a humorless laugh. "The only reason we aren't standing next to those poor wretches is because of Grandma Lorena's generosity. If not for her, we'd be homeless."

"I work very hard, young lady." Indignation flashed across her face. "Mother is helping us, yes, but I deserve some credit too."

I held back a sigh. She never liked to discuss Grandma's financial assistance. "I know you do, Mama, but you know as well as I do we would've had to sell the house long ago if Grandma hadn't taken over the mortgage payments."

Silence hung heavy in the room, as it always did when Mama and I discussed finances.

She pushed her potatoes around her plate before she sent an accusing glance my way. "Why do you always take her side against me?"

"What?" Where did that question come from?

"Mother can do no wrong in your eyes, and I can't do anything right."

I stared at her, wondering how the conversation had veered off so drastically. Mama and her mama didn't get along well. They didn't argue and fight; they simply avoided one another. I saw Grandma Lorena far more than Mama did despite us living just down the street, which caused jealousy to rise in my mother. Admittedly, it was far easier to talk to Grandma, simply because she let me share my thoughts and ideas and didn't pass judgment the way my mother did.

Clearly, though, Mama felt slighted, which was never my intention.

"Mama, I don't mean to make you feel like I don't appreciate everything you do. I know you work hard at the shop." She sniffled, a good sign. It usually meant mollification was near. "But I also appreciate everything Grandma does for us. I love you both."

She gave a small nod. "Thank you, Rena." Her gaze drifted to the study and the door that stayed closed most of the time. "I just wish things were different."

We finished our meal in silence after that, both lost in

thoughts better left unspoken. I volunteered to wash the dishes since Mama had cooked. She disappeared upstairs, and I knew I wouldn't see her again until morning.

As I cleaned things up, I thought back to Frankie's tiny kitchen, where she'd made my tea, her gnarled hand never slowing her down. I longed to run down the street and tell Grandma Lorena all about Frankie, but after the dinner conversation and Mama's hurt feelings, I felt it would be a betrayal of sorts.

The setting sun gave the house a gloomy feel as I made my way to my room. I returned to my Underwood and Frankie's story. Typing the words she'd spoken that day brought images to my mind I'd never experienced before. A Negro child beaten and bleeding. Slaves by the dozens laboring in the fields, some as young as Frankie's brother Saul.

I couldn't recall ever hearing such things in school when the topic of slavery was discussed. People who owned large parcels of land prior to the Civil War required vast numbers of laborers, the teacher said. Slaves had been brought over from Africa for that purpose. It never occurred to me to question whether they'd been mistreated or what a slave had to endure. Their existence was simply part of our country's history.

I continued typing.

Tears sprang to Mammy's eyes. She took me by the shoulders and gave me a little shake. "You ain't got no choice, Frankie. We is slaves."

I stared at the words.

No choice. Slaves.

They echoed through my mind, as though I heard Frankie's mammy's voice myself, growing louder and louder, until understanding began to dawn, filling every inch of my being.

"She was owned by someone," I whispered, shocked by the revulsion that swept over me at the very thought of such a thing. As I stared at the words I'd just typed, it suddenly seemed so absurd that the truth of slavery had evaded me for twenty-two years. I knew the definition of bondage, but until this moment I'd never put a face to it. I'd never met anyone who'd experienced it firsthand. "Frankie was *owned*," I repeated.

The reality of what that truly meant for thousands upon thousands of people overwhelmed me.

I sat back in my chair, unable to continue.

CHAPTER
EIGHT

Frankie was waiting for me when I arrived the next day.

"Mornin'." She stood on the porch in a faded-green dress and house slippers. When she waved to Mr. Norwood, I turned and saw him return the gesture. Our eyes met briefly before he drove off. He'd been quiet on the drive into town, which was fine with me. It allowed me to gather my thoughts and prepare the questions that would get the interview back on track. But now I wondered if he'd thought me rude.

I sighed. I couldn't worry about Mr. Norwood. I had a job to do.

"I wasn't sure you'd be back," Frankie said matter-of-factly. "Thought I mighta scared you off."

I faced her, surprised by her doubt. "You haven't finished your story."

She studied me a long moment before giving a slight nod. "Come on in. I'll get us some coffee fore we get started."

I followed her into the cozy home and deposited my purse, notepads, and a bologna sandwich wrapped in paper on the chair I'd occupied the previous day. The aroma of freshly baked bread filled my senses. "Oh, my, something smells wonderful."

We continued to the kitchen, where two loaves of bread sat cooling on the table.

"Jael is a fine cook, but she can't bake bread. She'd rather buy it at the market, but I don't like that store-bought mess. Tastes like cardboard to me."

I remembered Dovie's homemade rolls, and my mouth watered. "When I was growing up, our cook made the most delicious yeast rolls. They'd practically melt in your mouth."

"Baking bread ain't hard, but it takes patience to get it right. Young people these days don't slow down long enough to do nothin'. Always lookin' for the easy way." She moved to the stove. "Coffee?"

I nodded. "Please."

She poured two cups of steaming brew from a blue enamel pot on the stove and added a sugar cube to each after we discovered we both liked it sweet but without cream.

We took our drinks to the living room and settled in. I assumed she'd want to get right to her tale, but she didn't seem in a hurry to talk about the past and instead asked me about my family, a subject I wasn't too keen to delve into.

"Mama works as a seamstress. I have an older sister who's married and has three children." I paused, wondering what I could say about Dad that didn't divulge my true feelings of bitterness and disgust. "My father lost his business in the stock market crash. He hasn't found a new job yet."

Frankie sipped her coffee while I gave the brief answer. "It be hard times, for sure. I 'spect they appreciate you taking this job with the . . . What's it called? The Federal Writers' Progress?"

I held back a grin. "The Federal Writers' Project. It's part of the Works Progress Administration."

"Yes, I remember now. Has something to do with the president, though I don't see why he'd pay good money to have you come out and listen to my ol' stories." She shrugged and finished her coffee. "But," she said as she put her empty cup on the low table that separated us, "if he wants to, ain't gonna argue with that. You ready to start?"

I hurried to get myself organized, shuffling notes and wondering if I should press the issue of returning to the questions or simply let her continue the tale as she saw fit.

"Last night after you left, I got to thinkin' that maybe I shouldn't tell you 'bout all the ugly things I seen during slavery times."

My hands stilled, and I met her eyes.

"I got lots of stories that ain't as hard to hear as them like I told you yesterday. There was some good times, too, and funny things that happened. I thought maybe that's what I should tell you today instead of goin' back to them dark days."

We sat in silence with our own thoughts for a long moment. A rooster crowed somewhere in the neighborhood.

I knew it must be difficult for her to recall the painful past, and I certainly would never presume to insist she continue with what we began yesterday. But the reporter in me also believed her story—the true story—needed to be told. Especially after the eye-opening revelations I'd experienced last evening.

"Mrs. Washington." I hesitated, trying to find the right words. "I haven't been around very many black people, as you correctly guessed yesterday. Our housekeeper, Dovie, is the only one I've ever known, really." I paused. "People like me, like my family, we don't know much about what slaves experienced. I've never heard of children being beaten with no one held accountable, or being forced into labor at the age of seven. Even though slavery isn't legal anymore, I believe it's important to remember the past as it truly was, not as we wish it to be."

I didn't know if my speech made any sense, but I meant every word. In the twenty-four hours I'd known this woman, her life's story had touched me in a way I had not expected.

Another long moment passed before she nodded. "I 'spect you're right. We who lived through it don't talk 'bout it much. Times is still hard, but it ain't nothin' like back when folks could own you without you havin' a say. We was no more than a dog to some masters. Fact is, we wasn't treated as good as folks treat a dog these days."

She gave a slow nod. "I'll give you what you come for. The truth about slavery times."

With that settled, we both seemed to mentally prepare

ourselves. She to go back in time to hard, painful memories, and me to listen, learn, and perhaps come away with a better understanding of the cruelties and injustices some people experienced at the hands of others simply because of the color of their skin.

⸻

Despite my tears, screams, and protests, Mammy dragged me up to the big house the day after Miz Sadie beat me. My hand throbbed and my head ached, but Mammy said there wasn't nothin' to be done. I'd be whipped by the overseer if I didn't obey, and I'd seen enough slaves suffer that punishment to know I didn't want to ever experience it.

Aunt Liza met us in the kitchen. She looked at my bandaged hand, shook her head, and gently guided me toward the walkway to the main house. "Come on, chile. I take you on up to the nursery. Miz Sadie don't get outta her bed for another hour. We'll get you settled in with Miss Charlotte so things be nice an' peaceful-like when Mistress gets up."

With one last look at Mammy, who stood with her fist pressed against her lips and a sheen of tears in her eyes, I allowed Aunt Liza to lead me through the house and up a back stairway I'd never seen before. The only room on the third floor, the nursery was painted a pale shade of yellow with white, lacy curtains dancing in a gentle breeze coming through open windows. A child-size table occupied the center of the room, set with tiny dishes and cups. Three dollies sat in small chairs as though waiting for breakfast to be served.

Giggles came from an open doorway across from us. A moment later golden curls poked out, and I saw Charlotte peek around the doorframe. When Aunt Liza motioned to her, the girl came forward.

"Miss Charlotte, lookee who come to play dollies with you."

Charlotte's blue eyes were big and filled with curiosity. Her gaze strayed to my injured hand, and the same troubled look I'd seen on Master Hall's face after Miz Sadie hit me now appeared on Charlotte's. I found a measure of hope in it.

"You two girls stay put while I get your breakfast." Aunt Liza gave me a stern look. "Mind your manners, *Frances*."

I watched her exit the room with mixed feelings. I didn't want to be here, and I certainly didn't want to see Miz Sadie again. Yet excitement at being in Charlotte's nursery swirled through me too.

The bright space teemed with all manner of interesting toys and pretty things. I'd never seen anything like it, and I couldn't decide what to play with first.

"Does it hurt?"

Her quiet voice startled me. I turned to find Charlotte staring at me. She pointed to my hand when I didn't answer right away.

I shrugged, not certain if I should answer honestly or not.

"Mama shouldn't've hit you." She glanced at the door Aunt Liza had just disappeared through, then took a step closer to me. "I used to have accidents when I was little too."

Her lowered voice told me this bit of information was something only for me to know. While I appreciated her attempt to make me feel better, I didn't want her or anyone to think I wet myself all the time.

"I'm a big girl. Aunt Liza wouldn't let me use the outhouse yesterday."

Charlotte's face said she didn't believe me, but she let it pass. "Do you want to see my dollies?"

I did. I followed her to the table, where she picked up a beautiful doll with a painted-on face. Its dress looked similar to the ones Charlotte and I wore. It even had on snowy-white pantalets like those I'd soiled yesterday. Mammy washed them out, but they hadn't dried overnight. I wasn't wearing anything beneath my dress, and I hoped Miz Sadie didn't look to see if I had them on, otherwise she might beat me again.

"This is Mae. Papa bought her in Atlanta. He said she reminded him of me." She fussed with Mae's golden curls before returning the doll to her chair.

She picked up each of the other two dollies and told me their names, but she didn't offer to let me hold one. My fingers fairly itched to know what Mae's hair felt like, yet I knew Aunt Liza and Mammy wouldn't want me to touch anything unless I'd been given permission.

Charlotte moved through the sunny room pointing out painted blocks, carved wooden animals, and a miniature house filled with tiny furniture. She led me into the adjoining room, where she slept in a bed larger than the one I shared with Mammy and my siblings, all draped in yards of white fabric I could see through.

But it was the shelf near the window that captured my attention.

Slaves were not allowed to own books, but I'd heard Mammy and some of the grown folks talk about them. I'd never seen one up close before, so when Charlotte took a book from the shelf, the colorful drawing on the front held me in awe. I couldn't imagine how such a thing was filled with tales like those the old men sat around spinning.

"May I see it?"

My bold question went against every instruction Aunt Liza had drummed into me the previous day, but I didn't care. All I wanted was to know the feel of that book in my hands and to see those pretty pictures up close.

Without hesitation, Charlotte handed the treasure to me despite my lack of respect for the rules.

I cradled it in my hand as though it were a newly hatched chick. Two little girls graced the outside of it, seated at a table very much like the one in Charlotte's nursery. A dolly lay on the table while the girls looked at picture books. I tried to open it with my injured fingers, but they wouldn't cooperate. When I winced with pain, Charlotte reached over and parted it to reveal a boy playing ball with a big red dog.

"Mama taught me to read. Would you like me to read to you?"

With widened eyes, I nodded and handed the book back to her, too filled with wonder to speak.

She chose a different book from the shelf, carried it to the chairs near the fireplace, and settled on one of the pretty upholstered seats. I stood beside her where I could see the pictures. Charlotte began speaking slowly, using her finger to point to the funny marks at the bottom of the pages. Mammy sometimes talked about her desire to learn her letters, but I had no knowledge of such things and couldn't understand what she meant. Now as I watched Charlotte's finger move from one group of markings to the next, I realized she was forming words from what she saw on the page.

"'The Toadstool: "We won't worry . . . our . . . ourselves . . . with work," said . . . Dan . . . Dandelion. "Let us cl . . . climb up this great toadstool and have a dan . . . dance upon the top."'"

She looked up at me with a big smile. "See the toadstool?"

I nodded, my eyes returning to the drawing of two small children with upside-down flowers for hats playing beneath a huge toadstool. "I ain't never seen a stool that big."

Charlotte giggled. "It isn't big, silly. The children are small. They're elves." She closed the book and pointed to a picture of the funny-looking children and a toad sitting atop the stool.

I sat on the floor next to her chair while she read several more pages before Aunt Liza returned with a tray of delicious-smelling food, the likes of which I rarely saw unless it was a special day like Christmas. We left our reading to eat eggs, ham, and warm biscuits dripping with honey. When we finished, Aunt Liza carried away the dishes, and we hurried back to the chair and our book.

Charlotte had just begun to read about a pretty girl with butterfly wings when a loud gasp sounded at the door.

"What is going on here?" Miz Sadie's screech made us both jump.

Fear flowed through me as I bounded to my feet, looking for a place to hide from the mistress. I didn't know what had her riled, but I didn't want another smack from a poker. As Miz Sadie stormed into the room, I cowered behind the chair Charlotte vacated.

"Mama." Charlotte hurried over to Miz Sadie, a proud smile on her face as she held up the book. "I'm reading to Frances."

Miz Sadie yanked the book from Charlotte's hand. "Slaves are not permitted to read." Her glare moved from her daughter to me, and I slunk further behind the chair.

Charlotte's bottom lip trembled. "But I'm reading, Mama. Frances just looked at the pictures." She sniffled in much the same way I did when Mammy was cross. "I thought you'd be happy with me."

The ploy worked.

Miz Sadie's angry face eased some, and she reached to smooth Charlotte's curls. "Of course I am, my darling girl. I'm pleased you're practicing your reading." She cast a hard look to me. "But slaves are not allowed books."

Charlotte glanced at me, then at the book in her mother's hands as though she too was confused by the conversation.

"Put the book away, dear, and let me comb your hair."

Miz Sadie sent me one last glare, then seemed to forget I was in the room. She brushed Charlotte's yellow curls till they shone, all the while chatting about the day, Master Burton's new horse, and other topics I neither cared about nor understood. I simply stood where I'd been since she entered the nursery, fearful of moving lest I draw her attention.

When she at last exited the room without a glance toward me, I nearly collapsed on the carpet. My hand ached, and I suddenly felt tired, as though I'd walked a mile instead of standing perfectly still for nearly an hour.

"Let's go outside and play." Charlotte smiled with excitement shining in her eyes.

I nodded in agreement, even as a sudden thought occurred to me. "Where's Pauline?" I realized I hadn't seen the young woman charged with caring for Charlotte today.

"Papa sent her to the fields since I'm too old for a mammy now."

As we made our way to the door, I wondered if Pauline was glad she didn't have to work in the big house anymore. Even though Miz Sadie had been mean to me the previous day, I'd already begun to enjoy being Charlotte's companion. Not only had I eaten a fine meal and had the promise of playing with pretty dollies later, I'd been introduced to a treasure more wonderful than I could have imagined.

With one last longing look at the shelf of books, I followed Charlotte down the grand staircase, eager to return to the nursery later.

I knew one thing for certain, and I didn't care what Miz Sadie said about it.

I was going to learn to read.

CHAPTER
NINE

Frankie's eyes closed. I wondered if she'd nodded off to sleep again. It was after lunch but not quite time for me to leave. I'd wait to see if she awoke before packing up my things for the day.

After a few ticks from the clock on the wall, her eyes opened and she looked at me, with no hint of drowsiness to be found. "Mammy always told me I was stubborn. She was right. I knew I shouldn't touch Miss Charlotte's books, but I couldn't help myself. They seemed to draw me to 'em when I was left alone in the nursery while Charlotte went off with her mama or pappy."

She heaved a sigh. "Some months passed. Miz Sadie still didn't like me much, but she tolerated my presence when I accompanied Charlotte into the parlor. One day she took

Charlotte to town, which meant they wouldn't arrive back home until nearly dark. Aunt Liza put me to work cleaning the nursery, but once she left me alone, I took a book off the shelf and hurried outside with it. I had a good spot under a big ol' tulip tree that I liked, out of sight of the house and fields. No one would bother me there."

The room grew silent while Frankie stared out the window.

"Were you caught?" I asked, hoping to prompt her to finish the tale.

Her gaze met mine. "Not that day. I hid the book in a hollow spot at the base of the tree trunk. I snuck down there every chance I could to look at my treasure. I remembered some of the words Charlotte read to me that first day, and I tried to figure out the letters and what sounds they made. One day Miz Sadie said she was going visiting and wanted Charlotte to go with her. Soon as they left, I ran to my tree and book. The afternoon was warm, and I fell asleep. Next thing I knew, the overseer yanked me up and hauled me into the big house. Miz Sadie and Master Hall was there. She looked like a barn cat who'd caught a fat mouse when the overseer showed her the book."

I swallowed hard. Poor little Frankie. "Did she beat you again?" I whispered.

Frankie slowly shook her head. "I wish she had. I'd have taken a dozen beatings rather than what she planned. She ordered the overseer to chain me up in the barn until the slave trader could come an' fetch me."

I stared at her. A slave trader could mean only one thing. "You were sold because you looked at a book?"

"Yes'm." She took a shaky breath and turned away. "Mammy wasn't allowed to come see me, not even to say goodbye. I've often wondered what that day was like for her. A white man in a wagon come the next morning. He had two men and a woman chained in the back already. I'll never forget the look of despair on their faces. I screamed and fought when the overseer dragged me from the barn toward the wagon. Master Hall stood on the steps of the porch watching, that same troubled look on his face. I called for him to let me stay with Mammy, promising I'd behave. When his eyes met mine, I thought he might save me, but he didn't. He turned and went back into the house."

She pressed her lips together and shook her head. "That was the day I finally understood about slavery."

Frankie stopped talking then. We sat in silence a long time. I knew I should record her words, but I couldn't bring myself to write them down. The images they conjured were too hideous.

"I 'spect I might have done all right at the new place where I was sold if I'd had any sense, but I was so filled with hate and anger, no one could do nothin' with me." She heaved a sigh. "After I was caught stealing eggs, I was sold again. And again. I finally landed on a big place outside of Nashville. By then I'd discovered I could get extra food and privileges using my body, and I became pregnant when I was fifteen. It was a girl child, but she was tiny and sickly and didn't live long. I got pregnant three more times but lost 'em all. Master whipped me and said I was worthless if I couldn't bear chillens. I stayed away from men after that."

She paused. "That is, till I met Moss."

I looked up from my notebook where I'd begun recording her story again. "Moss. Who was he?"

"Moss lived on a neighboring plantation. My master paid the neighbor to use some of his slaves from time to time, especially during harvest. Moss come over with several others. He was handsome, and he knew it." She chuckled softly. "Moss and me became known as a pair. Slaves weren't allowed to marry, but that didn't stop us from taking up with someone we liked. One day Moss told me he was itching for freedom. Said he had a plan to run away and wanted me to go with him."

I felt my eyes widen as I wrote down her words.

"On the night we was to run off, I tried to get Moss to change his mind. I was scared, but he convinced me we could make it north. I thought about Mammy praying for freedom all those years before and wondered if maybe this was the answer. After everyone was asleep, we snuck out into the fields and started running. Someone must've seen us, for it weren't long before we heard the dogs." Frankie shivered and closed her eyes as though the yowling animals were just outside the door. "We ran for our lives, but in the end, Moss lost his. They shot him first, then let the dogs finish him off."

A lone tear ran down her cheek.

I couldn't move, couldn't breathe, couldn't speak. It

seemed unimaginable to me that this elderly woman seated in her cozy living room had once been a runaway slave, chased by dogs, and forced to watch her lover gunned down. What insanity had the world known to think such things were right?

"The beating I got when they dragged me back to the plantation nearly killed me." Her voice was hushed, the words measured. "There were many times afterward I wished it had."

———————

Saturday morning sunshine filtered into my open bedroom window, along with an unusually warm breeze for this time of year. No interviews were scheduled on the weekend, and I planned to spend the day typing up my notes. When Mr. Norwood drove me home yesterday evening, I didn't mention Frankie wasn't anywhere near the end of her story or that I'd assured her I would return as time permitted. After hearing her tale thus far, it didn't seem right to limit her to the generalities of the government questions. I had other interviews to conduct, which I would begin on Monday, but I found myself far too immersed in Frankie's life story to quit now.

There was something else I hadn't mentioned to him. As I listened to her tell of being sold and how Mr. Hall watched it happen without saving her, I suddenly had the feeling I'd heard the name Hall before. Not simply in passing or belonging to a school classmate, but closer, more familiar. I wasn't sure when or where I'd heard it though. I hadn't wanted to interrupt her emotion-filled story, but I hoped to ask Frankie some questions about the Hall family when I saw her again.

My thoughts strayed to Mr. Norwood as I made my way downstairs. He'd been quiet the first couple miles of our ride home, but after a while he started talking about growing up in Chicago. His stories of the boardinghouse his parents ran and the diverse clientele who stayed there intrigued me, and I found myself far more interested than I'd intended. When he said he wanted to be a novelist someday, I admitted I hoped to work for a large magazine in New York. We ended up having a pleasant conversation, and I wondered if perhaps I'd judged him too quickly that first day.

Mama sat at the kitchen table in her bathrobe with a cup of coffee and an old issue of *Ladies' Home Journal* when I entered the kitchen. "Do you want breakfast? I didn't have a chance to run by the market. We're out of eggs and milk, but I see you brought home a loaf of bread. Where did you get it? It looks homemade."

A small smile lifted my lips as I remembered how Frankie insisted I take home a loaf of her freshly baked bread when our time came to an end yesterday. "The woman I've been interviewing made it. I told her about Dovie's yeast rolls and how much I miss them, so she gave me some of the bread she baked."

Mama frowned. "We don't need to accept charity from strangers, Rena. I hope you aren't telling people about our circumstances."

I bit back words that would only cause an argument and moved to the stove to pour myself some coffee. "Mrs. Washington wasn't offering charity. She simply wanted to share some bread with me."

"Washington? You haven't told me why the government is interested in this woman's life. Who is she?"

Now I'd gone and done it. I still hadn't decided what to tell Mama about Frankie. When she learned I was spending time in Hell's Half Acre talking with former slaves, I knew I'd never hear the end of it. A well-bred young woman from Nashville's society wouldn't step foot in that neighborhood, let alone take a job that required doing so.

But more than the money I was earning, which would greatly help my family, I was gradually coming to understand how little I knew about the world I'd grown up in here in the South. I'd studied slavery and the Civil War in school, but the history I'd been taught never told tales like those I'd heard from Frankie the past two days. Slave labor was a necessity in those days, and they lived and worked on plantations and farms in much the same way laborers do today. Or so I'd believed.

Yet if what Frankie said was true—and I had no reason to think it wasn't—it put plantation owners like my ancestors in a completely new light. I didn't know much about their lives or how they'd treated their slaves, but according to Grandma Lorena, her grandparents and great-grandparents had owned a large number of slaves. Had they been benevolent masters? Or had they been the type that would beat and sell off children?

But I couldn't say any of that to Mama.

"She's seen a lot in her lifetime. Mrs. Washington is . . . is . . ." My heart pounded. Could I tell Mama the truth?

"Is what?"

The moment of bravery passed. "Mrs. Washington is 101 years old." A sense of shame engulfed me, but I simply couldn't bring myself to divulge the color of Frankie's skin. Not yet.

"My goodness. Does she still have all her sensibilities?"

"She seems very sharp."

The door to the study opened then, interrupting our conversation. Dad stepped from the darkened room, his hair and clothes disheveled. When his gaze landed on me, he seemed surprised. "What are you doin' here?" He glanced around, a confused expression on his whiskered face.

"It's Saturday. I don't have to work." My cool words hit their mark. Dad looked ready to retreat into his dungeon.

Mama stood and poured another cup of coffee. "Come sit down, dear. Rena was just telling me about the woman she's interviewing."

She carried the cup of steaming black liquid to the table. Dad gave a hesitant glance toward me, then moved forward. I had no desire to make small talk with my parents, let alone continue the conversation about Frankie.

I set my half-finished cup of coffee in the sink. "I have a lot of notes to type up." I headed for the doorway.

"Your mother says you're working for the government." Dad's bloodshot eyes met mine.

My spine stiffened. "I am. What of it?"

Mama sent me a pleading look. Dad and I didn't speak to one another often, but when we did, it usually ended in an argument and loud voices.

He shrugged and picked up his cup. "The government got us into this mess. Don't know why you'd want to work for them."

"If you're referring to our family's financial situation, the government isn't responsible." My ire rose at his lack of culpability. "I should think you'd be grateful the Works Progress Administration created jobs for out-of-work writers like me. They're helping individuals while at the same time doing something useful and beneficial for all of society."

He scoffed. "How is conducting interviews beneficial to society? You've always thought too highly of yourself."

My fists clenched. How dare this man who'd gambled away my future sit in judgment of me!

"For your information, the subjects of the FWP interviews are former slaves. President Roosevelt believes it's important to preserve their stories for the generations to come. I've learned more about slavery in the two days I've been with Frankie than in all the years I studied it in school."

Mama's eyes flew wide. "The woman you're interviewing is—?"

I lifted my chin. Ready or not, it was time to confess. "Yes, Mama. Frances Washington—or Frankie, as she's known—is black. She's lived through all kinds of terrible things, and it's important her story, as well as the others', are told."

My parents stared at me as though I'd taken leave of my senses.

Dad cursed under his breath and shook his head. "Now I've heard everything. The government paying good money to let those people tell tales about how whites did them wrong. I bet this woman has already filled your head with how poorly she was treated." His tone spoke his disdain.

"Oh, Rena." Mama's face went pale. "I had no idea you were involved in something like this. Why didn't you tell me who this woman was when I asked?"

I blew out my frustration. "Because of this." My wave encompassed them both. "Because I knew you wouldn't approve."

Mama huffed. "Of course we wouldn't approve. What would our friends say if they knew what you were doing?" She gasped. "Have you gone into this woman's house?"

I ignored that question and addressed her first. "What friends, Mama? No one cares about us, so why should I care what anyone might think?"

"Because we still live in this community, Lorena Ann. We attend church with some who wouldn't think too highly of these interviews." Mama shook her head, her anxiety mounting. "Peggy Denny will have a grand time spreading this news around. How could you do this to us? I won't be able to show my face once folks learn what you're involved in."

I stared at her. My father had bankrupted our family with dishonest schemes. My sister's indiscretion had forced her to marry a jerk who couldn't stay faithful. How was my job interviewing former slaves deemed worse than all of that?

Determined to put an end to the conversation, I stomped to the doorway. "Mrs. Washington is a very nice woman. Her life matters, just as much as yours and mine."

I didn't wait for a response and ran up the stairs to my room. I slammed the door in much the same way I'd done as a hot-tempered adolescent. It wasn't very mature, but their attitude toward Frankie infuriated me.

I flopped onto the bed, breathing like a bull ready to charge. Their disapproval was expected yet it still stung. Despite Mary's disappointing marriage and rowdy children, she'd always garnered praise from my parents. Mama cried buckets when Mary had to quit school, even though my sister cared little for studies. But whenever I voiced my displeasure at not being able to take classes in journalism at the university, Mama called me ungrateful.

With my eyes closed, I tried to calm myself. My parents' opinion of my job with the FWP didn't matter. I knew I was doing something that deserved more praise than what they were willing to give.

And yet questions silently filtered into my mind. Questions the brief conversation with them raised.

Why did I feel the interview with Frankie was so important? What made her life's story worthy of being told? By my own admission, I knew very little about what slaves endured during the period when owning another person was legal. Why should it matter to me now?

I rolled over and gazed out the window. The top of the magnolia tree filled the view, but it was Frankie's tiny backyard that came to mind. Even though she lived in one of the worst neighborhoods in Nashville in a small house without an indoor lavatory, she'd managed to make her little part of the world beautiful. She didn't have the benefit of gardeners like we'd had before the stock market crash. She just planted seeds and tended them with loving care.

I breathed out a sigh and sat up.

The life Frankie and others like her lived was as foreign to me as someone from China. Was that the reason I found myself interested in hearing what she endured during slavery? Simple curiosity?

I made myself give an honest answer.

Yes.

And no.

I couldn't explain it.

Something had stirred inside me when Frankie began telling her story. Something that had been dormant until that moment. It was almost as though I saw young Frankie romping through the plantation, carefree and happy, when her life was suddenly altered in the most horrific way. Obviously I knew she'd survived being sold and beaten, but I hungered to know the details. I wanted to know how.

How does one keep going after experiencing such horror and pain?

I thought about the past seven years. My life was nothing

like hers, my hardships no comparison, but I'd suffered. Or I thought I had until I heard Frankie's story.

I heaved another sigh.

My parents wouldn't understand my confusion, but Grandma Lorena might.

I looked at the clock. Grandma got her hair done every Saturday morning, then ran errands. I wouldn't be able to visit her until later this afternoon.

An idea sprang to mind.

I could visit Frankie and continue the interview. I'd told her I would come by as time allowed. With a strong need to get out of the house, now was as perfect a time as any.

I flew to the closet and dressed. Gathering my notebooks and pencils from the desk, I stuffed them into the canvas book bag I'd carried in school. I hadn't sneaked out of the house in years, but I remembered every squeaky floorboard to avoid lest I alert my parents to my departure as I made my way to the front door. They couldn't prevent me from leaving the house as they had back in my teenage years, but I didn't want to continue the argument over Frankie and the FWP interviews.

The day I started my job, Mama gave me several coins for the streetcar in case Mr. Norwood proved to be a man I felt uncomfortable riding with. The coins were still in my purse. For a brief moment I thought about calling him since he'd given me his telephone number at the boardinghouse where he was staying. I was certain he wouldn't mind giving me a ride if he wasn't busy, but I decided not to bother him on the weekend. Better to let him believe my interview with Frankie was finished.

The sun shone brightly, a glorious autumn day. I'd enjoy the short walk to the streetcar stop. I couldn't wait to get to Frankie's. I hoped I'd learn the secret to her survival today.

CHAPTER
TEN

The streetcar line ended at the state capitol building. I was the only white person to disembark with a dozen other passengers, each staring at me with suspicion in their eyes. I let them move on to their destinations, with one or two turning back to give me a last look, before I got my bearings. When Mr. Norwood drove me to Frankie's, he used the street that ran parallel to this one. I feared I would get disoriented if I took a different route, so I walked a block to the familiar path and headed into Hell's Half Acre.

It's strange how different the neighborhood seemed without the protection of a car and a man. I suddenly felt exposed, especially when residents who'd been going about their Saturday business turned to gawk at me. I nodded politely to two women sitting on a porch, but neither returned the greeting. When a little boy ran toward me with a friendly grin, his mother hollered for him to keep away. I told myself it was because I was a stranger and not because of my white skin, but I had to admit had the situation been reversed and a black person walked down our street, the reactions would be the same.

I sped up my pace when a group of five or six young men took notice of me. They were lounging on the steps of a house across the street, but when they spotted me, one of the men stood.

"Hey, lady. You lost?"

The others laughed and whispered while the bold one continued to watch me. My heart hammered in my chest as I drew even with them. I shook my head and kept my feet moving, praying they'd simply let me pass. Frankie's little house was around the next corner. I just had to get there.

"Where you headed, lady?"

I stole a quick glance over my shoulder to find the man's attention still on me. When he took a step into the street, my heart nearly stopped beating. My legs began moving on their own, going as fast as possible in my heeled shoes. Oh, why hadn't I worn my saddle shoes?

I didn't have time to think. I simply knew I had to get to Frankie's.

I rounded the corner and had a vague sense of spectators watching from the safety of their homes, but no one came to my rescue.

Frankie's yellow house shone bright in the morning sunshine. To my utter relief, she was there, standing at the front gate as though waiting for me. I rushed into her open arms and buried my face in her shoulder.

"What's goin' on? Rena? What you doin' here, chile?" She smoothed my hair while I tried to catch my breath.

"You know this gal, Mama Fran?"

The voice of the man. I shivered and tucked deeper into Frankie. She smelled of cinnamon and flour.

"'Course I do, Billy. She be a friend o' mine." Frankie's frail arms tightened around me. "What you mean scarin' her like you done?"

"Didn't mean to, Mama Fran. Figured she was lost. You know it ain't safe for someone like her to wander round down here. Just wanted to be sure she got to where she's going, is all."

I peeked out to look at him. He appeared genuine in his concern for me, which made my fear seem foolish. Shameful, even. I'd thought the worst of him when the truth was he'd only wanted to help.

Frankie thanked the young man, and he turned and headed back up the street.

"It's all right, chile." She smoothed my hair again. "He gone."

Slowly I came out of her embrace. My heart still pounded.

"Come on inside. We get you some water."

I followed Frankie up the flower-lined walk. A galvanized watering can sat abandoned, giving evidence of Frankie's mission before I charged into her day. We went to the kitchen, and she motioned for me to sit at the small table, where a plate of freshly baked cookies sat. My legs felt like jelly, and I gratefully slid onto the seat.

"I made them spice cookies for Pastor Silas over to the church. They're his favorite. I don't 'spect he'd mind if you had one, specially after having such a fright."

I shook my head, knowing I couldn't eat a bite. It would most likely come right back up, considering how upside-down my insides felt. "No, but thank you." I did accept the glass of water she held out.

After I took a sip, I closed my eyes, trying to put the incident into perspective. I'd never been so frightened in all my life. What if . . . if . . . ?

I shuddered.

"Now, now, you don't have to be afraid no more. Billy's a good fellow. He watches out for the young'uns and us old folks here in the Acres. He wouldn'ta hurt you."

She reached to wipe a tear from my cheek. I hadn't realized I was crying.

"Thank you." I choked on the words, my tears, my fear.

She gave me a little smile. "Funny thing is, I don't usually water my flowers till later in the day, but something in my spirit told me to go on out early this morning."

I offered a trembling smile. "I'm glad you listened."

She placed her gnarled hand on my arm. "Now, you tell me what brings you down here on a Saturday without that handsome fella drivin' you."

I suddenly felt like a fool for coming. "I . . . I just wanted to continue our interview."

Her dark eyes studied me a long moment before she nodded. "Let's go in yonder to the sittin' room. Jael's running
some errands this morning, but she ought to be back before
lunch."

We took our usual seats. As I pulled my notebook from
my bag, I inhaled a calming breath. I was safe in Frankie's
home, and I'd learned a valuable lesson.

Not everything was as it seemed here in the Acres.

With one last shudder, I looked up to find Frankie studying me.

"You know that fear you had a little while ago when you
thought that fellow was chasin' you? All raw and consumin'?"

I nodded.

"That's how I felt when them patrollers was huntin' me
and Moss. Fear like nothin' I'd ever felt before, not even when
Miz Sadie sold me away from Mammy. That kind of fear is
like a livin', breathin' thing inside you. And sometimes, it
don't never go away."

I knew exactly what she meant.

───────

The sound of moaning woke me up.

When it came again, I was surprised to find it originated
in my own throat. My eyelids felt heavy and didn't want to
budge, but I managed to open narrow slits and found myself
flat on my stomach, looking at the dirt floor of the cabin I
shared with six other slaves.

Confusion swirled through my mind, which, like my

eyelids, felt heavy. Had I fallen out of bed? I closed my eyes, trying to remember, but nothing surfaced. I had a sense something was terribly wrong, yet my head couldn't conjure up a reason for this feeling of foreboding.

Maybe I was dreaming. Moss once told me I talked in my sleep. Maybe I walked in my sleep too and had taken a tumble.

The nightmare became real, however, when I tried to rise.

Intense, red-hot pain shot through my entire body. I gasped, agony tearing through my abdomen with the slight movement. Bright stars filled my eyes, blocking out the cabin.

Have mercy, what happened to me?

"Help."

My whispered plea barely reached my own ears. I opened my eyes again, the stars fading. A shaft of sunshine came through a place in the log wall where the chinking was missing, telling me it was daytime. Everyone would be out in the tobacco fields, where I should've been. Why wasn't I?

"Moss?" My lips cracked, and I tasted blood when I ran my tongue across them. "Moss?"

Stillness followed.

A bird trilled outside.

No one answered. I would need to get off the floor myself.

Wave after wave of excruciating pain invaded every crevice of my being as I inched my body up into a kneeling position. My middle and ribs hurt something fierce, and they wouldn't support me without sending me into agony.

I slumped against the wall by the door, crying like a newborn baby. I had no idea what terrible fate had befallen me. All I could do was wait for Moss.

The next time my eyes opened, I found Bessy's young face close to mine.

"Thank the Lawd." My cabinmate turned to someone out of my view. "She wakin' up."

I hoped it was Moss. It was not.

Ophelia lumbered into my sight. It hurt to look up at her, but she didn't seem inclined to come down to my level as Bessy had.

She shook her head. "You a fool, girl." There was no sympathy in her thick voice. "I tol' you Moss weren't good for you, but you wouldn't listen. Now look at the mess you gone and got yo'self into."

I blinked, trying to sort out her scolding words. "Where is he?"

"Who?" Ophelia frowned. She and Bessy exchanged a look.

"Moss." It took all my strength to speak. The women didn't seem motivated to tell me what happened. I just wanted Moss to come and carry me to our bed, where I could sleep away the pain.

"He be dead, girl. You know that. Them dogs tore him to pieces."

I stared at the woman, thinking her mad. Moss wasn't dead. He—

It all rushed back to me then.

Our escape. The gunshot. The dogs. The beating.

The mournful sound that emitted from me would forever echo in my soul. I remembered. I remembered it all.

Ophelia ignored my cries, my shrieks of pain, when she and Bessy grasped me by the arms and dragged me across the room. I must have blacked out, because the next time I woke, I was in bed. Alone. Darkness had descended, and the small cabin was quiet except for the occasional light snores from the other occupants.

I lay there thinking about Moss, wishing I'd died with him. God must truly hate me if he left me here, broken and bruised, without Moss. The Almighty had taken from me time and time again—Mammy, my babies—to the point I quit believing in him altogether. The happiness I'd found with Moss ignited a spark of hope deep inside me, in a place I'd thought long dead. Hope that perhaps God was real and he might find me worthy of the love Mammy had always talked about.

As I lay there in misery, with my body and my heart shattered, I knew better. If God was real, he was a vengeful, angry god. Mammy'd been wrong to say he was love. What kind of love was it to enslave people simply because of the color of their skin? Love didn't kill. Love didn't maim.

The small flame that had ignited in my heart when Moss came into my world blew out. I stared into the darkness and knew.

If I lived through this, I would never again allow myself to hope.

For anything.

CHAPTER ELEVEN

The front door to Frankie's home opened, letting in a flood of sunshine. A pretty young black woman entered, carrying two sacks of groceries. She came to an abrupt halt seeing me there with Frankie.

"Jael, this is Rena, the gal I told you was interested in talking about slavery times." Frankie turned to me. "This is Jael. She takes care of me."

I stood, shuffling my notebook and pencil into one hand before I realized Jael wouldn't be able to shake mine even if I offered. "It's nice to meet you."

She closed the door with her foot and came into the room. "I'm pleased to meet you as well. Mama Fran can't talk 'bout nothin' else but this here interview you're doing."

"Can I help with your bags?"

Jael nodded. "That'd be nice." She handed me one of

the paper sacks before turning to Frankie. "They's all out of bacon, Mama Fran, but they had some ham steaks that looked good."

Frankie nodded. "Guess we'll cook some beans then. You get 'em soaking while Rena and I finish up; then we'll have a bite to eat."

Jael disappeared into the kitchen. I hadn't thought to bring a sandwich with me, considering my hasty exit from the house. I didn't want to be a bother. "I should probably go and let you get on with your day."

Disappointment flashed in Frankie's eyes. "I ain't got anything pressing to get done. When you reach my age, just rising out of bed is an accomplishment. But if you need to go, I won't keep you."

I held no desire to return home and face Mama just yet. Besides, I hadn't figured out how I'd get to the streetcar stop. Despite Frankie's insistence that Billy and the others were harmless, I wasn't brave enough to attempt walking through the infamous neighborhood alone again.

"If you're sure, I'd like to continue the interview."

Frankie nodded and settled back in her chair. "I don't like remembering the bad times, but the Lord has a way of using them to get you to where he wants you to go."

I carried the groceries to the kitchen, where Jael instructed me to set them on the table. I returned to the living room and took up my pencil and notebook again, pondering the bit of wisdom Frankie had just imparted.

Was that the key to her surviving slavery? Believing God

had a purpose in the midst of the pain? If so, how had she come by it?

"After the beating and Moss's death, I gave up on life. I wouldn't eat nothin', no matter what Bessy tried to poke down me. Ophelia and the others would've let me die, I guess, but Bessy fretted over me like a mama hen and eventually managed to get some broth in me." She stared off to the distance for a moment, remembering. "I can't recall how many days passed, but one afternoon Master came down to the quarter to see me. He cursed when he entered the cabin and found me lying in my own filth. Said he'd paid good money for me and wasn't about to let me die and waste it."

I wrote her words, disgusted by the man who'd owned her. Surely his heart had been made of stone.

"The next day Bessy and Ophelia washed me and got me into a clean dress. Soon as they was done, the overseer and another white man carried me to a wagon. I figured they'd dug a hole somewhere and planned to put me in it, but instead they drove me to Nashville to the slave market."

My head shot up. "The slave market? What's that?"

Frankie frowned. "The market was a place where us slaves was auctioned off. It was down on Cedar Street. We had to stand on a high platform while white men bid on the one they wanted to buy. Some of the big, strong men went for a thousand dollars or more, but I was so scrawny and weak, no one wanted me. I stood there in shame as the man in charge of the auction kept lowering the price, convincing me of my worthlessness."

A gasp came from the kitchen doorway.

"Mama Fran, you ain't worthless." Jael rushed to Frankie and embraced her. I'd forgotten the young woman was in the next room, no doubt listening to the troubling tale.

"I know that, baby girl." Frankie smoothed Jael's curly shoulder-length hair in the same way she'd smoothed mine earlier that morning. "I know that now, but I didn't then."

Jael moved to where she could look at Frankie, tears sparkling in her eyes. "I didn't know how much you suffered, Mama Fran."

Frankie patted her cheek and gave a brave smile. "Better me than you, baby girl." Her gaze returned to me. "About the time I thought no one would buy me, a short man in a tall hat bid ten dollars. Mr. Waters owned a big wholesale grocery business in downtown Nashville, right off Market Street, and needed someone to clean the warehouse and offices."

Jael settled on the floor, clutching Frankie's deformed hand, listening.

"I never would've dreamed it, but that man saved my life." Frankie chuckled. "He was a strange little man, but he wasn't cruel. He set me up in my own shed behind the warehouse. It had a small stove and a cot to sleep on. Twice a week a house slave would arrive with enough food meant to last me until he showed up again. I gained my strength back and determined I'd be a good worker for Mr. Waters rather than causing trouble like I'd done in the past."

"Were you happy there?" Jael asked.

I never would have dared to ask such a thing, but I had to admit I was curious to hear Frankie's answer.

She pursed her lips. "I can't say I was happy, but some of the anger and fire that had been a part of me was gone. Whether it was beat out of me or got buried deep inside, I didn't know. I kept to myself mostly and didn't speak to the warehouse workers much. At first, Mr. Waters locked the shed at night to make sure I didn't run off. After a while he must've decided he could trust me, because he left it unlocked and even allowed me to run errands for him. I'd never seen a city before, and I'd stare up at the tall buildings and all the white people wandering the streets."

Her gaze met mine. "I 'spect I would've stayed with Mr. Waters forever had the Federal Army not shown up and changed everything."

———

The three of us sat at the small table in Frankie's kitchen, eating cold fried chicken and slices of bread spread with sweet butter.

"Have you ever met anyone who lived to tell about the War between the States?" Frankie directed her question to me.

"My grandma was born right before the war began, so she doesn't remember anything about it. Some of my great-uncles fought in it, but . . ." I gave a small shrug, knowing my ancestors had been Confederates. I'd never been ashamed of that fact until this very moment. Had they, like the men who'd owned Frankie, believed it was their right to keep people in bondage? To beat innocent children? To murder?

Frankie nodded, no doubt guessing why I didn't finish my thought. "It's a terrible thing when countrymen fight against one another. Yet, if them Yankees hadn't come to Nashville, I would've been a slave a whole lot longer."

"Weren't you afraid of the soldiers, Mama Fran?" Jael's eyes grew wide.

Frankie took a bite of chicken before giving an answer. She wiped her mouth on a napkin, then sat back in the chair and looked out the kitchen window to blue sky. "I was terrified, baby girl. 'Course, they weren't the first soldiers I'd seen. Up till then, the Confederate Army held Nashville, so I was used to seeing soldiers in gray. We'd heard rumors the Yankees were coming, but I don't think we believed it until they were practically on our doorstep, camped right across the Cumberland. All them boys in gray hightailed it south, leaving the city unprotected. People filled the streets, running and screaming. Wagons piled high with household belongings clogged the roads headed out of town. Them that couldn't leave barricaded themselves in their homes."

She looked at Jael, then to me. "Mr. Waters was desperate to vacate the city and planned to take me with him. If I recall correctly, his wife had kin in North Carolina and they intended to go there. But he didn't want the Yankees to get hold of his inventory, so we were delayed while wagons were loaded with merchandise. He sent me to deliver a message to his family, telling them to start without him, but when I tried to get back to the warehouse, I couldn't for all the commotion. That's when I saw a line a mile long of soldiers in blue coats marching into downtown. A band of soldiers was playin' instruments, like it was a holiday parade."

Jael and I stared at Frankie in rapt attention.

"Did they hurt you?" Jael whispered, moisture forming in her eyes.

Frankie shook her head. "No, although I thought they might when they gathered us slaves up."

"Where did they take you?" I asked, my lunch forgotten.

"First, we were put in a camp not far from here. After a while, they moved some of us to an area south of the city and set up canvas tents. I heard later they called it a contraband camp, meaning we slaves were contraband because we'd run away from our owners." She shrugged. "I hadn't run away, but I never did see Mr. Waters again."

"Were you free?"

Frankie patted Jael's hand and smiled. "I was, baby girl. For the first time in my life, I was free."

They shared a triumphant smile that left me, a white woman, out. I'd never endured anything like what Frankie had, nor had I experienced racial discrimination as Jael most surely had. I couldn't possibly understand the depth of feelings that must have passed through Frankie when she realized she was no longer a slave, owned by another.

Frankie's smile faded. "Life inside the camp was good at first, even though it was cold and crowded. I think we were in shock for a time, before it finally sunk in that we were free. There was food aplenty in the beginning, and it felt like a celebration. Music and singing every night. Laughter. But after a while, folks began to get restless. They didn't like that the soldiers wouldn't let us roam around outside the camp. The men were forced into labor, building a big limestone fort up the hill from our camp and digging trenches around the city to keep the Confederates out. Rumors crept in that a group of soldiers abused some of the women."

Her voice dropped. "When a man was shot because he refused to work for the Yankees and tried to leave the camp, we started to wonder if we'd traded one master for another."

CHAPTER
TWELVE

"Thank you for giving me a ride."

I glanced at Mr. Norwood's profile as he maneuvered the car through Hell's Half Acre in the dim light of dusk. I'd stayed at Frankie's far longer than I intended. She'd offered to teach Jael and me how to make bread, and time slipped by as we talked and laughed and got flour everywhere. When I glanced out the window and noticed the sun dipping near the horizon, panic nearly overwhelmed me, and I wondered how I could reach the streetcar stop without drawing unwanted attention again, especially in the dark. After Frankie told Jael what happened that morning, she volunteered to run to Pastor Silas's house to use the telephone to call Alden. I never dreamed I'd be so happy to see his old Chevrolet coupe pull up in front of Frankie's house.

He glanced at me, his face a mask in the waning light. When he turned back to the road without a word, I got the distinct impression he wasn't pleased with me.

"I'll pay for the gas," I volunteered, thinking that was the problem. Or maybe I'd interrupted his plans for Saturday evening. Did he have a girlfriend? Was he annoyed at being late to meet her?

After a moment, his shoulders eased. "I'm not worried about the gas." Another glance. "You shouldn't have come down here alone."

His authoritative tone rankled, and yet I knew he was right.

He swallowed, making his Adam's apple bob. "You could've been hurt . . . or worse."

Now I understood. "Jael told you what happened?"

"Yes." He let out a sound of frustration. "What possessed you to think you could come down to Hell's Half Acre without an escort? A pretty white woman all by herself is asking for trouble in this neighborhood."

He thinks I'm pretty?

For some reason, that slip of information in the midst of such a serious conversation made me smile.

"What are you grinning about? I mean it, Miss Leland. Don't ever come down here by yourself again."

"I promise I won't," I said softly, duly reprimanded.

He seemed appeased by my answer. "What was so important that you had to come down here anyway? I thought you finished Mrs. Washington's interview."

Guilt pricked my conscience. "Well, not entirely."

His brows rose when he shot me a look.

"Frankie—that's her name—is taking her time telling me her story. I don't want to rush her, so I told her I'd come visit whenever I can." At the shake of his head, I hurried on. "I won't neglect my other interviewees, so you needn't worry. There's just something about Frankie's story . . ." I shrugged, unable to articulate what was steadily growing inside my heart. "Her courage, I think, is what I most admire. As terrible as some of the details of her life are, she doesn't wallow in them."

He was silent for a long moment before he conceded, "She sounds like a very interesting woman." At my smile, he gave a stern look. "But meeting with her is not worth putting yourself in harm's way. Next time you want to come down here, I'll drive you. Agreed?"

My grin widened. "Agreed, Mr. Norwood."

"Seeing as I'm going to be your private chauffeur, you might as well call me Alden."

Shyness suddenly stole over me with such an intimate turn in the conversation, but I countered with "Then you should call me Rena."

"So, Rena," he said with a wink, "tell me something about this Frankie of yours."

Over the remaining miles, I told him about Sadie Hall and Frankie's deformed fingers. I told him how Frankie was sold time after time and about Moss's murder. He asked several questions, revealing his own curiosity in the story as well as his knowledge about slavery. When we pulled up in front of my house, where lights glowed from nearly every window, I was sad to see our time together end.

"Can I ask you a question?" He turned to me.

"Yes."

"What did your father do before the economy tanked?"

I'd assumed he was still considering Frankie's life story, so his question caught me off guard. I hadn't shared many details about my family with Alden after his misguided observations that first day. Even though he'd apologized, and I believed him to be sincere, I didn't want to revisit the subject.

But he was becoming a friend, so I decided to be honest. "He owned several banks here in Tennessee. I never understood much about banking and investing, so it was a shock when he lost everything."

"I'm sorry." His eyes held sincere sympathy. "The crash was hard on everyone."

I could let the conversation end, and he'd be none the wiser about the circumstances of my father's fall from grace. But something made me want to continue. To let Alden see who I really was and form his opinions based on facts rather than fiction.

"It was a difficult time. October 29 is my birthday. I turned sixteen the day the stock market crashed. We were supposed to have a big dinner party with a hundred guests, but after the news came, Mama was scared to leave the house. You see, my father had mismanaged thousands of dollars belonging to the bank's customers. People we'd known for years lost their homes and were left practically penniless because of my father."

He didn't say anything. I couldn't tell what thoughts might be going through his mind, but I could well imagine.

"The big house you see here used to belong to my grandparents. My mother was raised in it. When Grandpa Jim passed away, Grandma sold it to us and moved down the street to a smaller house. After the crash and Dad's bank failures, she didn't want us to lose the house, so she took over the mortgage payments. If it weren't for her, we'd be homeless like thousands of others. Mama's salary at the sewing shop keeps food on the table, but that's about it."

We sat in silence for several long moments. Somehow, telling my sad tale was like letting a heavy weight fall from my shoulders. Yes, my father had done a terrible thing. He didn't go to jail, but he would always pay the price for his poor decisions. Yet his story wasn't mine. I was innocent in all that had transpired. Just because my birth date coincided with that fateful day didn't mean I needed to carry around unnecessary guilt or shame.

"I'm glad you heard about the job with the FWP."

I glanced at him to find a soft smile on his lips. "I am too." I gathered my things. "Thank you again for coming to my rescue, sir knight." My attempt at humor apparently didn't impress him, because he scowled.

"It's no joking matter, Rena. Hell's Half Acre earned its reputation legitimately."

I sobered. "I know. I learned my lesson."

Our gazes held, light from a streetlamp allowing me to see his face clearly. A hint of dark stubble peppered his cheeks and strong chin.

"Good night, Rena." Warmth washed over me with his tender expression. "I'll see you Monday."

I reached for the door handle. "Good night, Alden."

I watched him drive away, wondering why I hadn't noticed how handsome he was before. Even Frankie mentioned something about my handsome friend that morning when I'd first arrived at her house, frightened and out of breath.

"Rena? Oh, thank goodness you're home."

I turned to find Mama standing in the front doorway, her voice wobbly with worry. It hadn't occurred to me until this very moment I should have called my mother at some point during the day to let her know I was out and wouldn't return for a while.

"I'm sorry I didn't call. There wasn't a telephone I could use." I climbed the steps to the front porch and heard high-pitched children's voices from inside the house. A quick glance revealed my sister's old Hudson parked in the driveway.

"We were about to call the police, Lorena Ann." Mama's concern quickly turned to rebuke. "When Mother said she hadn't seen you all day, I was nearly frantic with worry. Poor Mary had to load up the children without their supper and come console me."

While I did feel bad about not calling, Mama's dramatics were a bit much. "I'm fine, Mama. Next time I'll let you know when I'm going out."

She frowned at me in the yellow porch light, then looked down the road. I followed her gaze to where Alden's car disappeared around the corner.

"Was that the young man from the FWP?"

I sighed. Here came the interrogation. "Yes. Alden Norwood."

"What were you doing out with him? You've been gone all day."

I weighed my next words. To lie and say I'd been with Alden would be far easier than enduring the lecture I knew would be forthcoming if I told the truth regarding my whereabouts. Yet I had nothing to be ashamed of.

"I went to see Mrs. Washington. We're not quite finished with her interview."

Mama grew completely still and stared at me. Finally her eyes narrowed. "Where does this woman live?"

I broke eye contact and moved toward the door. "Jackson Street."

Mama reached out to prevent me from entering the house. "Do you mean to tell me you've been going down to . . . to . . ." Her voice dropped to a low hiss. "You've been going down to Hell's Half Acre?" Her gaze darted around the darkened yard as though the neighbors had gathered on the lawn to eavesdrop.

"Yes, Mama. Mrs. Washington lives in a very nice house. She's planted all sorts of flowers and even has a vegetable garden. It's not what you think."

Her expression grew hard. "I've seen that neighborhood,

Lorena Ann. It's run-down and dangerous. What has gotten into you that you would not only disgrace us by spending time with unsuitable people, but also put yourself in harm's way by going down to that . . . that area?"

Mary appeared in the open doorway just then, two-year-old Buddy in her arms. The odor of a dirty diaper followed them. She glanced between Mama and me. "Where have you been, Lulu? Mama's been worried."

"She's been down to see *that woman*." Mama's lips pinched.

Mary frowned. "Mama told me about your job. Really, Lulu, couldn't you find something more respectable?"

"Yes," Mama said, crossing her arms. "Respectable. Maybe you'll listen to your sister if you won't listen to me."

The last thing I needed was a lecture given by my sister, who'd never held a job in her life. Even if Mama was right about Frankie's neighborhood being dangerous, I refused to quit the FWP, especially now that Alden had agreed to drive me.

I turned and stomped down the steps. "I'm going to Grandma Lorena's. You don't need to call the police."

Mama protested and Mary called me childish, but their words fell on deaf ears. I had to talk to someone, and only one person would do.

⸻

"Mama will make my life miserable unless I quit my job."

I sat across from Grandma Lorena at her breakfast table, feasting on her famous chicken and dumplings. She'd eaten supper earlier, but that didn't stop her from having a small helping to keep me company.

Grandma wore a thoughtful frown. "That would be a shame, Rena. I believe Frankie's story needs to be told. The others, too. Especially for the younger generations to hear."

My heart swelled with appreciation. "Thank you, Grandma. I don't understand why Mama refuses to see that. She's never met Frankie, and yet she's already made up her mind that Frankie isn't someone I should associate with."

We each took a bite of our supper before Grandma set her spoon down.

"I know it's hard for you to understand, but Margaret was raised in a time when white people didn't associate with blacks. Now, that doesn't mean she or any of us should think another person is any different because their skin is a darker shade, or that we're somehow superior because of our white skin, but some habits and beliefs are hard to change once they're set inside you."

I considered her words. "But you don't have any prejudices against a person because of the color of their skin."

A look I couldn't quite discern filled Grandma's face. "I certainly hope I no longer carry any in my heart, but shamefully, I admit there was a time when I thought like your mother."

Surprise surely shaded my face. "I don't believe that, Grandma. Not you."

"It's true. I'm not proud of the way I treated people who were different from me when I was younger. After Cornelia passed away, my mother hired other black servants. I took the notion that because I was white and the daughter of the mistress of the house, I was somehow better than them."

Her confession shocked me. I couldn't believe my sweet, loving grandmother—a pillar in the church and community—had at one time been exactly like my own mother.

"What changed your mind?"

A wry smile lifted her lips. "I'd like to say I had a revelation and came to it on my own, but it was actually your grandfather and his view of the world that helped me see how wrong mine was."

I hadn't known Grandpa Jim well before he passed away. I was only nine at the time. My memories of him mainly consisted of his contagious laughter and an ever-present spittoon to accommodate his chewing tobacco habit.

"Tell me about Grandpa."

Warmth filled her eyes. "Jim never met a stranger. His smile drew people to him like flies to a picnic. It didn't matter the color of the person's skin or their status in society. Jim was friend to everyone."

"How did you meet?" I couldn't recall the details of their romance, although I'm sure I'd heard the tale before.

"I was a student at Ward Seminary for Young Ladies," she began, taking on the same faraway look Frankie often wore when remembering days of old. "It was May of my second year of school. I was studying to become a teacher, because that was one of the few careers offered to women at the time."

I smiled, thinking of my grandma as a young woman.

"It was a Sunday afternoon, bright and warm. I'd been voted May queen, so I was to be honored during the parade through town for May Day. I rode in a wagon pulled by four beautiful but spirited horses. The young boy driving them was no match." She chuckled. "I've often wished I could've seen his face when one of the lead horses spooked and caused him to lose his grip on the reins. Those horses bolted down the street, not only endangering me and the boy, but everyone who'd come to see the parade."

I leaned forward, captured by the images Grandma's story spun in my mind.

"My young driver and I could do nothing but hang on for dear life, hoping the horses would slow eventually. Suddenly, from the corner of my eye, a horse and rider appeared."

"Grandpa?"

She nodded. "Yes, it was your grandpa. He came alongside the runaway horses and somehow managed to bring them to a stop. I know I should have been frightened out of my wits, but all I could think of when I saw my handsome hero was how glad I was those crazy horses had acted up."

We both chuckled.

"Jim volunteered to drive the wagon back to the school since the boy abandoned me as soon as we stopped. In the half hour it took us to reach the school, I'd fallen madly in love with him, and he with me."

A dreamy sigh escaped my lips at such romance.

"When Papa heard about the runaway wagon and how Jim saved me, he invited Jim to the house for supper. I was a bundle of excitement and wanted everything to be perfect so I could show him what a good homemaker I would make. When he arrived, I put on airs, barking orders at the servants and severely reprimanding a young woman when she spilled a bit of soup on the linen tablecloth. I believe I might have even said something about them needing to 'know their place.' By the end of the evening, I could tell something was bothering Jim. We sat on the porch, with the moon settling in for the night and offering a romantic atmosphere, but Jim was unusually quiet. When I asked what was wrong, I was not prepared for his answer."

I held my breath, even though I knew the story had a happy ending.

"'Lorena,' he said, just as serious as I'd ever seen him before or since. 'I fear I've made a terrible mistake.' I couldn't imagine what he meant, and I encouraged him to continue, not knowing that what he was about to say would devastate me. 'I didn't know you were of the kind to treat a person poorly because of the color of their skin. I'm sorry, but I won't be able to see you again.'"

She heaved a sigh. "He left then, and I didn't know if I'd ever see him again."

My heart ached for young Lorena Sue. "But you weren't truly prejudiced, were you?"

"I didn't think so at the time, but looking back I see that I was. I believed my white skin set me apart from a black person. That, somehow, I was better than they would ever be. It took losing Jim to open my eyes to the truth. Mama, of course, said Jim was a fool, and I was better off without him. She and Papa both encouraged me to forget Jim. A string of eligible young men began showing up for dinner, hand-picked by my parents, but my heart couldn't forget Jim."

I had never been in love, but I thought I could imagine the pain Grandma endured. "How long did Grandpa stay away?"

"Nearly three years passed before I saw Jim again. I couldn't tolerate any of the young men Papa brought to the house and decided I would never marry. By then I'd graduated with my teaching certificate, and Papa helped me get a position in a school for young ladies. Young *white* ladies, of course. But Jim's words had stayed with me, and I began to see our seg-regated world the way he did. When a young black woman petitioned the school for entrance, the headmaster laughed in her face." Grandma closed her eyes for a long moment. "I'll never forget watching that young woman walk away from the school. While the teachers and students mocked her, she held her head high with a dignity I found lacking in my own race. I later learned that same young woman went on to attend Fisk University and earned her master's degree. She's made quite a name for herself in Memphis, what with her involvement in the women's state convention as well as the National Baptist Convention."

"How did you meet Grandpa again?"

"After watching my colleagues treat that young woman so disgracefully, I knew I couldn't stay where I was any longer. I thought I'd like to teach in one of the schools for blacks, but Papa forbade it." She met my gaze. "I couldn't go against his wishes, as much as I wanted to. It simply wasn't done in those days."

I saw now why Grandma understood me so well. We were actually more similar than I'd ever realized.

"One day I heard about a rally for equal rights. I told Mama I was going to visit a friend, and I was, although I didn't know it at the time I spoke the untruth. When I arrived at the park, there was quite a crowd gathered. Someone was giving a speech, but I stood at the back and wasn't able to hear what was being said. I felt out of place even though there were many white people in attendance."

Her eyes misted over. "I couldn't believe it when I saw Jim walk toward me. He asked what I was doing there. When I told him I'd changed, his smile could have lit up the city."

I grinned. "He still loved you."

"He did. We talked for hours, and by the end of the day, he proposed and I accepted."

"What did your parents think?"

"They weren't overly excited, but Jim came from an old Nashville family, so they were satisfied with his pedigree and bank account."

Grandma's story had a happy ending. Even though I'd only been a child when Grandpa passed away, I'd seen the love they had for one another. It was evident in their conversations, their laughter. When Grandpa died of a heart attack, Grandma seemed lost. One day she arrived at our house with a smile and something else I didn't know what to call back then, but I did now. Peace. The pain of loss no longer filled her face. She still missed Grandpa fiercely, but she was able to move forward.

"With Margaret our only child, Jim decided we needed to help the children of Nashville who were less fortunate. He gave quite a bit of money and much of his time to some of the programs for the poor, oftentimes going into Hell's Half Acre."

I stared at her, unable to believe what I'd just heard. "Grandpa spent time in Hell's Half Acre?" At her affirmative nod, I asked, "Does Mama know?"

She sighed. "Jim took Margaret with him once when she was about twelve years old. He'd become acquainted with a pastor down there, and there was always a need among the congregation. That day it was a young mother whose husband had abandoned her and her four children. She needed some repairs done to their home. Winter was upon us, and the poor things were freezing. Jim provided the money to purchase the necessary supplies to repair the roof, but he also wanted to help with the physical labor. He thought it would be a good experience for Margaret to see the poverty that some people are forced to live in, hoping it would quell the selfish streak we were beginning to notice in her."

I tried to imagine Mama as a girl, seeing Hell's Half Acre for the first time. "I guess it was quite a shock for her, seeing that neighborhood."

"It was. Unfortunately, the time she spent down there with Jim did more damage than good. It seemed to solidify in her mind her superiority over the people who lived there rather than ignite any sympathetic feelings for their plight."

I glanced into the living room, where a black-and-white picture of Grandpa sat on the mantel. "I wish I could've gone down there with him."

"He would have enjoyed that. And he would have been so proud of you, Rena." When I turned to her, she smiled. "I believe you've inherited some of his spirit. Like your grandpa Jim, don't let anyone, not even your mother and father, keep you from doing what you know you're called to do."

I left Grandma's a short while later, full of wonder that my own grandparents had witnessed the inequality between the races and tried to do something about it. What if Mama had taken pity on the residents of Hell's Half Acre on that long-ago day rather than allowing her scorn to grow? How different would things have been for our family, our servants?

A question resounded in my heart.

Was I making a difference? Did my interviews with former slaves truly matter?

As my feet carried me home, I realized how desperately I wanted the answer to be yes.

CHAPTER THIRTEEN

Mrs. Patsy Hyde was a sweet elderly woman whose stories of her life as a slave were touching yet far different than those told to me by Frankie. Patsy spoke of her days as a child on the plantation with a fondness I wasn't sure what to make of, and I struggled to keep to the list of questions provided by the FWP. I wanted to ask about beatings and babies and freedom and how she truly felt about slavery. The things Frankie had willingly shared. But I didn't, and I felt strangely unsatisfied when I bade Mrs. Patsy goodbye.

Alden was waiting for me.

"How did it go?" he asked after I'd settled into the passenger seat.

I shrugged. "Good, I suppose. We finished her interview."

He studied me with eyes that grew narrower with each moment. "But you aren't happy with it."

How did he know me so well already?

"I wish she would have opened up more, that's all."

After a silent beat, Alden said, "You mean like Frankie."

I glanced longingly in the direction of Frankie's house a few blocks away and nodded. "Frankie is so honest in the telling of her story."

"And you don't believe Mrs. Hyde was honest?"

I looked at him, uncertain how to answer. "I don't think she lied, if that's what you mean. She was a young child when the war ended, like my grandma Lorena. Maybe she wasn't aware of all the terrible things that went on or simply doesn't remember them." I shrugged again, unable to believe my own assessment. Every slave, young or old, surely witnessed things that would stay with them the rest of their lives.

"I guess I know what you mean." He shrugged. "The people I've interviewed aren't nearly as open as your Frankie has been with you. I think she's a rarity among former slaves. You're lucky you've been able to hear her stories firsthand."

"Thanks." Before I could stop myself, I added, "Would you like to meet her?"

He'd just put his hand on the gearshift. He paused and glanced at me. A slow smile drew the corners of his mouth up. "You know, I think I would. I'd like to meet your Frankie."

I grinned, then glanced at my wristwatch. "I need to call Mama and let her know I'll be late; otherwise I'll never hear the end of it."

Alden drove past several businesses that most likely had a telephone installed. I pointed to an establishment with a number of cars parked in front. "Why don't we try that one?" But he passed it too.

When I asked why, he didn't look at me when he replied. "They aren't the type of place a lady would enter. Especially a white lady."

I gulped. After my frightening experience over the weekend, I certainly didn't want to bring unnecessary attention to myself ever again. I wasn't familiar with the types of businesses he referred to, but something in my gut told me I didn't want to become familiar with them.

We drove to a small grocery store not far from the capitol building. An older black man stood behind the counter. His ready smile disappeared at seeing us approach.

"What can I do fo' you folks?" His gaze darted beneath the counter for a brief moment.

"We'd like to use a telephone if you have one," Alden said, sidestepping in front of me.

I thought it quite rude, so I moved out from behind him. A look of annoyance flashed across his face before he returned his attention to the man, who seemed to regard me with a hint of humor in his dark eyes.

He pointed to a door behind him. "I got one in the office there you can use."

After calling Mama and making an excuse for not coming directly home, we headed to Frankie's. My thoughts, however, stayed back at the store.

"Why did you get in front of me when you were speaking to that store owner?"

Alden kept his attention on the road. "Because he had a gun underneath the counter."

I gasped. "How do you know that?"

"I saw him look at it when we walked in."

Part of me wanted to argue that he couldn't possibly know for certain a gun lay feet from us, yet hadn't I learned Saturday that life in Hell's Half Acre was far different from the life I'd always known? Alden had much more experience down here than I did, and I needed to trust him. Our situation reminded me a bit of Grandma and Grandpa's, with her learning from him.

Heat rushed to my face, and I turned so he couldn't see.

I did not have romantic feelings toward Alden as Grandma had for Grandpa, I reminded myself. We were strictly coworkers and possibly friends, nothing more.

And yet he'd shielded me with his own body.

The thought of such chivalry warmed me to my very core.

We arrived at Frankie's. Light shone from the living room window as the oranges and golds of dusk settled over Nashville. Somehow the run-down neighborhood looked more peaceful and less sinister in the evening light. Yet if a shopkeeper kept a gun hidden beneath the counter, all was definitely not well in this part of town.

"We won't stay long," I said and climbed from the car. "She and Jael are probably getting their supper ready." Someone in the house next door looked out the window, watching us.

Alden followed me up the narrow flower-lined walk.

A surprised look flashed across Jael's pretty face when she

answered my knock on the door. "Rena, Mama Fran didn't mention you were coming by." Her gaze took in Alden.

"She isn't expecting me, but I'd like her to meet my friend, if she's not busy."

"Come in." Jael ushered us into the small living room. The aroma of something savory came from the kitchen. "She's been napping, but I heard her stirring a while ago. I'll let her know you're here." The young woman disappeared down the hallway.

I turned and found Alden smiling at me. "What?"

He gave a slight shrug. "I can see you've become someone they trust. That's quite an accomplishment in such a short amount of time. Well done, Miss Leland."

His praise and the look he gave me sent a shiver running through me.

"Well, lookee who's come to visit." Frankie came into the room minutes later with Jael following behind. Her dress looked slightly rumpled from her nap, but otherwise she was just as spry and alert as ever. Her gaze settled on Alden. "And you brought your young man, too."

I was sure my face flamed red, but I nodded. "This is Alden Norwood. Alden, this is Mrs. Frances Washington."

Frankie gave Alden a good study. "I understand you work for the same organization as Rena."

"Yes, ma'am," Alden said. "I've been with the WPA over a year."

"And what do you think about the gov'ment spending all this time and money on us former slaves?"

I held my breath. I didn't think Alden would be caught off guard by such a direct question, but he hadn't planned for it either.

"I believe understanding events of the past can help us make the future better for everyone. Our generation," he said, glancing at me, "doesn't know much about slavery. Your willingness to share your story will not only benefit us, but it will touch the lives of many people for years to come."

After a moment, Frankie chuckled, and I breathed again.

"Young man, you should think about becoming one of them politicians that sits up yonder on the hill in that big ol' capitol building. You've got the knack for saying just what a person wants to hear."

Alden grinned, clearly at ease. "You're not the first person to suggest that, ma'am."

A sense of satisfaction crept over me, watching them interact.

"Have you two eaten supper?" Frankie asked.

"No, ma'am," Alden answered before I could say a word. "Something sure smells good."

Was he wrangling for an invitation?

"Well, you best join us then. Jael's got a stew on the stove and corn bread in the oven. She may not know how to bake a loaf of bread, but her corn bread melts in your mouth."

I glanced at Jael to gauge her reaction, but she simply smiled. "Mama Fran's teaching us about bread making, though, isn't she, Rena? Pretty soon our bread will be just as good as hers."

We all laughed and made our way to the kitchen, as though it weren't completely out of the ordinary for two young white people to take a meal in the Hell's Half Acre home of a former slave. I refused to even consider what Mama would say if she were to find out.

After Jael produced two mismatched chairs from somewhere in the house, I helped her get the meal on the table while Frankie conversed with Alden.

"You don't sound like you're from around here," Frankie said, motioning for Alden to take the seat across from her.

"No, ma'am. I'm from Chicago." He smiled up at me as I set a bowl of steaming stew in front of him. He'd removed his hat, and for the first time I noticed his eyes were hazel and not brown as I'd originally thought.

"Chicago." Frankie's voice drew his attention away, and I returned to where Jael stood at the stove dishing up more stew. "I knew some folks who went up north after the war. They didn't stay long. Said they nearly froze to death that first winter. They hightailed it back to Tennessee as soon as they thawed out." Frankie nodded her thanks when I set a bowl in front of her.

Jael and I each carried our own bowls to the table.

"It's an interesting place to live, but I must say I'm enjoying my time in Tennessee." His gaze flicked to me, bringing a hot flush to my face. Alden picked up his spoon. "This looks delicious."

He seemed ready to dig in when Frankie spoke. "Would you mind offering thanks, Mr. Norwood?"

It was now Alden's face that turned bright red. "I, uh," he stammered, more flustered than I'd ever seen him. "I don't usually . . ."

Thankfully, Frankie took pity on him. "That's quite all right, Mr. Norwood. I'll say grace."

I bowed my head, too embarrassed for Alden to look at him.

"Lord, we thank thee for your many blessings. I especially thank you for these fine young people you've gathered round my table. Bless this food to our bodies. Amen."

Jael rose to get the corn bread while I stared down at my stew, feeling awkward.

"I apologize for surprising you like that, Mr. Norwood." Frankie stirred her stew, letting the air cool it. "When you get to be my age, you try not to miss an opportunity to give thanks to the Lord for every little blessing. You never know when you'll find yo'self face-to-face with him." She chuckled, then took a bite of the meal.

Alden's tense shoulders eased with the sound. Jael returned with a platter of thick corn bread dripping with butter. Frankie's declaration of it melting in one's mouth wasn't vain boasting. I'd never tasted anything more delicious. Jael promised to share her secret with me.

Frankie asked about Alden's family and wanted to hear more about life in Chicago. He answered each of her questions, but the easygoingness from his previous interaction with Frankie had disappeared. He suddenly seemed reserved, almost shy about talking about himself.

If Frankie noticed, she didn't let on. "What is your family's religious background?"

It was almost as though the tables had been turned, and Frankie had become the interviewer. I glanced at Alden, wishing now we hadn't come to visit Frankie. I didn't know the answer to her question, but it was clear Alden was uncomfortable with the topic.

"My mother's family was Jewish, but she hasn't practiced since she was a child. Father was raised Catholic."

Frankie gave a thoughtful nod. "We never had a name for our religious beliefs back in slavery times. We weren't Methodist or Baptist the way folks are today. We didn't go to a church building or have regular meetings." She dusted corn bread crumbs from the table into her gnarled hand and deposited them into her empty bowl. "Mammy tried to teach us chillens about God, but I was too young to understand. After I was sold time and time again, I didn't think much about God since he didn't think much about me. I figured I was better off without such beliefs."

Alden frowned. "If you don't believe in God, why do you say grace?"

"Oh, I believe in God, Mr. Norwood. I sure do."

"Why? Like you said, if he does exist, he doesn't seem to care about us. What's the point of putting one's faith in something or someone who allows slavery and evil to exist?"

The question hung in the air.

Frankie seemed to consider her response before speaking. "I'll answer that question if you'll answer one of mine."

Alden nodded.

"Do you believe in God, Mr. Norwood? Not in religion, but in a Creator, a Father?"

All eyes turned to him. I wondered how the conversation had taken us down this dangerous path, and I hoped it didn't lead to hurt feelings or angry words. Religious discussions were not something we ever broached in my home. Ever.

"I don't, Mrs. Washington." Alden sat straighter in his chair and met Frankie's gaze. "I mean no disrespect to you or anyone who does. I simply find that the God of the Bible doesn't make sense or have any place in our modern world."

Several silent moments passed before Frankie gave a slow nod. "Yes, Mr. Norwood. I know exactly what you mean. The things Mammy told me about God didn't add up. Especially after living in slavery."

"Then why would you believe in God now? What happened to make you change your mind?"

Frankie's gaze narrowed on Alden. "I didn't change my mind, young man. It ain't as easy as that. When we're set in our ways, nothin' nobody says can make us change what we think or believe. It took something bigger than just preacher talk or words in a book. No, sir, I didn't change my mind."

"What happened then?" Alden asked.

Frankie sat back in her chair and crossed her arms over her chest, an impish grin on her face. "God showed me I was wrong."

———

My stomach roiled at the stench that came from behind the row of canvas tents.

Hot July air hung heavy and still over the contraband camp, trapping odors from makeshift outhouses and garbage piles like a cork in a bottle full of putrid milk. I was weary of the filth, the noise, and the drudgery of camp life. Conditions had steadily deteriorated in the four months we'd been kept here. Food was sparse and often inedible, and tempers, including my own, had risen.

Male laughter greeted me when I ducked into the small tent I shared with another woman. As my eyes adjusted to the dim light, I found my cot occupied by a writhing couple.

My blood boiled. "Get outta here!"

Nell, the laziest gal I'd ever met, struggled up from beneath the man. At least she had the sense to look embarrassed as she tugged the front of her dress closed. The man stood, adjusting his own garments. I'd seen him around camp the past weeks, pretending to have a bad leg in order to avoid working for the Yankees, building their fortifications and digging trenches to keep the Confederates at bay.

"I told you I don't want no men in here." I glared at Nell until her gaze dropped to her bare feet. She couldn't be more than sixteen years old, but I wasn't about to share this cramped, moth-eaten, smelly tent with a gal who ended up in the family way and brought a screaming baby into the mix.

"Now, Frankie, you don't gotta be cross at Nell here," the man drawled, offering me a sugar-sweet smile and showing off even white teeth. No doubt it was the same smile he gave every other gal in camp, worming his way into their beds.

I narrowed my glare on him. "Don't speak to me. Don't look at me. And don't ever come into this tent again, or I'll tell them soldiers you ain't got no hurt leg. You been making them look like fools for believing your pathetic story 'bout how you injured your leg runnin' away from your massa." My eyes traveled his length. "I seen you plenty of times when the soldiers ain't looking, walking around without a limp."

A flash of concern crossed his face before he masked it. "My leg ain't none of your business. 'Sides, I really did hurt it comin' up from Georgia."

I took a step toward him. "You make it my business if you come back to this here tent. Understand?"

He only hesitated a moment before he walked out the canvas opening without another word.

"Why you gone and done that, Frankie?" Nell whined after he'd disappeared. "Hank said we gonna marry once we get up North."

I turned to face her, wondering that a gal could be so addlebrained. "He ain't gonna marry you, chile. He's been with half the gals in this camp. The only thing he gonna give you is a sickness in your body if you keep company with the likes of him."

Nell pouted but wisely remained silent. I stripped the rough blanket off my cot and carried it outside. No telling what varmints that man might have left on it. While I hung it across the rope stretched between our tent and the neighboring tent, a ruckus from across camp reached me. Excited voices, laughter, calls. I couldn't see what was happening, but I noticed most everyone headed in that direction.

Nell exited the tent. "What do you think all that's about?"

"How am I to know, girl? Best we see for ourselves."

We joined the throng of mostly women, children, and old men moving in the direction of the entrance to camp. When we reached the edge of the gathering, all I could tell was two or three covered wagons had arrived. As people shifted for a better view, a white woman in a black dress and bonnet climbed upon one of the wagon seats. But instead of settling in to drive the team of horses, she turned to face us.

"Ladies and gentlemen, my name is Illa Crandle."

Her strong voice reached me where I stood, and a hush went through the crowd. She wasn't tall or handsome, but something about her demeanor commanded attention.

"I come from Philadelphia, where many of us have been fighting against slavery for a long time."

A murmur lifted from those nearby. Like me, they'd probably never heard a white person speak about ending slavery. Not even the Federal soldiers milling around spoke of it. They were simply here to defeat the Confederate Army and bring the Union of states back together.

"We've come," she said, her gaze sweeping those standing near the wagons, although I couldn't see who she spoke of, "to join arms with thee. We hope to establish schools and churches, and it's our desire to help prepare thee for life away from slavery. God willing, this war will end soon, bringing with it freedom. Freedom to make thy own choices and to live where thee wishes."

It took a moment for her words to seep in, but a cheer eventually went up from the crowd. Beside me, Nell hollered and jumped like a tree frog, but I stood unmoving.

Why would I put my trust, my hope, in a white person? Illa Crandle's speech sounded nice, but I didn't need a white woman's help. I didn't need anyone's help. As soon as the white man's war ended, I planned to shake the dust of Nashville off my feet and never look back. Where I would go was still a mystery, but it would be my decision, not some white woman's.

I turned and headed back to the tent while the crowd pressed forward to hear more of Illa Crandle's promises. Her words were wasted on me. When I approached the entrance, a rustling noise came from inside. With a jerk, I opened the flap, and my mouth slackened.

There stood Hank, a burlap sack holding my meager possessions in his hands.

"What do you think you're doin' in here?" I marched in and snatched the bag from him. "You got no business comin' in here, rifling through my things."

Neither Nell nor I owned anything of value, but I still felt violated. Anger rushed through my blood.

"I told you never come to this tent again." My glare went from the bag in my hand back to him. "Worthless. That's what you is. While that white woman out there prattles on about freedom and ending slavery, you in here stealing what little we got."

I turned my back to him. "I guess them Yankees be right glad to hear your leg is all healed up and you can start digging them ditches."

I hadn't taken two steps toward the tent opening when I felt his arm snake around my neck and yank me backward. I landed on the dirt floor at his feet, the breath knocked out of me.

"You best shut that mouth o' yours, woman. Or maybe I'll shut it for you." Gone was the even-toothed smile from earlier. Now he snarled at me like a rabid dog.

Although I'd received my share of beatings in the past, I wasn't prepared when his boot slammed into my jaw. Stars filled my eyes, and I tasted blood. Before I could gain my bearings, he kicked me again and again.

I had one last thought before I blacked out.

I was going to die before I'd truly lived.

CHAPTER FOURTEEN

I woke to activity and voices around me, but I couldn't see a thing.

At first, I thought I'd gone blind, but with a little work I was able to force my eyelids open enough to let in the tiniest hint of light. Pain shot through my head, and I quickly shut my eyes against it.

Was I back on the plantation? Had I received yet another beating? *"When are you gonna learn, Frankie?"* Mammy used to say. It was a question I still asked myself all these years later.

"Thy eyes are quite swollen, my dear."

The voice was kind, yet I couldn't place it.

Familiar sounds reached me. Conversations. Laughter. A stern command. I realized then I wasn't on the plantation. I was still in the contraband camp.

"Here," the voice said. "Have a sip of water to quench thy thirst." Blessed moisture touched my tongue, but she took it away before I'd had my fill.

The voice of the mercy giver didn't belong to Nell or one of the other women from camp I'd become familiar with. I tried once again to see who spoke, but the same pain prevented me from seeing anything.

A cool, damp cloth went across my forehead and down my cheeks, soft and soothing. Whoever tended me had a gentle hand. I couldn't begin to guess who it was.

"Thy wounds shall heal, but I wonder if thy spirit shall require more from the Lord than what I can give thee."

The words failed to make sense, and I was too weary to ponder their meaning. I hoped whoever saw to me wouldn't leave. Despite the raw pain swirling throughout my head, oddly enough I felt safe.

I drifted to sleep and awakened again some time later to the same voice.

"I have some broth for thee, my dear."

The stranger proceeded to carefully lift my shoulders and wedge a pillow in to prop me up. I didn't cry out for fear she'd leave me alone. I wished I could see who the woman was because I couldn't begin to guess. No one in camp had ever demonstrated this kind of concern for another.

"Who are you?" My hoarse voice was unrecognizable.

A soft laugh. "Eat first; then we'll talk."

She spooned delicious warm broth through my swollen lips until I was pleasantly sated. A sip of cool water followed.

"My name is Illa Crandle. I'm with the Religious Society of Friends in Philadelphia."

Surprise washed over me. The white woman I'd seen on the wagon. What was she doing in my tent?

I tried to force my eyes open, but they wouldn't respond. "What do you want with me?"

"Only to serve. Thy friend Nell found you. We brought thee here to tend thy wounds. Does thee recall what happened?"

I did.

Hank had done this to me, but I wouldn't tell the Crandle woman. It was none of her affair. As soon as I mended, I'd get my revenge on Hank.

"Thee should rest." I felt movement beside me and heard the rustle of her skirts as she stood. "I will return later. Perhaps thee will feel more like talking then."

She spoke in low tones to someone nearby, but I couldn't make out the words. I wondered what the extent of my injuries were and who else knew about the beating.

When the room grew quiet and I felt I was alone, I let my bruised body relax, but my mind swam in a murky pool of emotions. I'd been robbed and beaten by my own kind, yet a white woman caringly tended my wounds. Anger and hatred for Hank swirled through me while confusion over the Crandle woman's kindness threatened to edge it out.

Helplessness washed over me, and I hated myself for it. Ever since the day I was sold away from Mammy, I'd despised helplessness. When overseers beat me and chased me down like an animal, I'd been helpless. When men used my body for their own pleasure and babies died, I'd been helpless to prevent it from happening.

But the one thing I'd fought to maintain control over was my emotions. No one could force me to love or hate. They were mine to decide. I wasn't about to allow this white woman to steal that away from me, no matter her attentive ministrations.

The next time she came to visit, I refused to speak or eat. I thought she would leave in a huff, but the minutes ticked by with only the soft sound of her breathing to let me know she still sat next to my cot.

Finally my taut nerves had enough. "Leave me alone."

It seemed an absurd thing to speak into the silence, considering she hadn't uttered a word or attempted to touch me.

More silence filled the space between us before she spoke. "When I was a girl, I found a robin with its wing broken. My father told me the poor thing would die, but I refused to accept that." She chuckled softly. "Papa always said I was stubborn. I put the bird in a cage and tended it. By some miracle it survived. I cried the day Papa said it needed to return to the wild."

Despite my declaration of wanting to be alone, I waited to hear the end of the story.

"I carried the cage to the edge of the cornfield. When I opened the door, the robin didn't fly away. For a moment I thought she wanted to stay with me, and that filled me with great joy. But suddenly she found the opening. I'll never forget watching her take flight, as though she'd never been injured. She soared higher and higher before she finally disappeared into the woods."

She paused a moment before adding softly, "I only wish to help thee take flight."

The next day I let her spoon broth into my mouth. I allowed her to bathe my face and arms. She didn't speak and neither did I, but the silence wasn't heavy. I still couldn't make out her face, yet I knew her hands well.

On the third day, I opened my eyes to her happy smile. "Good morning."

She looked different than what I remembered from the day she arrived at camp. That day she'd worn a large black bonnet and a black dress. Today she wore a simple sheer day cap over her graying hair and a dark-blue dress without the adornments most white women preferred.

"Perhaps today thee will want to rise from thy bed."

I did, but I didn't want her to believe she had charge over me. Even in my helpless state, I refused to surrender to the whims of a white person.

While she fed me, I glanced at my surroundings, surprised to find myself in a well-made tent. It was far larger than those we slaves occupied. A curtain separated my bed from the rest of the space, but I could see past it to two cots with colorful quilts, along with several trunks and a small writing desk and chair. Boxes and crates sat neatly stacked, and I wondered at their contents.

My study of the tent continued until my breath caught,

and I found myself staring at a stack of books sitting on the ground near the desk.

The Crandle woman turned to see what had captured my attention. "Ah, I see thee has noticed the books for our school." She faced me again. "One of the most vital skills we wish to impart to freemen and -women is the ability to read and write. Some believe school is only for children, but I daresay every adult can benefit from learning their letters."

I stared at her, not believing what I'd just heard. "You gonna teach slaves to read?"

She smiled. "Yes. Young and old alike. Reading is not only for pleasure; it will be essential to securing employment and assuring one is not being taken advantage of. There are those who don't believe thee and thy friends should learn to read, but I am not among them."

Memories flooded my mind, taking me back to the day the overseer found me with Charlotte's book. I'd longed to know what the letters and printed words meant back then, yet that book had cost me dearly. Now this white woman and her kind were offering to teach slaves to read. I wasn't sure what to make of it.

"Would thee be interested in learning thy letters?"

My attention jerked back to her.

Although she looked nothing like my former mistress, all I could see was Miz Sadie's wide, pale face, smirking as the overseer dragged me from the house.

"No." I turned away, my appetite gone. "I ain't interested in your books."

She stood after several moments. "I understand. But if thee changes thy mind, thee is most welcome to look through them. We have some on science and history, as well as story-books. The illustrations are quite good."

I didn't acknowledge her comments, and she finally turned and left me alone.

She and several other white ladies came and went from the tent throughout the day. A younger version of the Crandle woman brought me a noon meal consisting of bread soaked in milk and small bites of boiled chicken. Although my jaw was quite sore and swollen, thankfully it hadn't broken.

Nell came to visit me that afternoon. Her gaze darted around the spacious tent before she settled on a chair next to my cot.

"Miz Crandle made the Yankees put Hank in one of their prisons."

This news surprised me. "How'd she know it was him who beat me?"

"Someone seen him leaving the tent and come and told her. When the soldiers went looking for him, they found him with your bag."

I chuckled, then grimaced at the pain it caused. "Guess he's wishing he was digging them trenches right about now instead of sittin' in a Yankee prison."

Nell shrugged. A moment later, however, tears sprang up in her eyes. "I sorry, Frankie. It's my fault he beat you. If I had listened to you, this woulda never happened."

I almost reached for her but stopped myself before the

pain got too bad. "It weren't your fault, girl. He made up his own mind. Just watch yourself, you hear? Men like that are worthless. Next time it be you all bruised up, or worse."

She nodded, then glanced into the other area of the tent. "Miz Crandle gonna start up a school. Says we all need to learn to read and write so's we can make something of ourselves after the war ends. Sam already knows how to read real good."

I didn't care to discuss the school, so I settled on a new topic. "Who's Sam?"

Nell sighed and took on a silly look in her eyes. "He be the most handsome man I ever did see. And he's free. He come with Miz Crandle from Pennsylvania. He's been reading to us from the Bible in the evenings. I tell you, it's something listening to him read."

A free black man. There hadn't been many of those in Nashville before the Federals arrived. It was far too danger-ous to be free in the South. You could be snatched up and taken to auction. But now that the Union Army occupied the city, quite a few freemen had turned up and were working for the army building fortifications around the city. Yet from Nell's description of and ridiculous mooning over this one, I'd just as soon pass. I had no need for a man, free or slave, who had book learning.

I shooed her away, suddenly exhausted. Nell promised to return, no doubt still feeling guilty for bringing Hank to our tent. My eyes drifted closed and I dreamed about Charlotte's book. I woke with a start to the dim light of dusk.

"I'm sorry to wake you, ma'am."

The deep voice surprised me. A large figure on the other side of the curtain moved to the table. He struck a match and lit the lantern. When he lifted it, illuminating his face, I knew immediately who the man was.

Sam.

The freeman.

Nell was right. He was the most handsome man I'd ever seen.

And I didn't want anything to do with him.

———

Alden picked me up the next evening after work and drove to Frankie's. She'd invited us to join her and Jael for supper again, and I was anxious to find out more about Sam.

"Why do you think Frankie was afraid of Sam?"

Alden maneuvered the car through the darkening streets of Hell's Half Acre. Thick clouds had filled the sky all day, giving the neighborhood a shadowed, ominous feeling tonight despite soft light coming from windows.

He glanced at me. "What makes you think she was afraid of him?"

"I don't believe she thought he would hurt her or anything like that, but she was definitely afraid of him."

He chuckled. "Women are a mystery. You tell me why she was afraid."

I grinned. "I haven't figured it out yet." After a moment, I sobered, remembering Moss and how he was murdered right in front of Frankie. "I'm sure it must've been hard to imagine happiness after all she'd been through. She'd lost her mother, her babies, and a man she loved. I think it would be terrifying to care for anyone after all that."

We parked in front of Frankie's yellow house. She was waiting for us.

"Jael is helping a friend tonight with her sick little ones." She ushered us into her small living room. I noticed the kitchen was dark.

"Mrs. Washington, we don't want to be a bother. We can come back another time."

"It's no bother to have you young people here." She winked at Alden. "Especially if you help get a meal on."

I smiled. "We'd be happy to." Alden echoed his agreement.

We moved to the kitchen. It was decided a meal of pancakes and fried eggs—courtesy of a neighbor's chickens—would suit us all, and we set to work. I was surprised to find Alden quite comfortable in the kitchen. After stoking the fire to life, he volunteered to cook if we ladies would get the batter mixed, explaining that he'd often helped his mother prepare meals in the boardinghouse.

Frankie sat at the table and directed me to where the flour and other items were located. It felt a bit strange prowling through cabinets that didn't belong to me, but she seemed unconcerned by it.

"We had flapjacks nearly every day while I was living in the contraband camp. That and watery soup. I imagine it cost the Yankees a pretty penny to feed all of us. We didn't have no way to buy our own food, being that we'd been slaves up until the minute the Yankees arrived. I heard there were other contraband camps around Nashville and more throughout the state. Also heard rumors that the commander of our camp was stealing food meant for us and sellin' it at a store he opened in town." She shook her head, disgust written on her face. "Life wasn't pleasant in camp, but I guess I should've been a bit more grateful than I was at the time."

"How long were you in the camp?" Alden asked from his place at the stove. Eggs sizzled in a large frying pan, sending out a delicious aroma.

"The Yankees marched into Nashville in February of 1862. The war ended in April 1865."

Alden gave a low whistle. "Three years is a long time to live under those conditions."

Frankie nodded. "It was. The tents they gave us was the sorriest things you ever did see, with black mold growin' and holes that let in the cold, rain, or heat, depending on the time of year. Disease and sickness was rampant. Rashes, lung sickness, fevers. They even had to make a separate camp for those with smallpox. Too many folks died that shouldn't have. But after Illa Crandle showed up, things got a mite better. She knew how to handle them Federals in order to get what she wanted."

Frankie's voice and expression softened. "And for reasons I'll never understand, that woman was determined to make something of me. I just didn't know what."

CHAPTER
FIFTEEN

After I healed, I thought Illa Crandle would leave me alone. I was wrong.

I sat on a stump outside our tent in the bit of shade it offered, the afternoon heat nearly suffocating. Spring rains and cool air were but a memory, replaced with the meanness of summer. Nell and the others disappeared each day, spending time at the newly formed school that met in the shade of one of the few oak trees left standing. One of Illa's helpers served as the teacher, and their laughter and excitement often reached me.

But I had no desire to join them. Let *them* suffer the consequences of book learning.

A shadow fell over me. "Hello, Frankie." Illa stood between me and the sun. "I've found thee a job. 'Tis a blessing, to be sure."

I tilted my head and gazed up with half-closed eyes. "I ain't got need of a job."

What I needed was for the woman to leave me be. She'd pestered me every day since I left her tent. *"Frankie, how does thee feel?" "Frankie, thee best eat some of this soup." "Frankie, Frankie, Frankie."* I'd just about had enough of it and found myself practically hiding when I knew the woman was around. I was grateful she'd tended me when I was down. Even I wouldn't have done such for a complete stranger, especially if the roles had been reversed and a white person had been hurt. But I wasn't some child in need of a mammy. A white mammy, at that. I didn't need her fawning over me anymore.

"I hope thee will change thy mind. They'll pay for thy work."

My head jerked up. The woman had my attention despite my previous thoughts. "Who?"

She knelt in front of me, the delicate white fabric of her day cap peeking out from beneath the rim of a sturdier black bonnet that kept the sunshine from her face. "The army."

I scoffed. "The army don't pay for nothin'. They just order us around, like we was their slaves."

For months I'd watched soldiers load up every able-bodied man and boy from camp and force them to labor, day after day, as woodcutters, haulers, and corders. Conscripted, the army called it. Slavery without ownership, I called it. Nashville had been scalped of its trees, large and small, old and young, to provide material to build fortifications, housing for the officers, and forts, including the one just up the hill from our camp. Hour upon hour these conscripted men and boys toiled, the work as hard and exhausting as anything they'd done as slaves. I listened to their stories and complaints at night around the campfires, with most admitting some of the white soldiers from the North were almost as bad as the plantation owners. And as far as I knew, not one of them had received the promised payment for their work.

"They'll pay." The Crandle woman gave a firm nod of confidence. "I've seen to it."

I eyed her, wondering for the hundredth time why this white woman cared so much about us slaves. Why she cared about me. She could be back home in Pennsylvania, with food aplenty and the war far away. Who in their right mind would leave a comfortable life to come here?

I finally huffed, knowing she wouldn't leave me be unless I addressed her offer. "What do I have to do?"

"Laundry."

Oh, lawsy. Had the heat caused the woman to become addlebrained?

Everyone had seen the huge vats outside the soldiers' camp. Dozens of slave women worked over hot fires, washing sheets, blankets, and clothes for the Yankees. The backbreaking work wasn't something I'd wish on anyone. There were simply too many soldiers and too much laundry.

I shook my head. "I ain't interested."

"Thee would not be doing laundry for the whole company. Thee would only work for the officers and then only for those who haven't taken houses or hotel rooms in town."

Despite my firm resolve against the job, my mind quickly tallied the men at the fort and in the garrison who wore uniforms distinguishing them as officers. Far fewer than the hundreds of enlisted men who roamed the area.

"Why can't the gals over to the soldier camp do their laundry?"

"The officers prefer to keep their things separate."

That made sense. I considered the offer, but I wasn't convinced. It still meant I'd be out in the heat of the day, bending over a hot cauldron, washing white men's clothing. "How much they pay?"

"They'll pay four dollars a month."

In spite of myself, I felt a thump of excitement grip my heart.

I'd never been paid for work. Some slaves I'd met in camp told of masters who allowed them to earn a bit of money hiring out to others or selling crops they grew on their own time, but I'd never even held a coin of my own. Only on rare occasions had Mr. Waters sent me on errands that required money. He'd count out the coins, put them in a pouch, and tell me not to open it. Not even when I reached my destination was I to take them out. I'd simply hand the pouch to the store owner, never touching the money.

How did one know how much each gold piece was worth? And what about paper money? There was so much I needed to learn about the world before I was turned loose in it. Maybe it wouldn't be so bad doing the officers' laundry if I knew I'd get paid for it. The thought of having my own money was tempting.

Illa waited. I mulled it over again and again. Finally I drew a breath. "I'll do it," I said and quickly clamped my mouth closed, afraid I might take the words back.

My agreement must have surprised her, for her graying brows disappeared beneath her bonnet. A moment later, a smile spread across her face. "Thee does keep me on my toes, Frankie." She stood. "We'll get thee started tomorrow morning. It's best to work in the early hours, before the day gets too hot."

Had any other white woman said such a thing, I would have laughed, imagining she knew nothing about work and hot days. But I didn't laugh at Illa. She worked harder than most slaves. She tended the sick, held colicky babies, helped cook meals, broke up arguments, and did anything else that needed doing. She'd quickly earned the admiration of most everyone in the contraband camp as well as many of the soldiers.

Sam approached us then, much to my chagrin. He smiled, tipped his hat, and sent me a polite nod. "Miss Frankie. Sure is hot out here. Might should join them others under the tree where it's a bit cooler."

I barely acknowledged him before turning away. I wasn't sure why, but I disliked the man greatly. He was too courteous. Too handsome. Too . . . everything.

"Frankie has agreed to become the laundress for the officers," Illa said, pleasure in her voice.

I didn't look at her or Sam.

"That's mighty fine news. I'm sure they'll appreciate your work."

It seemed rude to completely ignore him, so I gave a quick

nod without looking up. I stood and dusted off my hands. "I best get inside, out of the sun."

"I'll meet thee at the officers' quarters at dawn." I found a smile on Illa's face. "The morning air will do us good after all this heat."

Without meaning to, my gaze shifted to Sam. His grin revealed teeth as straight and white as Hank's. I guessed he was mighty proud of them since he showed them off all the time.

Before he could say anything else, I ducked into the tent, belatedly remembering why I'd abandoned it earlier. The air was stifling. I'd wait until they walked away before going outside again.

I lay down on my cot, thinking it'd be cooler if I could just be still awhile. I closed my eyes, feigning sleep should anyone peek inside the tent. My mind, however, whirled like a twister.

I had a job. A real job. For the first time in my life, I'd be paid for my work.

My eyes flew open. Panic surged ahead of my elation.

I'd never dealt much with the soldiers. They weren't too friendly, and Nell and I determined it best to keep our distance. Would the officers be demanding and cruel like a master? What if I ruined their clothes? Lye soap wasn't always dependable. And what of their blue jackets? Surely the wool they were made from couldn't be washed. How would I ever get them clean?

Sweat broke out on my forehead.

What punishment would I receive if I couldn't do the job

properly? Would they beat me like an unsatisfied master? Send me to prison with Hank?

My heart hammered.

Maybe I shouldn't have accepted the job. I'd never tended a white person's laundry before. Not even for Mr. Waters. He and his family had house servants who took care of their personal needs. I'd simply cleaned the warehouse and offices and run an occasional errand.

"You're a smart girl, Frankie. Ain't nothin' you can't do if you set your mind to it."

Mammy's voice in my head stilled my racing thoughts.

Mammy'd always said things like that, trying to teach me even though I was so hardheaded. I couldn't recall what I'd been trying to accomplish on that long-ago day, but her encouragement returned to me as clear as the blue sky above. In the short time I'd had with her, she'd tried to instill in me a confidence that seemed in direct contrast to our position as slaves. I knew she'd been an obedient servant to the Halls, but her desire for freedom and hope for a better life for her children never waned. Maybe confidence in oneself had nothing to do with what other folks thought or did. Maybe it was deep down inside you, just waiting to be let loose like a spring of water gushing to the surface.

What would Mammy think of me hiring myself out to wash Yankee officers' drawers?

I chuckled, then sobered.

I'd been thinking about Mammy a lot lately. When I first came to the contraband camp, I searched for her. Every day

I'd ask newcomers if they knew Lucindia from the Halls' plantation, but no one ever did. I dreamed of finding her once we were truly free, no matter how long it took.

I sucked in a deep breath and blew it out.

Mammy would want me to take the job. "I'll make you proud, Mammy," I whispered into the hot breeze coming through the flap.

The next morning, I was up long before the sun. Snores came from Nell's side of the tent as I tiptoed outside to greet the day. I hadn't left the contraband camp too many times in the months I'd been here. I had nowhere to go. While we weren't required to carry a pass as we'd needed to when we were slaves, the soldiers guarding the entrance to camp made certain to ask me my business before letting me go any further. Miz Illa said the soldiers were there to keep us all safe from our former owners and those who'd want to steal us away to sell us, but I couldn't help but feel like I was doing something wrong by leaving camp each time I passed their stony faces.

The soldier camp was located between the contraband camp and the fort. I made my way there, feeling the outsider. No one bothered me, and some of the men even tipped their heads politely as I walked past, but mostly I was ignored. I saw several women from the contraband camp already busy cooking over fires or carrying baskets of laundry.

True to her word, Illa met me at the far end of the soldier camp where the officers lived. Those men didn't sleep in canvas tents like the enlisted men. Cabins and a number of larger buildings had been constructed for their use.

"Good morning, Frankie." Illa's bright smile rivaled the sun just peeking over the eastern horizon, tinging the sky with shades of pink, blue, and gold. "I'm happy thee did agree to this job. I think thee will find it rewarding in the long run."

I followed her to the back of one of the larger buildings. Several big kettles hung over bricked circles where the remains of fires lay. I counted five in all. Beyond that, lines were strung in rows for clothes to dry on.

"There are baskets in each of the men's quarters where they leave their laundry." She pointed to the cabins. "Thee will want to make note of which basket belongs to whom, to avoid getting them mixed up."

A thread of trepidation began to wind itself through my stomach.

I hadn't thought about the laundry itself and how I'd know what shirt belonged to which officer. I'd need to be extra attentive when gathering the dirty things.

"There's plenty of soap, although I daresay it's the strongest lye soap I've used. Take care with thy hands when using the washboards, and use the paddles as much as possible." She motioned toward the big kettles. "Sam will be by to help tote water and get the fires going this morning."

To this I jerked my head toward her. "I don't need his help."

Illa ignored my hard tone. "It's quite a chore hauling all that water by thyself." Her gaze drifted to my poor hand.

"I don't need his help," I repeated, my shoulders stiff.

A moment passed before she gave in. "Very well. If thee

changes thy mind, he'll be around. He also works for the officers, running errands, tending their horses, and such."

"I thought he worked for you."

"No. Sam escaped from a plantation in eastern Tennessee ten years ago and found his way to Philadelphia. When he heard about our mission here in Nashville, he wanted to join us."

Now that was a wonder, I thought. An escaped slave risking the threat of being recaptured to help those still in bondage. It didn't make me like him any better, but I had to admit to a bit of admiration for anyone who would do such a thing.

Illa left me then, and I set to work hauling bucket after bucket of water to fill the kettles. The pump wasn't far from where I was to work, but the buckets grew heavy once they were filled. I wouldn't ask for Sam's help, though. Once I had all five kettles full, I got the fires blazing. I'd need a lot of hot water for washing, but I planned to rinse everything in cold water. It would save time, effort, and wood.

Once I had everything ready for washing, I ventured to the first cabin. I knocked on the door, but no one answered. I looked around. Was I supposed to just walk into the private quarters of a Union Army officer without supervision? No one seemed to care that I stood at the door. The soldiers went about their business, leaving me unnoticed.

I reached for the knob and gulped. With one last look around, I opened the door and peeked inside. A cot similar to my own was neatly spread with an army blanket. A small desk sat in the corner, piled with maps and papers. Pegs held miscellaneous items of clothing. In the corner to my left sat the laundry basket, just as Illa described.

I hurried in, snatched up the basket, and was back outside before anyone could say I'd lingered. I wouldn't want to be blamed should items go missing.

Over the course of the morning, I repeated the process a half-dozen times. Only once was the owner of the laundry in residence. A young lieutenant sat at his desk writing a letter when I approached his open door. He barely acknowledged me and simply pointed at the basket in the corner when I said I'd come for it.

Heeding Illa's advice, I devised a plan to keep the laundry and the owner straight in my mind. The cabins were laid out in a neat row, so that was the order in which I washed, rinsed, and hung the laundry. After my initial misgivings about washing the men's personal garments, I soon was so busy, I didn't even notice what item I was scrubbing.

I saw Sam in my comings and goings. The ever-present smile remained on his face as he greeted the officers, soldiers, former slaves. It didn't matter who he happened across. They were all treated to that smile and a polite word.

By midafternoon, with the sun beating down and heat coming from the fires, exhaustion swept over me. I hadn't worked this hard in ages. Not even when I'd labored in the tobacco fields. My body wasn't used to physical labor, and the muscles in my back and arms screamed their discomfort. I knew I'd feel the misery in the morning.

One scraggly tree remained nearby, and I sat beneath its

pitiful offering of shade. I'd washed all the officers' shirts, socks, and underthings and had them hanging out to dry. I could only hope my tired brain remembered whose was whose once they came off the line and I pressed them with sadirons. I still needed to empty the kettles and bank the fires, but my aching back demanded I stay where I was.

"We sure could use some rain right about now."

I looked up to find Sam a few paces away. He wasn't smiling, although he wore a pleasant expression despite trails of sweat dripping down the sides of his face.

He held out a canteen. "Thought you might like some cool water."

My first reaction was annoyance. Why did he presume to know what I might need?

But then I realized how thirsty I was. I hadn't taken time to drink or eat anything all day, focused as I'd been on doing well my first day. No wonder I felt light-headed.

"Much obliged." He handed me the canteen, and I drank until there wasn't one drop left. I gave a slight shrug as I handed the empty container back to him. "Guess I forgot all about drinking anything in this heat."

He nodded. "Wouldn't want you to get sun sickness." His glance went from me to the lines of clean laundry flapping in the hot breeze. "You sure been workin' hard. The men, they 'ppreciate a hard worker. They got rid of the last woman 'cuz she was lazy. I see they don't have to worry about that with you."

Despite my dislike for the man, his compliment eased some of my worry. "I just hope I don't get their drawers mixed up when I put 'em away."

A deep chuckle rumbled in his chest. I couldn't help but enjoy the sound.

"I'd be right pleased to empty them kettles for you, Miss Frankie, while you tend to other things."

I didn't want to become beholden to this man, yet my weary body couldn't muster the strength to finish the job. I'd let him do it—this once—but I didn't want him to think it was a favor to me.

"Suit yo'self." I gave an uncaring shrug. "I've got some tidying up to do, and I want to check one of the shirts that needs mending."

A grin lifted the corners of his mouth. "Yes, ma'am."

He set off, a spring in his step despite the heat. I watched him take the thick rag I'd used to keep my hands from getting burned and lift the heavy kettle as though it weighed but a pound or two. The muscles in his arms bulged and strained, but he gave no indication the task was difficult.

I dragged myself to my feet and cleaned up the laundry area. By the time he finished with the last kettle, I was ready to find my tent.

"It'd be my pleasure to walk you home, Miss Frankie." He tipped his head politely and smiled. "I'm going that direction myself."

While I was grateful for his help with the kettles, I had

no desire to spend time with the man. "I'm sure I can get there fine on my own." Begrudgingly I added, "Thank you for emptying the water."

I started toward the contraband camp, hoping he'd stay put. I'd gone several paces when I heard, "I'll see you tomorrow, Miss Frankie."

Curiosity made me turn around.

That big ol' smile stayed in my mind the rest of the evening.

CHAPTER SIXTEEN

I groaned when I saw Mary's car in the driveway after Alden dropped me off at home.

We'd ended our evening with Frankie a bit earlier than I would have liked. She nearly dozed off while telling her story, so we'd excused ourselves, promising to come again over the weekend.

I glanced down the road. I could slip over to Grandma Lorena's and no one would know. Frankie's mentioning of Sadie Hall once again had me thinking about the familiar name. Maybe Grandma could help with the mystery.

Voices and laughter came through an open window in the house.

If they would simply leave my job and Frankie out of the conversation, I wouldn't mind visiting with my mother and sister. Contrary to how it appeared most of the time, I did love them.

I quietly entered the house and set my things down in the living room. Light from the kitchen spilled into the adjoining dining room, dark since it was long past the supper hour. After the stock market crash, we'd had to sell some of our possessions, including the silver and Mama's china. It still made me sad to see the empty hutch in the corner as I made my way toward the kitchen.

"She needs a husband. How is she ever going to find one if she keeps this up?"

Mama's voice lifted above the chattering and giggles of the children. I wondered which of Mary's friends they were discussing. Not many of her classmates remained unattached, but there were some who seemed resigned to spinsterhood.

"Have you met the man who's driving her downtown? Norwood something, isn't it?"

Mary's question brought me up short just outside the kitchen entrance. They were talking about me, I realized.

"No. She won't bring him to the house." Mama gave a disgruntled sound. "I can't imagine he's much of a gentleman if he won't climb out of that car of his and come to the door."

"He isn't picking her up for a date. They work together."

Silently I thanked Mary for understanding.

"Still," she continued, "it would be nice for him to meet you and Daddy."

I rolled my eyes. Didn't they have more important things to discuss than my relationship with Alden?

"How can she meet eligible young men if she's spending all her time in—" Mama paused, then hissed—"that neighborhood? Oh, the very thought makes me ill. That place isn't fit for anyone, but especially not *our* kind."

"It does seem odd that she enjoys interviewing those people. Other than Dovie, I don't think Lulu has ever spoken to a black person."

"Of course she hasn't." Mama sounded offended. "We raised you girls to know your place in society. She won't have a prayer of a chance at a good marriage if word gets out about this. I can imagine what Peggy Denny will say if she learns about it. It won't matter to her that the job is only temporary. No. She'll let everyone know *where* Rena has been spending her time and with whom."

Just then the sound of small feet approached. My niece appeared in the doorway and looked up at me. "Mommy," she bellowed, loud enough for the neighbors to hear, "Auntie Rena is here."

I'd been found out. I had no wish to defend myself against their gossip, but it was too late to escape to my room. I breezed into the kitchen and forced a smile to my lips. "What a nice surprise to find my sister, niece, and nephews here."

A look of guilt flashed across Mama's face, but Mary eyed me as though she knew I'd been listening to their conversation.

"I thought you were going to *that woman's* house for dinner." Mama sniffed as though the odor from Frankie's house might have followed me home.

"We did, but she was feeling a little tired, so we didn't stay long."

Buddy toddled over to Mama and lifted his arms. She bent to pick him up and wrinkled her nose. "You, young man, need your diaper changed."

Mary started to her feet, but Mama waved her back into her seat. "I'll take him upstairs and give him a bath. That way he's all ready for bed when you get home." She gave Mary a pointed look. "You and your sister can have a chat."

She carried Buddy out of the room, with James and Holly on her heels, begging to take a bath too. Their voices faded as the group noisily climbed the stairs.

Before Mary could say anything, I held up my hand. "I don't want to hear one word about my job with the FWP, about Mama's opinion of it, or about what Peggy Denny might have to say."

Mary's brow shot up. "You needn't be so rude, Lulu. I knew you were listening to us. I was simply going to ask how your day went."

She seemed genuine, so I let my hand drop. "I had a good day. The woman I interviewed was a house servant before the war. It was interesting to hear how her life differed from those who'd worked in the fields."

Mary sighed. "Homer's daddy wants to hire a housekeeper for us, but Homer said he doesn't want a strange black lady going through his things when we aren't looking."

That was all she had to say? "What does that have to do with the woman I interviewed?"

Her face went blank. "Well, nothing, but when you mentioned she was a house servant, it reminded me about our need for a housekeeper. I told Homer we could hire a white maid, but he said that was an even worse idea."

My blood boiled. I wanted to punch my brother-in-law and shake my sister. "I'm talking about slavery, Mary. These people weren't hired to do a job; they were forced to do it. They didn't have a choice. If they didn't comply, they were beaten and eventually sold to someone else."

Mary frowned. "Why are you suddenly so concerned with slavery? Mama is worried about you, and now I see why."

"Because I care about someone other than myself?"

The barb struck its mark. "I care about my family, Lulu. I have three children who depend on me for everything. Their father is—" She clamped her mouth shut and looked away.

Guilt washed over me. I shouldn't have baited her. "I know, Mary. I'm sorry."

"You don't know everything," she whispered, tears swimming in her eyes when she looked up at me. "I'm not sure how much longer I can stay with Homer."

We stared at each other. Her quiet words shocked me, and she seemed a little surprised that she'd voiced them aloud. "You're thinking about leaving him?" While I felt she should have dumped the jerk long ago, this was serious.

Her slim shoulders lifted in a shrug. "I'm just tired of it, Lulu. He's always out with his buddies, drinking and gambling. I know he's been with other women, too."

I sank down into the chair across the table from her. "Oh, Mary."

"I'm not an idiot, you know. I'm aware of his wild ways. I kept hoping Papa Whitby could talk some sense into Homer, or at least control him somehow with money." She wiped a tear that trailed down her pale cheek. "He was fired from his job yesterday. I haven't told Mama yet."

I reached to grasp her hand in mine, something we hadn't done in years. The sisterly action brought fresh tears to her eyes. It would be silly for me to offer any advice, being that I wasn't a wife or a mother. What would she do if she left her husband? How could she raise three children on her own?

We sat in silence for several minutes before she squeezed my hand and stood. "Don't mention any of this to Mama. I wouldn't want her to worry. Not yet, anyway."

I nodded. "I'm not making much with the FWP, but if you and the children need anything . . ."

She gave a sad smile. "Papa Whitby has always been generous with me and the kids. We'll be fine."

After Mary took her children home, I bade Mama good night and went to my room. I was too keyed up for bed, so I reached for my notebook and found the pages I'd filled at Frankie's. Her story of life in the contraband camp came alive in my mind, and I began to wonder about its location. More than seventy years had passed, so evidence of it would most likely be long gone. Still, I'd like to know more about it.

I turned to a clean sheet of paper and jotted a note.

Where was the contraband camp near Nashville?

More questions flooded my mind, and I wrote them down as well.

Where was the Halls' plantation? What was Sam's last name? Is anyone from the camp still alive?

I tapped my pencil on the notebook, wishing I had answers to the questions. With a flop onto the bed, I stared up at the ceiling.

When had Frankie's story become much more than an interview for the FWP? I thought back to the day I met her. I'd been shocked to discover she was 101 years old. She'd seen so much in her lifetime. Even more than Grandma Lorena. Frankie's stories of being sold and beaten were horrible, yet her courage to survive it all touched me somewhere deep, in a place I hadn't realized existed until I met her.

Wasn't that what life was about? To know and be known. To offer encouragement to others and share the burdens we all face. No matter the color of one's skin, weren't we all supposed to care about each other? My own sister was suffering, but I'd shown her little compassion over the years. Accusing her of being concerned only for herself was like the pot calling the kettle black, as the saying goes. Ever since the stock market crash, I'd wallowed in my own self-pity. My job at the newspaper allowed me some semblance of redeeming the life I'd lost, but then I was fired. The position with the FWP had initially been about doing something that would bring me back to feeling like the me I'd lost seven years ago.

But Frankie and all she'd lived through deserved more than that. Maybe time and maturity helped me see this more clearly than I would have years before. Certainly had the earth-shattering events of October 29 not happened, I would have never taken a job such as the one I now held. I wouldn't have ever considered going into Hell's Half Acre, escorted or not. The plight of the slave from bygone eras would've remained as foreign to me as it was to my mother. I would have never met Frankie Washington and heard her story.

I sat up and stared out to the night sky, astounded where my thoughts had led.

I'd never dreamed this possible, but I'd just discovered something good actually came out of the crash and all the changes it brought to my life.

———

I had a request for Alden when he arrived Saturday morning to take me to Frankie's.

"Would you mind if we stopped at the library?" I knew we weren't far from the stately white limestone building on Eighth Avenue. "There's a book I'm interested in reading."

"Sure. What's the title?" He turned the car toward the library.

"*Uncle Tom's Cabin* by Harriet Beecher Stowe."

He nodded. "I think that's a fine idea. My mother has a copy. I read it as a teenager, and I believe it helped me understand slavery even more." He glanced at me as we pulled into the parking lot. "When President Lincoln met Mrs. Stowe, he credited her as the author of the book that helped start the war."

I remembered hearing about *Uncle Tom's Cabin* in school, but it wasn't a book my teacher recommended. As a student, I hadn't given it any thought, but recently I began to wonder about the story. Like Alden said, even President Lincoln was said to have read it. I was curious if any of the things Frankie had shared were similar to what the characters in the fictional tale experienced.

The sharp-nosed librarian scowled when I asked for the book. "What is a young lady like you doing reading such things?"

I simply smiled. "Learning." From his place next to me at the counter, Alden covered a laugh with his hand.

The librarian huffed before turning to search her card files for the location of the book. When she went to retrieve it, the young woman left in charge of the desk came over. She glanced from side to side as though making sure no one was listening, then leaned over to whisper, "There's an excellent biography about Mrs. Stowe, if you're interested."

I nodded eagerly, and she went off to find it as the older woman returned, her face pinched like she'd eaten sour grapes.

"I don't know why we have this book on our shelves. Literature like this only stirs up things best left in the past."

Like Mama, this woman wouldn't be convinced of the benefits of the FWP slave interviews, so there wasn't any point in explaining my motivation in asking for the book.

Thankfully, the younger woman returned with the biography, and the sour-faced librarian left me in her care.

"I admire Mrs. Stowe's writings," the young woman said as she jotted my name on the paper lists of those who'd checked out the books prior to me. There weren't many.

"Thank you." I gathered the books. "I'm sure I will too."

Alden had a surprise for Frankie and me when we arrived at her house a short time later.

"I brought a camera today." He took a shiny black box from its leather case. Two glass lenses on the front reminded me of an owl's big eyes. "The Works Progress Administration hopes to collect as many photographs of former slaves as possible to go with the stories."

Frankie eyed the strange-looking contraption. "Well, now, I ain't had my picture made since I was a young woman. Them cameras look different these days. It's smaller than the ones I remember."

Alden nodded. "It's very easy to operate." He opened the top and tinkered with a knob, explaining the process, before meeting her gaze again. "Would you be willing to have your picture taken?"

At first, I wasn't sure she would comply. But after a long moment, a slow smile slid up her face. "I 'spect if the gov'ment wants a picture of ol' Frankie, I shouldn't deny them that pleasure."

While Alden scouted the best lighting for the picture, Frankie invited me back to her bedroom. "I'd like to freshen up a bit. You can come on back and help, if you care to."

I followed her down the narrow hallway to the room on the right. I'd only peeked in the door that first day in my quest for a bathroom. Now I had time to take in the details, few as they were.

"I suppose my dress will have to do, but some years ago I was given these earrings." She opened a plain wooden box on top of a dresser and took out two silver hoops. "I don't wear such things these days, but when I was younger, I enjoyed dressing up every now and then." She handed the earrings to me. "Would you help get these on my ears? I'm afraid my poor old hand can't manage it."

I took the hoops from her and set to work. I'd helped Grandma Lorena with her jewelry many times. It felt right somehow, being that close to Frankie, helping with a task familiar to women of all colors.

When I had the earrings in place, she glanced in an old mirror on the wall, its worn silvering distorting the edges. "You probably think I'm silly, me an old woman, fussing about a picture," she said, using a small comb to straighten her short white hair.

"I don't think you're silly at all." Our gazes met in the glass. "I'm glad Alden thought to bring a camera."

"You two seem to be gettin' along."

Heat rushed to my face. "We're becoming friends."

She turned to me, a half smile on her lips. "Mm-hmm. Friends is good."

We returned to the living room only to find Alden on the front porch.

"The light is perfect out here." He indicated the chairs on the porch. "Mrs. Washington, if you'll have a seat, I'll step down off the porch and take the picture looking up at you."

Frankie settled in the chair and turned to face Alden while I moved out of the way. Her hands rested in her lap, with her right hand covering her gnarled fingers. A plain gold band I'd never noticed before sparkled in the sunlight.

Alden looked into the camera, tried various angles, but eventually frowned and shook his head.

"Perhaps you should look at Rena," he said, motioning to where I stood on the walk amid the flowers, just down from the porch steps.

She nodded, turned her head, and faced me. I thought she might smile, but she took on a pensive look. Before Alden could snap the picture, Frankie brought her right hand up and covered her lips as though deep in thought.

I heard the camera click.

"Perfect." Alden cranked a lever and smiled.

Frankie continued to stare past me. Only after I returned to the porch did she seem to shake herself out of her reverie.

"Funny, I hadn't thought of that photograph in years."

Alden glanced at me. I shrugged. "What photograph is that, Mrs. Washington?"

"A photographer came to the contraband camp sometime after Illa Crandle got me the job doing laundry. One day she gathered a group of us slaves to have our picture made." She chuckled. "We had to stand still for the longest time before that man came up from beneath his black cloth and said he was finished. We couldn't figure out how the thingamajig worked or if he was just fooling with us. Years later, a professor put out a book about the war here in Tennessee. He was giving a speech at Fisk University, and I went to hear him. Would you believe he had a copy of that picture?"

"Do you recall the name of the professor?" Alden asked, his eyes sparking with interest.

Frankie shook her head. "No, that's been too many years ago. But I was right happy to see that photograph. I'd forgotten some of the people in it, but Miz Illa and Nell were there."

"Was Sam in the picture too?" I asked. I wasn't sure if the familiarity we'd experienced in her bedroom gave me courage, but I couldn't leave this question unanswered.

A soft smile parted her lips. "Yes, Sam was there. And wouldn't you know, he was the only one smiling."

CHAPTER
SEVENTEEN

Sam.

I couldn't seem to get away from that man. If I needed water, he was there to haul it. When I accidentally let my fires go out, he had them blazing in minutes. Despite my gruff words, ugly glares, and downright rudeness, the man would not take the hint and leave me alone.

"Folks is talkin' about you, Frankie."

Nell and I sat on our cots, wrapped in blankets to ward off a chilly October wind blowing outside the tent. Illa Crandle wouldn't allow labor on Sundays, so the day was ours to enjoy despite the turn in the weather.

"What do I care?" I pretended nonchalance, but inside, I fumed. I didn't like being the subject of gossip.

"Folks is wonderin' why you so mean to Sam when it be clear as day he likes you."

I scoffed. "That man likes everybody. He ain't got no special feelings for me."

"That's not what people are sayin'."

"Best you not listen to tittle-tattle, girl. Nor spread it."

We sat in silence before Nell continued the conversation. "Why don't you like Sam? Ain't no one nicer than him."

I didn't want to discuss Sam with anyone, let alone Nell. But I knew she wouldn't leave it alone, so I decided to be honest. "I don't like him because I think he's fake. I think he's like one of them porcelain dollies with a painted-on smile." I gave her a pointed look. "Just like Hank."

Nell shook her head. "Oh no, Frankie. Sam ain't nothin' like Hank."

"How would you know? You couldn't tell Hank was a good-for-nothing when he was laying on top of you."

Hurt crossed Nell's face. "Maybe not, but I know Sam ain't anythin' like him. You should come to the Bible readings he gives. It ain't just for those of us takin' lessons at the school."

Nell and the others talked nonstop about the readings when Sam first arrived. They discussed fascinating stories I'd never heard of, with floods and kings and healings, but I refused to join them each night after supper. While a crowd gathered around Sam and his black book, I went back to the tent to fall into bed after a long day of scrubbing and pressing officers' clothes.

Sometime after Nell's and my discussion, curiosity got the better of me. When a group gathered around Sam after supper, I hung near the back, hoping to go unnoticed. I had to admit it was something special to hear a black man read.

I never thought I'd live to see a day like such, and it brought up feelings I didn't want to contend with.

The next day, Sam came to me while I was up to my elbows in a tub of hot, sudsy water.

"Miss Frankie," he said, twisting his hat around in his hands and acting more nervous than I'd ever seen him. "I has something to say."

I straightened and wiped my hands on my apron. "Go on then. I's busy and can't stand around jawing all afternoon."

He nodded, then took a big breath. "You ain't gonna like this much. I keep tellin' the Lord he's made a mistake, but he ain't backing down."

I frowned. Had he gotten into the whiskey some soldiers illicitly sold to folks in the contraband camp? I'd never known Sam to be a drinking man, but he was sure acting soused. "What foolishness are you talkin' about?"

"Ain't foolishness, Frankie. When I was back in Philadelphia, the Lord told me I'd find my wife in Tennessee."

My eyes widened. Surely he didn't mean—

"And I have." His gaze landed on me.

I took a step back, worried he might try to grab me.

"But the thing is," he went on, as serious as one could be, "I don't want to get married until we're free. Truly free."

"I thought you were free," I said, although I hadn't intended to enter the crazy conversation at all.

He nodded. "I declared myself free when I escaped from the plantation and made it to Philadelphia. But if my former master found me now, he'd have the legal right to take me

on back as his slave. Same as you. Same as all these folks."
Distress filled his face. "It ain't true freedom, what we have
now, Frankie. If the Yankees lose this here war, I 'spect it'll
mean trouble for us. We could hightail it north, but that won't
solve the real issue. I want us to start our new life together
as man and wife as a *free* man and woman."

While I couldn't fault him for his convictions, I was not
the woman for him.

"That all sounds fine and good, but you best keep looking
for that wife. I ain't never getting married."

A slow smile curled his lips. "You can argue with me,
Frankie, but you can't argue with the Lord."

I watched him walk away, a feeling in the pit of my stomach
that Sam knew something I didn't. It wasn't a good feeling
at all.

Fall turned to winter, and life in the camp wore on. Every
so often I'd find a gift from Sam lying on my cot or beside the
container of lye soap in the laundry area. Just small things at
first. A pretty maple leaf. An extra hunk of cheese wrapped
in cloth. Nell swooned when she discovered he'd left me a pair
of warm gloves.

"That man be crazy in love with you, Frankie." She sighed.
"I wish someone would love me like that."

Usually I rebuked such talk. I didn't like discussing Sam,
mostly because I didn't want anyone to know my feelings
toward him had softened since he'd declared he was going to
marry me. Truth be told, I sometimes found a secret smile
on my lips when I considered the prospect. But more often

than not, fear gripped my insides when our eyes met across the camp and Sam sent me his special smile. It wasn't the big grin he wore when talking with others. It was softer, less showy. Intimate.

What if I gave my heart to Sam and something terrible happened to him? If the Confederates won the war, none of us slaves would be free. Who knew where we might end up when it was all over. I couldn't bear watching him sold away—or worse. No, it was best to keep my distance. To keep telling myself and everyone else that I didn't care about Sam. Maybe if I said it enough, my ol' fool heart would listen.

Christmas Day arrived, bright sunshiny but cold as ice. Everyone had the day off, and we enjoyed a fine dinner of roasted wild goose and turnips provided for us by Illa's Friends Society. After such a big meal, I thought to take a walk and stretch my legs. When Sam appeared by my side, I couldn't refuse his company on a joyous day like this one.

"I dream about celebrating Christmas in my own home someday," he said, surprising me with his sentimental thoughts. I'd never once considered such a thing. Christmas had always been for white people.

"What would you have?"

He grinned. "*We'll* have us a big tree, tied with pretty ribbons and candles. There'll be presents under the tree for all the chillens."

I stopped walking. "All the chillens? How many young'uns you planning to have?"

"As many as the Lord gives us."

I let the comment pass. He'd taken to using *us* and *we* when he talked about the future. It aggravated me at first, especially when he accompanied it by saying the Lord told him such and such about me and him. But over the months, I'd grown used to it, and it didn't bother me as much. I still didn't plan on marrying the crazy man, but I'd come to the conclusion he was harmless.

We climbed halfway up the hill behind the camp. The fort the army built lay at the top. We stopped and looked out over Nashville. From our vantage point, it looked like a completely different city than the one I'd lived in after Mr. Waters bought me. Most of the trees were gone, having been used to build several forts and barricades to protect the city from attack. Rumors constantly circulated about the Confederates' determination to retake Nashville, but other than an isolated skirmish now and then, they hadn't come close enough to try. Still, despite the daily demands and drudgery of camp life, the future seemed precarious. Nothing was certain.

"I have something for you, Frankie."

Sam's voice drew me from my thoughts. I turned to find him holding a small paper-wrapped parcel tied with string.

"I can't—"

"Now, before you go and start an argument, let me tell you the story behind this gift."

I hid my smile. He knew me so well already.

"When I first got to Philadelphia, I was full of confidence. I'd escaped slavery and beaten the odds. I tried to get work, but no one would hire me. Day after day I searched for a job, but nothing turned up. Soon, I was starving, but I couldn't bring myself to steal like some escaped slaves did to survive. It was near Christmastime, and I didn't have nowhere to sleep. I feared I'd freeze to death if I stayed still too long, so I started walking, not knowing where I was going. It got dark, and I crawled up on the steps of a building to get out of the snow."

He glanced up to the clear sky, no doubt thankful for warm sunshine on his face now. "Turns out it was the home of Miz Annabelle Gaddis. She was a Quaker woman, like Miz Illa. She took me in and had her cook set me down to a meal. There were servants aplenty, but she offered me a job to earn my keep. On Christmas Day, she gave me this." He handed the parcel to me. "Said someday it would mean more to me than silver or gold."

I looked at the wrapped package. "I can't take somethin' that means so much to you." I offered it back, but he shook his head.

"I want to give you more than silver or gold, Frankie." His soft voice struck me in a place I thought long dead. Tears sprang to my eyes, and I looked away.

At his prodding, I untied the string and let the brown paper fall away. There in my hands was a small book. Its black leather cover bore cracked edges and looked worn, but the gold lettering on the front fairly sparkled in the sunshine.

I stared at it, my mind traveling all the way back in time to the day I stole Miss Charlotte's book and held it in my hands. Oh, how I wished I'd thrown it in the fire that day.

"Miz Annabelle taught me to read," Sam went on, unaware

of the painful memories his gift unleashed deep inside me. "This here is a book of Psalms from the Bible. Many are written by a man named David. He was a king long ago. The Psalms tell us all about God and how we can trust him. David says God is our heavenly Father who loves us. For slaves like us who ain't had a father or someone to care for us, I find that comforting."

My breath came heavy. I stared at the book, torn between the desire to hug it to my chest as a treasure or throw it into the Cumberland River as a curse.

I lifted my eyes to Sam, angry that he'd caused such confusing emotions to swirl through me. "What am I supposed to do with a book? I can't read it."

My harsh words and ungrateful attitude didn't affect the peaceful expression on his face. "I'll teach you to read."

Tears welled in my eyes, betraying me. I pushed the book into his chest. "I don't want your book. I don't want to read. And I sure don't want your God. Can't you just leave me be?"

I turned and ran. I couldn't see where I was going through my tears. I only knew I had to get away. From Sam. From memories. From everything. The feelings he and his book wrought inside hurt too much.

The hem of my dress caught on a low stump, and I fell, bruising my knees. I covered my face with my hands and wept. For Mammy. For the innocent child I'd been before I was ripped from her. For my babies. For Moss. It all came out, like floodwaters that had been dammed up too long. Loud wails spilled forth, and I couldn't've stopped them even if I'd tried.

I didn't know how long I knelt there on the frozen ground,

but eventually my tears ceased. My breath hiccuped, the only evidence of my heartache. I lifted my face to the sunshine, wondering what Sam must think of me now.

The answer was there when I stood and started back to camp. He was kneeling on the ground a short distance away, the small book in his hands. Tears wet his cheeks and his eyes were closed, but his mouth moved in silence. I knew he was praying. For me.

Our gazes met when he looked up. He slowly got to his feet and faced me. "You don't have to be afraid no more, Frankie."

Of all the things he could have said to me, those soft, unexpected words were exactly what my weary heart needed. Without thought or hesitation, I fell into his waiting arms.

He cradled me a long time, swaying in the cold breeze. Then he started talking.

"Don't you see, Frankie? The day I landed on Miz Annabelle's doorstep changed my life. I thought I found freedom when I ran away from my master, but it weren't mine. Not yet. Freedom comes in knowing the truth of God. He loves each of us the same. He loves you, Frankie."

I shook my head, my cheek rubbing against the rough fabric of his coat. "That ain't true," I said, yet wishing with all my heart it was. I pushed out from his embrace to look him in the face. "If God loves me, why'd he make me a slave? Why'd I get sold away from my mammy? I seen terrible things done to folks, Sam. Folks like you and me. If your God loves us, why does he allow all this misery?" I waved my hand to encompass the contraband and soldier camps in the distance.

I shook my head again. "You're a fool to trust him, if he's there at all."

"The apostle Paul said, 'We are fools for Christ's sake.'" A content smile lifted his lips. "I guess I'm in good company." He looked down at the small book still in his hands, then up at me. "Please take this, Frankie. Don't none of us know what tomorrow holds. It'd give me a measure of peace in my heart to know you have it should something happen to me."

My body and emotions were spent. I didn't have the strength to argue with Sam anymore. I sure didn't want to think about something bad happening to him and the regret I'd feel if I didn't do this one thing for him. I accepted the book. Neither of us said anything more as we returned to camp.

When I reached my tent, I was grateful to find myself alone. I couldn't have tolerated Nell's chatter right now. Without looking at it or turning even one page, I shoved the book under my cot and tossed a soiled apron on top of it.

I appreciated Sam's kindness, his words of comfort, but I didn't want his book.

It could stay under that cot until the end of the war, for all I cared.

———

Alden volunteered to drive to the drugstore near the capitol building and pick up some chicken salad sandwiches from the lunch counter. Jael arrived home in time to join us, and the four of us talked and laughed and enjoyed sharing another meal around Frankie's tiny table.

"I hope you don't mind my asking, but did you ever learn to read?" Alden said as he stood to help Jael clear away the dishes. She stacked them on the counter and they both returned to the table.

Frankie leaned back in her chair. "Reading was forbidden for a slave. It's hard to imagine these days, what with schools and colleges teaching our young folks to read and write and do sums." She smiled at Jael. "I'm right proud of all the progress we've accomplished since the war ended."

I opened the notebook I'd left nearby and jotted down her words. Had she forgotten Alden's question? I was about to repeat it when she continued.

"I realize now I *was* afraid." She rubbed her deformed fingers in an unconscious manner. "A book had cost me dearly. As irrational as it might seem now, I feared Sam's book would bring all kinds of trouble if I learned to read the words on them pages."

Jael reached over and put her hand on top of Frankie's.

"Illa Crandle was a stubborn woman. About as stubborn as me." We all smiled at that. "Sam must've told her about the book, because one day she came up to me and said, 'Frankie, I'm gonna teach you to read whether you like it or not.' Well, you can imagine I had all kinds of things to say about that, but sure enough, she began showing up while I had my hands full of hot, soapy laundry. I couldn't run away and had to listen to her talk about letters and the sounds they make. She'd spell *kettle* and *soap* and *water*, telling me what letters they had in them and drawing them in the dirt."

Frankie closed her eyes. "I can see that woman even now, with her hands on her hips and that big ol' black bonnet keeping the sun out of her eyes. Before long, I had an itch for learning. Nell brought home one of Illa's books, the same books I'd seen when I was recovering from Hank's beating. She was just learning, so her reading wasn't too good, but she'd recite her letters and such until I'd tell her to hush. I'm certain Illa put her up to it."

"Illa sounds like a woman after my own heart," Alden said with a laugh.

Frankie pursed her lips. "She knew she had me the day I corrected her when she misspelled a word. 'Course, I didn't realize at the time she'd misspelled it on purpose."

I chuckled. Illa did sound like an interesting lady.

"I couldn't attend the school since I had a job, so Illa began tutoring me after supper. Before long, I was reading. I read all the books on her shelf. When the officers heard I'd learned to read, some of them offered to let me borrow books they had with them."

A frown creased her face. "Sam was the only one who didn't celebrate my book learning. He'd kept his distance since Christmas, and I couldn't blame him. When I'd see him around camp or near the laundry area, he was as polite as always, but he'd stopped talking about our future together. I tried to convince myself it didn't matter, but inside, I felt as though I'd lost somethin' special."

Sam and Frankie's story reminded me of Grandma Lorena and Grandpa Jim's. Like Sam, Grandpa had loved people for who they were, but both Frankie and Grandma had lessons to learn before love could grow.

I stole a peek at Alden, warmth filling my cheeks as I wondered if there were lessons I could learn from him.

"One day I was in my tent alone. It was Sunday, and Nell and the others were at the service Illa and her helpers conducted. I was poking around beneath my cot, looking for something I'd dropped, when my fingers found the book Sam had given me. My breath caught when I pulled it out. I don't suppose I'd truly forgotten about it, but finding it that day was like finding a great prize."

Frankie lifted her hand to her face, and I realized a tear had slipped down her cheek.

"I sat on my cot with that book in my lap. *Book of Psalms*, it said in gold letters right across the front. I carefully opened it, marveling that I held my very own book in my hands. A book no one could take from me. I began reading and reading and reading. When I came to the Twenty-third Psalm, I couldn't get past it. I read those lines over and over, and every time it was like sunshine pouring into a dark place."

She looked at each of us, smiling with glistening eyes. "I understood then. I understood what Mammy tried to teach me about God and his goodness in spite of us being slaves. I understood that the masters who beat me and sold me weren't anything like God the Father. They was sinners, just like me. I understood that bad things are gonna happen in this world and that we'll all walk through the valley of the shadow of death. But I needn't live in fear anymore. The things I endured in my pitiful life as a slave didn't mean God isn't good or that he don't love us."

We sat in silence for several long moments, the impact of her words resonating within me. I'd blamed God for the stock market crash and the changes it forced upon me. I'd blamed him for my parents' failures and even for Mary's pitiable marriage. Yet was it fair to foist guilt upon God for every bad thing that happened? Didn't the decisions of individuals play a role in the outcomes?

"When I saw Sam the next day, he knew something was different. We talked a long time. 'You've made peace with God,' he said, and I guess I had. We settled into an easy friendship and spent most of our free time together, reading and talking. I had my job and nearly bawled the first time I held my own gold coins. Life in camp wasn't always pleasant, but I 'spect I was happier than I'd been in a long time. Days passed, then weeks and months. Before I knew it, I'd been in that camp two and a half years."

She paused and looked out the window. The sky had grown dark with clouds.

"I'll never forget the day a rider came tearing into the soldier camp. It was November of 1864. I was putting away laundry in the commanding officer's quarters when this young fellow barreled in, his face drained of color. I can hear his words to the general even now. 'Sir,' he said, all out of breath. 'The Army of Tennessee is on the move, and they're headed for Nashville.'"

CHAPTER
EIGHTEEN

Chaos.

Pure chaos erupted after the messenger delivered the news to the commander. Like a beehive that'd been split open, folks swarmed about camp, shouting, crying, arguing.

Should we run? Should we stay put? Would the Yankees protect us from the Confederates? No one knew the answers to any of the questions, leaving people terrified and on edge.

"What's gonna happen, Frankie? I don't want to go back to my massa."

Nell's eyes were wide with panic as we sat in our tent, wrapped in blankets, more to ward off the chill of fear than the mild November weather. Voices full of anger and uncertainty ebbed and flowed past our canvas home as folks sorted out their options, but we'd retreated to the tent after searching in vain for Sam or Illa Crandle among the crowds. I hoped

Sam would seek me out soon and that he'd have the answers we all sought.

A tear slid down Nell's smooth cheek. It occurred to me I'd never thought to ask the girl what her life was like during slavery. From the look of terror in her eyes at the prospect of going back, I guessed it was as bad as mine had been.

"Ain't no way to know what's gonna happen, girl," I said, giving her a stern look. "But I'll tell you one thing. We ain't going back to our masters. The Yankees and Miz Illa won't let that happen."

I prayed my words held truth. In the midst of the bedlam, I'd heard some folks say they'd rather die fighting the Rebs than go back into slavery, and I suppose somewhere inside me I felt the same way. A number of men decided they'd join the army right then and there. While I hadn't been mistreated by Mr. Waters, I had no desire to go back to being his slave, living in a shack behind his warehouse. I'd tasted freedom, and I had no intention of giving it up.

Things eventually grew quiet outside. Tangible fear had a way of silencing a soul, and I imagined folks had hid themselves away like Nell and me. There wasn't anything to do but wait. Wait for the Army of Tennessee to arrive. Wait for the Yankees to keep us safe . . . if they could.

When I heard Sam's voice sometime later, my body sagged with relief. Nell had fallen into a fretful sleep, so I walked with Sam to the edge of the contraband camp. Up the hill, Fort Negley buzzed with activity. Soldiers ran hither and yon, moving cannons into position, carrying supplies, and watching the southern horizon for the Confederate Army.

"Are they really coming, Sam?"

I didn't have to explain who I meant. His grave nod indicated he knew. "Hood's army is camped down near Spring Hill. He chased Schofield's men out of Columbia and now they're headed north."

"They're coming to Nashville then."

"It appears so."

We stood in silence, watching the soldiers prepare for battle. I didn't know why I'd thought the war would never reach us. Maybe because life had fallen into a comfortable routine. It wasn't perfect, but I was content here in the contraband camp, waiting for freedom. Yet with the Confederate Army practically on our doorstep, freedom seemed farther away than ever.

"What will happen now?" I sounded like Nell. Sam wouldn't have all the answers, but he might have some.

"Miz Illa is preparing for the wounded we'll receive. Even though there are already military hospitals around the city, it's feared they won't be enough. Makeshift hospitals need to be stocked with supplies and bandages made. She'd like your help."

Guilt washed over me. I hadn't considered the men who might die or be wounded in the fighting. I'd only been concerned for myself. "I'll come."

He took hold of my poor hand and kissed the back of it,

seeming not to care that my fingers were deformed. "I'm going to help the officers in whatever way I can."

Worry filled me at the thought of Sam anywhere near the battle.

"You get to the fort as soon as the shooting starts, you hear me?" He gave me a hard look, meant to keep me from arguing. "You get up there and stay until it's done."

I nodded. Fear clogged my throat.

We walked back to my tent. Before leaving, Sam sent me that special smile he reserved only for me. "When this is over, Frankie, you and me is getting married. I won't take no for an answer."

My eyes followed him as he walked toward the limestone walls of the fort, and I marveled that God had brought such a good man into my life. "Take care of him," I whispered.

Two evenings later we heard distant cannon fire echo in the south just as the sun set.

A shout went up. "Franklin is under attack." Fear shone in every eye when Nell and I hurried out of our tent. We all stood around, listening. The battle lasted five long hours, and then all was silent.

It was still dark when Illa came to wake me the next morning. "There's been a terrible battle in Franklin. Thousands are dead and thousands more wounded. I'm going to help. I need you to continue our preparations here. I fear Nashville will not escape the hand of death."

I roused Nell and we made our way to town without trouble. The soldiers were far too busy preparing for Rebs to worry about us women. Schofield's army had hightailed it to Nashville during the night, and the streets were crawling with more Federal soldiers than I could count, crowding the camps, forts, and city.

Over the past two days I'd joined Illa and dozens of other volunteers at several hospitals that had been set up throughout the city in office buildings, factories, hotels, and even churches, taking inventory of supplies needed to care for the large number of wounded we expected to receive. Walking through the city, I recalled how Mr. Waters had feared the Yankees would take over his warehouse, and I imagined it now filled with rows of cots instead of groceries.

Although it was the army's responsibility to supply the hospitals with doctors, medicines, and food, we spent the day tearing sheets into bandages, scrubbing floors, and assisting Miz Michaels, the matron in charge, with anything else needed. Her staff scurried about, and I found myself wondering what it would be like to be a nurse.

When I found Miz Michaels at the end of the long day and let her know we were leaving, I said, "When the wounded arrive, I'd like to help."

She studied me, a grave look on her face. "Until you've seen it for yourself, you can't imagine the horror left in the wake of battle. Most of the men who will come here won't survive. Many will lose arms and legs. Infection, gangrene, and dysentery are daily struggles. A hospital is no place for anyone with a weak constitution."

I stood my ground. "I've seen plenty in my day. No one would ever say I had a weak constitution."

After a lengthy silence, she conceded. "If what we've heard about the number of wounded in Franklin is to be believed, I fear what we can expect once the fighting recommences here. Everyone who is able and willing to help will be welcomed."

Illa didn't return the following day, so Nell and I stayed in camp. I still had my job working for the officers, and plenty of laundry awaited me. A drizzling rain plagued us all morning, and by noon word came that thousands more Federal soldiers had arrived by boat during the night. Nell and I joined others from the camp and climbed the hill, with the fort towering over us, to look across the city to the Cumberland. As far as I could see, the wide river teemed with vessels of all sizes. One fellow nearby said the ships were military transports and ironclad gunboats, the best the Federal navy had to offer. I shivered, thinking what kind of damage guns from a ship that size could do.

It wasn't long before the soldier camp and fort overflowed with even more men in blue uniforms. A general named Thomas was now commander of all the troops in Nashville, and I heard one of the officers say they numbered nearly sixty thousand strong. I couldn't imagine the enemy going up against such a force, yet scouts continued to deliver messages letting the officers know the Confederates had taken up positions south of the city.

Three days after the Franklin campaign, I trudged through thick mud and rain after long hours of scrubbing filthy laundry. All I wanted was my cot, but getting across the soldier camp proved difficult. Thousands more canvas tents had sprung up since that morning, like weeds in a garden. It seemed there wasn't a square inch of muddy ground that didn't have a tent or a soldier occupying it.

Along with the hordes of new soldiers came dozens of women, white and black alike, known as camp followers. I kept my head down and didn't acknowledge the painted ladies who wore revealing dresses despite the chilly December air.

Two years ago, white women who made a living selling their bodies to the soldiers had been rounded up and shipped north in hopes of stemming the sickness the men were contracting at an alarming rate. They were quickly replaced with black gals willing to do whatever it took to survive, thus not solving the problem at all.

Seeing these new arrivals and knowing the reality of their miserable lives, I felt a gratitude swell inside me that I wasn't counted among them.

Near exhaustion and soaked to the bone, I finally found my way to the contraband camp, eager for dry clothes and my bed. Nell's voice greeted me, but it was Sam's smile that made my heart leap.

"Hello, Frankie." He stood in our tent, covered from head to toe in mud.

"Land sakes, what've you been doing? You carrying around half o' Tennessee on your back."

He chuckled. "They have us digging trenches west of the city."

"I thought they'd taken care of that years ago."

"They did. There's seven miles of trenches to the south and west, but the new man in charge wants more."

I wished Nell wasn't sitting here listening. I wanted to ask Sam all kinds of questions about the Franklin battle and if he'd heard when we might see fighting here in Nashville. But I didn't want to frighten her further. She'd had nightmares ever since hearing Miz Michaels talk about amputations, disease, and such.

"I can't stay. We can see the Rebs putting up breastworks. They ain't more than a quarter mile from the Yankees' line. I'm to drive one of the wagons to haul supplies down yonder for the soldiers."

Disappointment washed over me. I'd hoped Sam was no longer needed by the army. I hated to think of him in harm's way. "Have you had word from Miz Illa?"

He shook his head. "I worry she might not be able to get back, what with Hood's army camped between Franklin and here."

I hadn't considered that. Concern for the kind woman appeared on each of our faces.

He donned his dirty, bedraggled hat. "I best be getting back." I followed him to the opening in the canvas. Before ducking out into the rain, he turned and whispered, "Remember what I said. Get to the fort when the fighting commences."

I nodded, and he was gone. Not long afterward, the rain stopped and the cannons began. Thankfully, they quieted after a short time, but it served to put everyone on edge.

While we stood in line for our supper—a thin, watery gruel—I noticed it was mainly women and children in camp, many new faces among them. Like Sam, the men and older boys had been conscripted to reinforce fortifications around the city.

Sometime after we'd crawled onto our cots for the night, we woke to loud, earth-shattering blasts. I wrapped myself in my blanket and poked my head out the tent. Stars twinkled in the black sky, but shouts filled the air.

"The gunboats is firing!" someone yelled.

I wondered if we should make our way up the hill to safety behind the fort's walls, but it didn't seem as though the Confederates were firing back. At least not with anything as powerful as the Yankees. The boats on the Cumberland roared their guns all through the next day. Nell and I stayed in our tent, and I finally asked about her life in slavery. Her story held as much sadness as mine. Her master had used her body for his own pleasure, and she'd delivered two babies before she was fourteen years old. Both had been sold away from her to cover the man's shame. I couldn't imagine that sort of pain. I thought about the babies I lost. Somehow it seemed easier knowing they were dead rather than living in bondage where I couldn't protect them.

"What do you want to do when the war is over and we're free?" I asked, hoping to lighten the conversation.

A small smile touched her lips. "I'd like to find me a good man and have a house of my own."

I hoped her simple dream came true.

"What about you? You gonna marry up with Sam?"

The thought of such a thing scared me to death. Not because
I didn't care for Sam. I did. Somehow, he'd wormed his way
into my life, and it saddened me to imagine freedom without
him. But everything I'd ever loved had been taken away from
me. I worried if I let my heart open up and truly allow love for
Sam to grow, something terrible would happen to him.

I shrugged and turned away. "He's a good man, but I don't
know that I'm the marryin' kind." I stood, ending the conversation. "I'm going for a walk."

I wandered over to the soldier camp, thinking I'd sort the
officers' laundry and prepare for work on the morrow. If
the battle wasn't going to commence anytime soon, the men
would need clean clothes.

A commotion caught my attention. I joined a group of
people watching as four dirt-caked men wearing Confederate
gray were marched at gunpoint toward a wagon.

"What's going on?" I asked the woman beside me.

"The Federals captured some prisoners."

The men wore defeat on their pale, thin faces. I noticed two
of them were barefoot even though December was upon us.
For just a moment, a hint of sympathy swept through me. I'd
heard rumors about Camp Chase, the Union prison up north.
As one might expect, prisoners of war weren't treated kindly.
But these men being loaded into the wagon had chosen to fight
for the Confederate cause. Were they slave owners? Had they
been cruel masters like the man who'd owned Nell or like the
Halls, who'd left me with a crippled hand and no family?

My sympathy evaporated.

Some of the folks nearby spat at the wagon when it passed, and I found myself joining in. Let the devil have those men, I thought. They deserved no better than what they'd given.

I attempted to reclaim my normal routine over the next three days while we waited. Nell volunteered to help me with the officers' washing, and I was grateful for the company. The report of guns could be heard throughout the sunny days from skirmishes fought in the south, and we learned several men had been wounded and were taken to a hospital in town. We still hadn't heard from Illa, and her absence troubled me. I gathered enough courage to ask one of the officers if Illa could get through the Confederate line if she tried to reach Nashville, but he thought it highly unlikely. The Rebs wouldn't let anyone sympathetic to the Federals—woman or otherwise—cross their line.

On Thursday we awoke to a bitter wind blowing in from the north. Despite the change in temperature, cannons continued to roar and the pop of gunshots echoed until dark. The next day brought a sleeting rain that eventually turned to snow. Nell and I hunkered down in the tent most of the day, shivering and wrapped in thin blankets. When we did venture out, it was to huddle over one of the many campfires dotting the land. I recognized wooden fences and even bits of furniture being used for fuel. With most all the trees long felled for breastworks and forts, precious little remained to provide warmth in such frigid weather.

Tempers flared under the hard conditions. Residents of the contraband camp as well as the hundreds of soldiers were ill-prepared for such intense cold. Arguments broke out over which blanket belonged to whom or who let the fire die down. With so many mouths to feed, food was rationed. I took the gold coins I'd buried beneath my cot and went to town, despite the ever-present fear of gunfire. I found a baker I remembered from my days working for Mr. Waters. The man had always been kind toward me, and I trusted him to be honest now since I'd never bought anything with my own money. He traded two coins for a loaf of bread and some salted meat he'd managed to keep out of the hands of the soldiers. I thanked him and hurried back to camp, surprised by how many men in blue uniforms I passed on my way. I supposed many of them had never been to Nashville and were determined to see the sights in spite of the imminent battle. Rumor had it the cannons weren't the only thing booming. The city's saloons and broth-els saw steady business with the influx of soldiers.

Two more days went by with little change in activities. We began to wonder if there would ever be a battle, or if the two sides would continue to simply hold their ground. The wait-ing wore on our nerves inside the contraband camp, but the soldiers seemed to take it in stride. After nearly four years of war, they'd surely seen their share of waiting.

Each day I searched for Sam, but each day I was dis-appointed. I hoped he was staying warm and dry. The air still held a heavy chill by Sunday afternoon, but folks seemed to settle in for a day of rest. Even the guns had grown blessedly quiet, giving us a much-needed respite from the relentless fear of war.

I decided to walk to the fort and take a look around. Sam felt we'd be safe there once the fighting began, but I'd never stepped foot behind the high limestone walls. It seemed best to acquaint myself with the layout before things grew dire.

I climbed up the hill to the sally port, the only entrance into the great fort. The wooden gates were closed, and without Sam or Illa to accompany me, I didn't have the courage to approach the guardhouse. I walked the perimeter of the huge wall instead, scouting the best place for Nell and me to hide when the shooting started.

Atop Saint Cloud Hill, the view from the fort held beauty despite the impending battle. The whole country surrounding the city, on both sides of the river, looked like one big tented field. Thousands of cheerful campfires sent smoke into the clear sky, offering warmth and comfort, belying the uncertainty of the soldiers' tomorrows.

To the north, the Cumberland River teemed with war vessels and ships, their masts waving in the cold breeze. Hills, barren and stripped of trees, dotted the horizon in all directions. I saw the newly finished capitol building gleaming in the sunshine, strong and sure. To the south, a half mile across Franklin Pike, Fort Casino buzzed with activity. I couldn't make out details, but I imagined their artillery looked similar to that of Fort Negley.

Out of breath, I stopped and leaned against the high wall. I hadn't taken much time to consider the fort all these years, despite living in its shadow, but I marveled now at the workmanship. I'd witnessed men, two at a time, hauling these thick limestone blocks up the hill, where they were laid out in such a way folks referred to it as an enormous star. Although I couldn't see it now, I knew a tall wooden stockade and towers occupied the center. Should the enemy breach the walls, the stockade would act as the last defense for the men inside. Soldiers stationed high above me manned cannons at the ready while others served as lookouts and guards.

A flapping sound drew my attention. I looked up and saw a large flag hoisted high on a pole, snapping in the stiff breeze, declaring to the world this was Union territory that would not be easily taken. As I stared up at the Stars and Stripes, I couldn't help but hope it'd still be flying once the fighting was over. A shiver ran through me, and I refused to even consider what it would mean to have the fort taken by Confederates.

I headed back down the hill, satisfied Nell and I could find adequate shelter on the north side of the fort if and when the battle began. A group of young soldiers came toward me, chatting and laughing. Since I was the one who didn't belong, I stepped off the path to let them pass.

"Ma'am." The fellow at the back of the group tipped his soldier hat politely as he passed me.

I noticed something shiny fall to the ground, but he kept walking, unaware. I went over and picked up a brass button, stamped with the emblem of the Union Army.

"Sir," I called. He turned, and I held up the button, identical to the dozens I'd sewed onto the officers' coats the past two years. "I believe this fell off your uniform."

He looked at his coat, surprise on his face. When he

approached, he said, "I thank you, ma'am. I've been meaning to mend that loose button ever since we got off the boat."

I handed it to him and waited for him to turn away.

"I'm Albert Underwood, with the Ninth Indiana Light
Artillery." He indicated his companions further up the hill.
"We thought we'd take a look around the fort."

"Pleased to make your acquaintance, sir." For some reason, I thought about this boy's mama and what she might say
to him if she knew he'd face the enemy soon. "You take care
of yourself when the fighting starts."

Appreciation filled his youthful face. "I will, ma'am."

I watched him go, praying God would keep Albert Underwood safe.

On my way back to camp, I passed the graveyard where
the bodies of more than seven hundred slaves had been laid
to rest. Men and women alike, they'd died from illnesses that
continued to plague camp or from injuries acquired during
the building of the fort. I couldn't help but wonder how many
more graves would be added once the fighting began.

The following day brought more cold air, snow, and hundreds of soldiers mounted on horseback. Rumors abounded
that the cavalry crossing the river meant a move toward
battle was imminent. Yet despite the snow turning to rain the
next day, the soldiers remained in camp.

Finally, on a foggy morning three days later, cheers went
up as line after line of soldiers marched out of camp, headed
south. By noon, the air was filled with smoke from cannons
and guns, the sounds of them a constant echo in the hills. Nell

and I took our blankets and meager possessions and made our way up the hill to the fort. Many others from the contraband camp were of the same mind. Although we weren't allowed to take shelter inside the stockade, we hid ourselves against the north walls, away from possible Confederate gunfire.

Each blast from the cannons shook my insides. I pushed my fingers in my ears, but it did little to keep the fury of war from rattling my brain. As the sun set, a welcome quietness settled over the fort. Shots could still be heard further south as the Federal Army pushed the enemy back, but the battle had seemingly left us and the fort unscathed.

Nell and I had scarcely made it to our tent when an urgent call drew me back outside.

"The hospitals are flooded with wounded," a white woman I'd never seen before shouted. "If you're willing and able, come quickly."

CHAPTER NINETEEN

I rose early Sunday morning despite staying up late reading *Uncle Tom's Cabin*. Although different from Frankie's true-life tales, the story invoked the same feelings of injustice deep inside me. I could well imagine how the country, especially those in the South, received this book when it was first published in 1852. Northern abolitionists were incensed at the treatment of slaves while those in the South cried foul at being portrayed so harshly.

Alden planned to pick me up at ten and drive me to Frankie's. He couldn't stay, he'd said with disappointment in his eyes, but he'd happily return to drive me home later. I tiptoed down the stairs, breathing a sigh upon finding the kitchen still dark. Mama hadn't been pleased that I'd been gone all day Saturday, so I hoped to appease her by having breakfast ready when she woke before breaking the news that I planned to be gone today, too.

I opened the refrigerator and took out the necessary items for breakfast, noting the barrenness of the shelves. Mama usually went to the market on Saturday, her day off from the shop. Had she not gone?

The aroma of coffee filled the kitchen when she appeared in the doorway an hour later, dark circles beneath her eyes.

"My goodness." She seemed genuinely surprised to find pancakes and fried eggs ready.

"Good morning. I thought I'd make you breakfast." I smiled from my place at the stove, my peace offering displayed on the table. I poured her a cup of coffee and doctored it with a splash of milk. "Come sit down."

After a moment, she settled at the table. "This is a lovely surprise, Rena. Thank you."

I sat in my usual chair on her right. "I know I haven't been around much lately. I thought we could talk over breakfast."

She sent me a look of suspicion but delved into the meal without further comment. We talked about the mild weather and how the flower beds in the backyard needed to be readied for winter. She asked a few questions about Alden, and I shared what I knew about his life in Chicago.

Mama glanced at the clock. "We'd best get ready for church. Mary and the children are coming by after the service. It would be nice if you'd spend some time with your niece and nephews for a change."

I hated to spoil her good mood so soon, but it couldn't be

helped. "I'm not going to church this morning. I promised Frankie we'd try to finish her interview today."

Mama's face hardened. "You're going to skip church to go down to Hell's Half Acre? Quite ironic, wouldn't you say? Doesn't that woman believe in honoring the Lord's Day?"

"Mama, Frankie is 101 years old. She rarely leaves the house. But I know her to be a woman of faith. She told us just yesterday about the day she made peace with God."

Mama harrumphed. "What could she possibly have against God?"

I took my time answering, not wanting to end our discussion in an argument. I simply wanted Mama to see the truth about slavery and what the FWP was trying to do with these interviews. "She was a slave, Mama. Owned by another human being. She suffered at the hands of her owners, including a disfigurement and being sold away from her family. I imagine I'd be angry at God if that had been my life. Don't you?"

The kitchen remained silent. Finally Mama's shoulders eased some. "I suppose there are aspects of slavery that I've never considered. But it all happened so long ago, I don't see the need to dredge it back up. Going down to that neighborhood and talking with that woman will not change the past, Lorena Ann."

"I know that, but maybe it can change the future for the better."

She gave a humorless laugh. "The only future it will affect is yours. Once people find out where you've been spending your time, no young man worth his salt will be willing to court you, mark my words."

I thought of Alden, his rapt attention on Frankie as she told us her life's story. I had to fight the smile his name brought to my lips these days. "Mama, if a young man can't see that what I'm doing has merit, then he isn't the kind of man I want to spend time with." I reached out and put my hand over hers, waiting until her gaze met mine. "You don't need to worry about me. I promise. I'm finally doing something I truly enjoy, and I'm getting paid to do it. That's something to be happy about, isn't it?"

After another long silence, she sighed. "I'll be glad when this job is finished. I need you." She glanced to the closed door of the study. "Your father is ill. I tended him all through the night."

"What's wrong with him?" Other than the usual drunkenness and all the wonderful ills that came with it.

"He's having pain and swelling in his abdomen, as well as severe nausea."

A hint of worry edged its way past my normal apathy. "Do you think it's serious?"

"I don't know. I hope to see Dr. Ridley at the service today and talk to him about it."

I glanced at the refrigerator, realizing this was the reason Mama hadn't been to the market. "I'm sorry I wasn't here to help, Mama."

She studied me a long moment. "What is it about this Frankie that you find so fascinating you keep going back?"

I gave a slight shrug. "She lived in a time I've only read about. She experienced things we never will. Just yesterday she told us about the Battle of Nashville. I barely remember reading about it in school, and yet Frankie's telling of it made me feel like I'd experienced it myself." At the look of horror on Mama's face, I chuckled. "I don't mean the gore and all, but the emotions of waiting for the battle to begin, the frigid weather." I recalled Alden's and Frankie's discussion about the rebuilding of the Civil War fort. "Did you know the Works Progress Administration is rebuilding Fort Negley? Won't it be wonderful to see what it looked like and walk around inside?"

Mama made a sound of disgust. "We lost the Battle of Nashville, Rena. Why on earth would we want a reminder staring down on us from atop a hill in the middle of town?"

I realized then Mama and I would never see eye to eye on the past.

Mama left for church an hour later. She checked on Dad and found him sleeping peacefully. I felt a twinge of guilt for not volunteering to stay home until she returned, yet the thought of dealing with my father sent me hurrying to leave the house when I heard Alden's car pull into the driveway.

Frankie was waiting for me when we arrived at her house. "Is Alden not coming inside?"

"No," I said, hoping my disappointment wasn't too obvious. A friend from the Works Progress Administration had asked to meet with him, although Alden didn't say why. I turned to see him wave to Frankie before he drove away.

"Well, it's just you and me then. Jael is at the church. She loves singin' in the choir and teachin' the kiddies in Sunday school." She noticed the small sack I carried. I'd asked Alden to stop at the market so I could purchase the makings for a meal of pork chops and vegetables.

"I'd like to make lunch, if that's all right with you."

She gave a deep chuckle. "Don't no one ever have to ask if they can cook a meal for me. I've had plenty-a time in the kitchen and I'm more than willing to let you young folks take over."

After putting the groceries away and pouring us each a cup of coffee, we settled in the living room.

"I can't remember where I left off yesterday," she said, staring out the window. "After you children left, my mind kept a-going. It's hard to turn off the memories once they start flowing."

I took out my notebook and turned to the last page. "You said a white woman you'd never seen before came to the camp to ask for volunteers to help in the hospitals."

"Oh yes, I remember now." She shook her head, squinting as though seeing the past in her mind's eye. "That Miz Michaels was right. You can't imagine the terrible things a bullet or a cannonball can do to a body. Nell wouldn't go with me, which was just as well, but me and some others climbed up into the wagon the woman brought. We drove into town, not knowing what we was getting ourselves into. You'd have thought it was market day, the streets were so crowded despite darkness falling upon us. Dozens and dozens of army wagons called ambulances flew hither and yon, bringing in the wounded and going back out for more."

She took a sip from her cup, then set it down on the low table between us. Her eyes squeezed closed, and I wondered, not for the first time, if remembering all the hurt and pain from the past was good for a woman her age.

"I never left the hospital once I stepped inside. For days I had me no knowledge of what was going on outside the walls of that old gun factory. I couldn't have told you what time of day it was until someone lit the lamps when night fell again. Can't recall eating, sleeping, or even going to the privy, but I guess I did." She met my gaze, an anguished look in her eyes. "If I'd known what was ahead of me the day that woman came calling for volunteers, I would have turned tail and run."

———

Blood.

Blood everywhere. On everything, staining the wood floors, the walls, me.

"More light! I can't see a thing."

The army surgeon bellowed even though I stood across the table from him. He didn't look at me but stayed focused on the soldier whose leg he'd just sawed off. Thankfully the patient had ceased his screaming once the chloroform took effect, but there were plenty of agonizing cries echoing throughout the building to prevent his from being missed.

I held the kerosene lantern higher, my arms aching, while keeping my eyes averted from the ghastly scene below. It was well past midnight, I guessed. I'd arrived at the hospital sometime after the guns had gone quiet, and now streams of wounded and dying men continued to flood through the door downstairs.

"Clean this man up. Then come assist me with the next one." The gray-haired man dipped his hands in a basin of red water, seeming not to notice the color of it, before moving away to the next moaning patient.

I didn't answer. I couldn't. I was simply too exhausted. I just stood there with the lantern in my hands, illuminating pools of red on the long table and the ash-colored skin of the man whose life had just been altered.

"Here, let me take over."

I turned weary eyes to find a white woman next to me. She wore an apron over her dark dress, now covered with blood. I'd seen her downstairs when I first arrived. Her authoritative voice went out over the masses as she directed men carrying in the wounded, pointing some up the stairs to surgery while others had to wait their turn.

I handed the lantern to her.

"There's coffee downstairs. And sandwiches. Get some rest. I'm told the fighting will resume once the sun is up, which means we'll receive more men come daylight."

I nodded and left the room. My stomach roiled at the sight of the buckets of blood-soaked rags in the hallway, awaiting someone to rinse them so they could be used again and again. The smell of blood, gunpowder, and death hovered in the air.

Panic and nausea rose up in me.

I had to leave. To slip away into the darkness and never return. I'd seen too much. Too many men lost their limbs. Too many men lost their lives.

When I reached the bottom of the stairs, the sight that met me stilled my feet.

The wounded filled the converted gun factory, covering every inch of space. Some men lay still as death while others moaned and cried out in pain. Nurses and volunteers flitted around, tending the men as best they could, but there were simply too many in need of care.

One older woman eyed me from across the room. "You here to help?"

I shook my head and bolted forward before she could argue. The door opened as I reached for the handle, and a soldier with a wounded man in his arms blocked my way.

"Help him," he begged, his fear-filled gaze landing on me. "He's my friend, and he's hurt bad."

Blood oozed from a wound in the man's gut onto the floor. His eyes were rolled back in his head, and I knew he wouldn't make it. None of the surgeons would even try to save him.

"I can't," I hissed and stumbled out the door into the cold night. I hurried down the wide steps to the street, intent on escape, but something solid on the ground nearly tripped me. I leaned closer and gasped.

A body lay at my feet, staring into nothingness.

As my eyes adjusted to the darkness, I found more bodies rowed up outside the hospital as far as I could see in both directions. Women with lanterns cared for the living among them. Men with stretchers carried off the dead into the night.

Hot tears rolled down my cheeks, turning icy in the frigid air.

How could I run away and abandon these poor wretched souls? They'd fought for my freedom, whether they intended to or not. Too many had died already. There weren't enough volunteers and doctors to keep up with the steady flow. They needed help. From anyone willing to give it.

I looked to the stars above me, my breath forming puffs of steam. "I can't do this no more," I whispered. "I can't."

"Ma'am?" a soldier nearby called out, his voice weak and his pale face illuminated by feeble light coming from the window. Blood and dirt caked his uniform, yet his youthfulness reminded me of Albert Underwood. "Ma'am, may I have some water?"

A simple request. Just something to moisten his parched lips. A task that would bring a small measure of comfort while he lay on the hard, frozen ground, wounded and unsure of his tomorrows. Could I ignore him and walk away?

I sent one last fleeting glance south, toward the contra-band camp, before nodding. "I'll get some water."

I turned and trudged back inside the hospital.

———————

Day and night came and went. I lost track of how long I'd been tending the wounded. The battle had raged for two bitterly cold days before the Confederates retreated, with Federal troops on their heels. While folks in the city celebrated our survival, those of us in the hospitals knew the cost.

I sat beside the bed of a bearded soldier, his head and arms swathed in bandages, spooning broth into his mouth. Neither of us spoke. I found most of the men preferred silence to pointless chatter. A cough now and then or the low murmurs of conversation—these had replaced the terrible groans and cries of the wounded fresh from battle. Now the long process of healing must begin.

It rained hard during the night. A light drizzle continued to fall outside the window. We'd managed to get the remaining men inside before they were soaked, although a great number were beyond help.

I learned that the white woman I'd seen the first day was Miss Annie Bell. A nurse whispered that Miss Bell had been at other battles, including Gettysburg, and her esteem of the woman rang clear in her awed voice. It reminded me of how I'd felt helping Miz Michaels prepare for wounded at the hospital in her charge, two streets over. That these women were willing to give of themselves so deeply to help strangers was a mystery I still hadn't solved, yet here I stood among them.

"No more." The soldier turned his head away from the spoon I held. He closed his eyes, effectively dismissing me.

"I'll be around if you decide you want more." I stood and headed to the makeshift kitchen for another bowl of broth for another wounded soldier. So many weren't able to feed themselves because of lost limbs, broken bones, or burns. I'd seen several of the men look at my deformed hand, and I wondered what they were thinking.

"You're doing a fine job."

I turned to find Miss Bell watching me from the stairwell. She came down the remaining steps. I noticed she'd donned a clean apron but still wore her soiled dress.

"Thank you, ma'am."

"It isn't easy caring for the men. They've seen and done things most of us will never experience. It will take time for them to heal, inside and out."

I'd never been a soldier in war, but I'd had my share of battles. I knew what she meant. "Yes, ma'am."

She studied me. "Frankie, isn't it?"

I nodded.

"When the war is over, Frankie, you should consider becoming a nurse. I believe you have what it takes."

I watched her walk away, astonished by her words. She might not be so giving of compliments if she knew I'd considered abandoning her and the wounded men the first night of the battle. Still, I tucked the kind words into my heart.

The following day I was cleaning the wound on a soldier's leg when I felt someone behind me. I turned. "Miz Illa!"

I scrambled to put the basin down without spilling dirty water on the patient, nearly giddy with relief at seeing the woman. I hadn't realized how important she'd become in my life until she wasn't there. "Land sakes, we been worried 'bout you. We looked for you before the fighting started, but the soldiers said no one would be able to cross the Confederate line."

Illa gave me a weary smile. Exhaustion marred her face. "For a time, I was plenty worried about myself, but we managed. We tried to get back, but as thee has said, the Confederates wouldn't allow us through. A farmer just south of Nashville took us in and gave us refuge. We hid in his cellar during the worst of it."

I had so many questions and things to tell her, but now was not the time. "Sam sure will be happy to know you're back. Last time I saw him was before the fighting started. I keep watching for him, but . . ."

My words trailed off. Her expression said she had news. "Miz Illa? You know something 'bout Sam?"

"Oh, my dear." Her lips trembled. "I'm sorry to tell thee, but he was badly wounded in the battle."

I held my breath as my heart beat with fear. *Please, God, no.*

Tears came to her eyes, and she reached for my hand. "Thee must go to him, Frankie. I don't know how much time he has left. He's dying."

In that moment, imagining life without Sam, I thought I might die too.

CHAPTER TWENTY

A knock at the door interrupted us. It was just as well. Frankie had grown quiet, her face cloaked in the pain of remembering that terrible day. She didn't seem to know someone was at her door, so I moved to open it.

Alden happily greeted me. "Hello." His smile faded when I didn't respond. "What's wrong?"

I glanced back to find Frankie's eyes closed. I didn't know if she'd fallen asleep or if she'd closed them to keep painful memories away. Turning back to Alden, I motioned him onto the porch and gently shut the door behind us.

"Frankie just told me Sam was wounded in the battle. Illa said he's dying."

Alden's shoulders slumped. "That's awful."

Pangs of grief swirled through me, which seemed irrational

considering the events of Frankie's story happened over seventy years ago. Yet Sam had become a real person to me, and I mourned him.

"I thought you wouldn't be free to visit today," I said, changing the subject away from so much sadness.

"Tom, my friend, had to get on the road back to Memphis before it got too late." He seemed eager to say something.

"And?"

He grinned. "And he thinks he can help me get a job with the Works Progress Administration here in Nashville. A permanent position."

I gasped. "Truly?"

"The WPA has a number of projects here, including rebuilding Fort Negley. I'm not sure what the job would be, but I told him I'm interested."

"That's wonderful news." I couldn't keep excitement from my voice.

A look of satisfaction filled his face. "I hoped you'd be happy."

Our gazes held for a long moment before I felt heat creep up my neck. Embarrassed, I turned away. "Come in. You're just in time to help make lunch."

He chuckled and followed me inside. Frankie was alert once again. Her face lit up when she saw Alden.

"Well, lookee who finally come to see me."

He went over to her, bent low, and kissed her cheek. "I came as soon as I could."

A happy smile replaced the previous sadness in her eyes.

It warmed my heart when Alden knelt beside her and told her about his possible job. I left the two of them conversing and went to the kitchen. I wasn't sure when it happened, but we'd all somehow become friends. The thought pleased me.

I was chopping carrots and potatoes to go with our fried pork chops when he came to help a short time later.

"Frankie's gone to lie down for a bit," he said as he washed his hands at the sink. He took a towel from a hook and met my gaze. "She told me about Sam. She said she'd finish the story after lunch."

"It's so sad. I don't understand things like that."

"Like what?" He removed the paper wrapping from the meat and seasoned the chops with salt and pepper. I still found it amazing that he knew his way around the kitchen. As far as I knew, my father hadn't ever cooked a meal in his entire life.

"Frankie had already suffered so much. Why couldn't she enjoy some happiness with Sam?"

We worked in silence for long moments. Finally Alden said, "I suppose you mean God should have allowed her some happiness."

I met his gaze. "Yes, I do. God is all about love and goodness. Why did he let slavery exist in the first place?"

He chuckled. "You're asking the wrong guy. I'm not sure I believe in God."

I recalled him saying something similar to Frankie several days ago. "I think there is too much evidence around us to rule out a Creator. Look at us, how complicated our bodies are. And all the different animals, and plants and flowers, and fruits and vegetables." I held up a long carrot. "How did all this come to be without God?"

He leaned against the counter, one corner of his mouth tipped up. "Again, you're asking the wrong guy. Your argument makes sense, but it still doesn't answer your questions. If God does exist, why is there so much pain and suffering in the world? Why doesn't he just wave his hand and make everyone's lives full of happiness?"

I'd wondered the same thing many times. When the stock market crashed and my life imploded, I'd asked God why. But after meeting Frankie and hearing her stories, I realized my family and I hadn't truly suffered. We still had a beautiful home, food on the table, help when it was needed from Grandma Lorena. My father's failures were responsible for any losses we endured. They were not God's fault.

"I don't suppose we're going to solve life's mysteries before lunch," I said, pleased at finding him so easy to talk to, no matter the subject. Unlike Dad, Alden didn't argue to make his point.

Our conversation drifted to other subjects while Alden got a fire going in the stove furnace. He fried the pork chops, and I boiled the carrots and potatoes. It's funny how comfortable I felt in Frankie's kitchen, cooking on her outdated stove. Almost as though I were a member of the family rather than a stranger who'd arrived on her doorstep a little more than a week ago.

When she entered the kitchen an hour later, lunch was

ready. "My, look what you young'uns have done. It sure smells good."

The three of us sat at the table. Frankie bowed her head and we followed suit.

"Thank you, Lord, for the bounty from your hand. Bless these two fine folks who cooked a meal for an old woman. Amen."

As we ate, Alden regaled us with stories of his life in Chicago. He told about the strange man who'd come to stay at his parents' boardinghouse when Alden was just a boy. The man turned out to be a bootleg whiskey runner and was using the boardinghouse as his hideout. One day when the man was out, Alden poked around his room and found a stash of liquor. When he carried a bottle downstairs to ask his mother if he could have some, she nearly fainted.

"Father didn't want to call the authorities. He was afraid it would cause trouble for him, so he told the man to leave and never come back. We heard later the fellow opened a distillery in Kentucky as soon as Prohibition was over and is doing quite well. He even sent Father a case of whiskey as thanks for not turning him in."

We laughed in unison.

"I've never been one to partake in strong drink," Frankie said, "but we used plenty while I was working in the hospital after the fighting was done. There wasn't enough medicine to go around to relieve the men of their pain. All we had to ease the suffering was whiskey." She sighed. "Let's clean up and then I'll tell you about Sam."

Alden and I insisted on washing the dishes while Frankie put the leftovers in the icebox. Jael, she said, usually went to a friend's home after church, but she would enjoy the meal for supper.

We settled in the living room, me with my pencil and notebook ready, and Alden with his long legs stretched out in front of him as he sat on the sagging sofa.

"When Miz Illa told me Sam was dying," Frankie began, her voice subdued, "I wanted to curl up on the floor and have a good cry. It didn't seem fair, him not even a soldier. But she wouldn't let me fall apart. 'He needs thee, Frankie,' Illa said. 'And thee needs to tell him how thee feels before it's too late. Otherwise, thee will live with regret the rest of thy life.'"

———

I climbed down from Miz Illa's wagon in front of a large building on College Street. I couldn't recall what it had been before the war, but now it housed Hospital Number 16. Many black men had joined the army, willing to fight for their own freedom. Sadly, over two hundred lost their lives in a peach orchard south of the city in the fighting. Many others were brought here.

We walked down hallways, turning this way, then that, before we came to a partially shut door. She held me by the shoulders, as though trying to impart strength upon me.

"Be as encouraging as thee possibly can. He needs to see thy smile, hear thy laughter. Thee does not want him facing death amid gloom and doom."

I stared at her. What she asked was impossible. "I can't do it, Miz Illa. My heart hurts too much." Tears welled in my eyes, blurring my vision.

"Yes, thee can. I'll be nearby should thee need me."

She pushed the door open the rest of the way and offered me a sympathetic smile. My feet felt wooden and heavy, but I made them move forward. Two dozen or so beds with men occupying them lined the walls. I hadn't thought to ask what Sam's injuries were. Would I still recognize him?

At the very end of the row, I saw him, a blanket tucked beneath his chin with only his face visible. His eyes were closed and his skin had a gray tinge to it. I could detect no movement whatsoever.

Was I too late?

Before I had a chance to turn and run from the room, his chest rose and fell ever so slightly. Then again. He was alive, and all the fear I'd bottled up since he walked away from my tent before the fighting started came out in a feral sob.

His eyes slowly opened. Seeing me, he tried to smile, but a grimace came to his face instead. "Frankie," he whispered. I could tell it took every ounce of strength to speak that one word.

"Oh, Sam." I fell to my knees beside his cot. I didn't know the extent of his injuries, so I didn't reach for him.

"I told him I couldn't go without seeing you."

His voice barely made it past his parched lips, and I had to lean in to hear. "You ain't going nowhere. You're gonna stay right here and get better."

He shook his head. "It's time."

I realized then he meant it was time for him to die. For some crazy reason, that ignited my anger instead of my fear.

"You listen to me. You is gonna get well. You promised me we'd marry up when the war was over, and I'm holdin' you to it."

A hint of a smile raised the corners of his mouth. "We woulda had us a good time, Frankie." He sounded weaker, if that were possible.

Tears sprang to my eyes. "You hush now and get some rest."

His gaze locked on mine. "I don't regret it, Frankie. That boy. I don't regret it." His eyes fluttered closed and his body went limp.

"Sam?" My heart dropped to my toes.

"He's still with us," Illa said from behind me. "He's been in and out of consciousness since they found him on the battlefield."

I turned and gaped at her. "On the battlefield? What was he doing there?"

"He volunteered to help carry the wounded from the field."

I looked at Sam's ashen face again. "Fool man," I hissed. "Why didn't you stay where you'd be safe?" Hot tears streamed down my face and dripped onto my dress.

"Sam saved many lives, Frankie."

I stared at him, wishing I could see that maddening smile again. "But now he's gonna die because of it." His words came back to me. "What boy is he talking about? What doesn't he regret?"

Illa sat on the edge of Sam's bed near his feet. "From what I'm told, Sam saw a young soldier go down during the height of the fighting and rushed to pull him from harm's way. The Confederate who shot him charged forward with his bayonet at the ready. Sam didn't stop. He hoisted the young man onto his shoulders and tried to make a run for it, but the other man was faster. He stabbed Sam several times. When they found him after the shooting ended, he'd crawled on top of the young man to shield him."

My chin trembled as I fought sobs that threatened to explode from me. Sam was a hero. And now God was going to take him away from me, just as he'd taken away everything I'd ever loved.

Illa left a short time later. She was needed back at the hospital where she'd found me. I knew I wouldn't leave Sam's side until his spirit slipped away. Nurses and volunteers came and went from the ward. No one checked Sam's bandages, and I knew they expected him to die. I took it upon myself to bathe his face, wondering for the first time what it might have been like to be Sam's wife.

Time passed, but Sam didn't awaken again. His breath grew shallow and labored. I couldn't sit here and watch him die. I needed a distraction. Glancing about, I saw a burlap sack underneath his bed and tugged it out. Inside were Sam's worn hat and his Bible, muddy and wet but still intact. I guessed he'd had it on him when the enemy tried to end his life. I carefully opened the small book, the pages parting on their own to the Psalms. How Sam loved the poetry of those words. We'd talked about them many a time over the years, relishing their beauty and discussing their meaning.

I stopped at the Twenty-third Psalm, Sam's favorite.

"'The Lord is my shepherd; I shall not want.'"

A lump formed in my throat and my lips trembled. I could almost hear Sam's deep voice reciting the words.

"'He maketh me to lie down in green pastures: he leadeth me beside the still waters. He restoreth my soul: he leadeth me in the paths of righteousness for his name's sake.'"

Tears choked me, but I kept going. "'Yea, though I walk through the valley of the shadow of death, I will fear no evil.'"

I slammed the book shut.

I didn't want Sam to walk through that valley. Why must he? He was a good man. He loved his neighbor better than anyone I'd ever seen. Be they white or black, it didn't matter. Sam deserved to live. I was the one who should die. I was selfish and mean-spirited. The world wouldn't miss me the way it would miss Sam and all his goodness.

"Take me," I breathed. With my eyes squeezed tight, I started rocking where I sat. "Take me, take me, take me." Over and over, I whispered the words until my body and my mind were exhausted.

I fell in a heap on the floor beside Sam's bed and clutched his cold, lifeless hand. If the Almighty was going to take Sam tonight, I was determined to go too.

CHAPTER TWENTY-ONE

"Frankie."

I heard Mammy calling. "I'm coming, Mammy."

"Frankie."

I opened my eyes, expecting to see Mammy's face above me. I found Illa instead. She helped me sit up, my body unusually stiff and sore, and it all came rushing back. Panic surged through my heart.

"Is he . . . ?" I couldn't look at the body in the cot next to me.

A soft smile touched her lips. "No, he's not. In fact, he's a bit improved."

I scrambled to my feet, not believing her. But she hadn't lied. Sam's breath wasn't shallow as it had been last night, inching ever closer to the death rattle. His face had lost its grayish hue, although his coloring wasn't back to normal either.

"The doctor wants Sam's bandages changed and the wounds cleaned." At my hopeful look, she cautioned, "We still don't know if he'll live, but we mustn't let infection set in."

Together, we cleaned Sam's wounds. I didn't know how he'd survived such a brutal attack. He'd lost so much blood, it was a wonder he had any running through his veins. Throughout our ministrations, Sam remained unconscious, which was a blessing. After we had him tucked back under the covers, Illa departed, promising to check on us later that afternoon.

I found a straight-backed chair in another part of the hospital and set it beside Sam's bed. I spooned thin broth between his parched lips, bathed his face, and read from his Bible. Some hours later, with a weary body and mind, I closed the book and rested my eyes.

"Ma'am, would you keep reading?"

I turned to find the man in the bed across from Sam's looking at me. A blood-soaked bandage covered half his face.

"I ain't never heard a black woman read before," he said. "It does my heart good to listen to the Book read by you."

The awe in his voice humbled me. "Miz Illa taught me after the army took Nashville."

"I'd never knowed it. You read real good for such a short time."

I glanced at the book in my lap. Sleep beckoned, but I couldn't bring myself to deny his request. "Any particular story you want to hear?"

"A preacher man came to the plantation once and talked

'bout what heaven gonna look like. It seemed too good to be true."

I knew those verses. Sam and I had discussed them on many occasions, wondering at the beautiful images they conjured in our minds. It seemed fitting in a hospital with death all around, the men's thoughts would turn toward heaven. Perhaps we all needed a reminder of what awaited on the other side of this life.

I turned pages until I found the twenty-first chapter of Revelation. "'And I saw a new heaven and a new earth,'" I began, "'for the first heaven and the first earth were passed away.'"

I read for another hour. When I finished with one passage, someone else in the room asked to hear such and such story. After I closed the book and said I needed to take a break, most every one of those men thanked me, a measure of peace on their faces that hadn't been there earlier. I realized, too, the fear that had held me captive since coming to Sam's bedside left while I was reading.

With one last look at Sam's closed eyes, I made my way outside for a breath of fresh air. The sun hung low on the horizon. I longed for my cot, yet I didn't want to leave Sam. What if he woke up?

A young woman I'd seen working in the hospital stood on the step, looking at the sky. When she turned to me, her eyes weary, she nodded a greeting.

"I's just listening for the guns."

Her words took me by surprise. In my worry over Sam, I'd near forgotten the fighting might continue. But as I strained my ears, all I heard were wagons, voices, and normal sounds of the city settling in for the night.

"Is that your man in there?"

I wasn't sure how to answer. My feelings for Sam were too big and too confusing to explain to this stranger. "He's a friend."

She nodded. "I hope he makes it."

"Thank ya."

"I ain't seen my man since the fightin' commenced. I keep hopin' he'll turn up. . . ." She shrugged and returned her gaze to the sky.

I knew the dead were still being buried, black men among them. But our people didn't have the benefit of a marked grave like the white soldiers. I silently prayed her man wasn't among them.

After making use of the indoor privy, the likes of which I'd never seen before, I returned to Sam's room. A lone lantern sat on a table near the entry, casting shadows over the beds. Some of the men slept; some stared at the ceiling. I settled next to Sam's bed, grateful no one had carried off the chair while I was gone.

I dipped a cloth in the basin of water and gently washed Sam's face.

"You gotta wake up now, Sam." I kept my voice low, not wishing the others to hear me but hoping Sam could. "The Yanks is chasing the Rebs south. I heard they's down in

Columbia. Makes me wonder if they'll keep going till they get to the shore in Alabama."

Did his eyelids flutter?

I leaned in close. "Miz Illa made it back from Franklin. Said things was fierce for a time, but now she's back, working hard as ever. She's over to the hospital on Front Street, but she comes by here to check on you."

I waited.

My shoulders sagged when no response came. A heavy sigh escaped my lips. "Sam, you gotta wake up. You gotta get better. You made me a promise, and I'm gonna hold you to it."

I rested my head near his heart, comforted by the steady beat beneath the blanket. As long as there was breath in his body, I wouldn't give up.

It was some hours later when I woke with a start. Had someone spoken to me? Called my name?

I sat up. The room was dark save the lone lantern. The other men continued to sleep. No one stirred. I must have been dreaming.

When I turned back to Sam, I found his clear gaze fixed on me. "Sam," I breathed.

A slight movement to his lips confirmed I wasn't imagining. "I always keep my promises."

Before I knew what I was doing, I planted my hands on either side of his face and kissed him. When I moved away, his smile deepened. "That there is what I been waiting for."

Weakness kept his words from going beyond me, but it didn't matter. He was awake and talking.

I fought tears that threatened to spill over. "I wouldn't be surprised if you went out on that battlefield just so's you could end up here, worrying me to death."

He chuckled, then grimaced. A reminder to both of us his wounds were far from healed.

"Did we win?"

"Yes. The Confederates are on the run."

He nodded and closed his eyes for a long moment before meeting my gaze again. "Did the boy live?"

The man amazed me. Despite nearly dying, his thoughts were on someone else.

"I don't know."

He was quiet for a time before he noticed his Bible in my lap. A knowing look came to his eyes. "You been reading God's Word."

It wasn't a question. I looked down at the book. "The others like hearing the stories."

Sam's gaze went beyond me to the darkened room, where beds were mere shadows. "How many?"

"Two dozen in this room. Lots more in the hospital." I knew he'd want to hear the whole story. "The Federals lost about four hundred men, but there's nearly three thousand wounded. That don't include enemy soldiers. They say the prison hospital over on Cherry Street is overflowing."

He closed his eyes. A lone tear slipped from beneath his lashes. "Why do men do it, Frankie? Why are they so bent on killing each other just so's they can claim to be the victor?"

"I don't think even they know why they do it. Someone

gets a hateful idea in their head; then they convince others on it. Like a disease spreading."

We sat in the stillness of our thoughts for a long time before Sam said, "You need to go to them."

I puzzled over what he meant. "Go to who?"

"The wounded over in the prison hospital."

I nearly tumbled out of the chair, shocked at such a fool thing for him to say. "I ain't going to help those men. What they ever done for me but keep me in slavery? I'm staying right here till you're well. You ain't getting rid of me that fast."

I thought he'd laugh at my joke, but he didn't. He didn't even smile. "I mean it, Frankie. I don't know why, but you gotta go to them. You gotta." He tried to rise up, but his face contorted with pain.

"Sam, be still or you'll open your wounds." I gently pushed him down. Surely the pain must have him confused. I didn't want to upset him further. "We'll talk about it later. Right now, you gotta get some rest."

He settled back on the cot and closed his eyes, seemingly appeased by my words. I sat in the dark room, listening to his even breathing when he eventually drifted to sleep. While I was grateful he'd finally awakened, he had a long way to go to full recovery. Infection killed many and was still a real threat.

But along with worry over his well-being, I was baffled by his adamancy that I go to the prison hospital. Why would he insist I go there? I'd seen several hundred Confederate prisoners marched into Nashville, covered in mud, with their heads hung low. Some were transported in wagons, their uniforms bloody and their faces pale. No doubt the prison hospital was brimming with fallen Rebs, but I had no desire to attend those men. They deserved to die, and nothing Sam said would change my mind.

Illa arrived with the sun. Sam woke in time for her to feed him a breakfast of watery porridge while I fought to keep myself awake.

"Why doesn't thee get some sleep, Frankie?" Her eyes held kindness as well as concern. "I'll stay with Sam until the doctor sees him."

I wanted to argue and declare myself fit to remain by his bedside, but I knew I wasn't. I could barely keep myself upright. Finally I consented. "I'll be back soon as I rest a bit."

Sam's weak smile assured me he understood.

I walked out of the hospital into a bitterly cold day. Puddles laced with a thin sheet of ice and frozen mud gave evidence of a heavy rain during the night, although I'd never heard it come or go. I pulled my coat tight, the threadbare garment inadequate against such frigid air, and trudged through the mess as fast as I could. I was numb by the time I reached my tent. There was no sign of Nell, and I hoped she'd taken over my duties as laundress for the officers like I'd asked. Even with most of the army marching south, there were still men in camp who needed clean clothes.

I crawled beneath the blanket and curled into a stiff ball. Although my tired muscles eventually relaxed in exhaustion, my mind wouldn't settle. Sam's words kept me awake longer than I liked, making me angry.

"I ain't going to that prison hospital," I hissed into the silent tent, the words puffs of white on the cold air. I flopped over and presented my back to the opening as though some unseen person stood outside, beckoning me to go tend wounded Confederates.

"Leave me be!" I shouted and squeezed my eyes closed. "Ain't nothin' you or Sam says is gonna change my mind."

CHAPTER
TWENTY-TWO

Jael arrived home. She had news.

"There was an incident on the streetcar." Her somber tone told us all was not well. "A gal got on at Cherry Street. The conductor wouldn't take her ticket book. Said she had to pay the fare, but she didn't have it. Her employer bought her the book so she could go home every Sunday to check on her girls and not worry about carrying fare."

Alden shook his head, disgusted. "I've seen this happen before. That conductor should be fired."

"Those of us on the streetcar got nervous when the gal and the conductor starting yelling at each other. Some of the white passengers got off."

Frankie reached her hand out toward Jael, who came forward to take it. "I'm sorry you got caught in all that mess, baby girl."

Jael sniffled, and I realized she was quite shaken by the confrontation.

"What happened to the woman?" Alden asked.

"A kindly old gentleman offered to pay her fare, but she refused. Said her book was good enough. When the conductor threatened to throw her off the car if she didn't pay, she threatened to tell her employer about him." Her eyes widened. "I thought that man was gonna hit her right there in front of us all. I guess some of the people who'd gotten off notified the police because an officer arrived about then. He dragged the woman off the car, kicking and screaming. The conductor laughed, then turned to those of us still seated and said he hoped we learned a lesson today."

My blood boiled at the injustice, yet what could I say to Frankie and Jael? A white man had done this to a black woman, simply because he could.

I remembered the man who'd boarded the streetcar with me the day I learned about the job with the FWP. Laws forced him to sit in the back while I was free to sit wherever I pleased. I recognized now how unfair it was to treat people as though they were inferior simply based on the color of their skin, but it shamed me that it had taken so long.

"I wanted to stand up and say something in that woman's defense," Jael said, her eyes welling with tears, "but I was scared."

Frankie tugged Jael down into an embrace. "You done the right thing, baby girl. It wasn't your fight. There may come a day when you gotta stand up for yo'self, but today wasn't it."

They stayed in one another's arms for a long moment, with Frankie whispering words I couldn't make out. I glanced at Alden, wondering if we should leave, but he was looking at the floor, hands clenched. In the short time I'd known him, I'd learned the inequality of the races didn't sit well with him. No doubt he wished he could locate that streetcar conductor and share a choice word or two.

Jael sniffled again before rising to her feet. "What are you all talking about?"

"I was just telling Rena and Alden 'bout the time after the fighting stopped here in Nashville. Sam was still in the hospital, but it looked like he might recover." A deep frown filled Frankie's face. "But the better he felt, the more that man kept on me about going to work in the prison hospital and caring for the men there."

"You mean the Confederates?" Jael's mouth hung open. "They didn't deserve any kindness."

After what she'd witnessed on the streetcar, I couldn't blame her for her strong opinion. The thought of a black person coming to the aid of the very people who'd kept them enslaved surely seemed offensive.

Frankie sighed. "There were so many prisoners, the folks tending them couldn't keep up. I thought poorly of anyone who went to help, but Sam wouldn't let up. 'You gotta go to them, Frankie,' he'd say every day. 'One of them prisoners needs you.'" She shook her head, her face pinched with aggravation as though Sam had just spoken the words.

"Why did Sam think a Confederate needed you? You didn't know any, did you?"

"None that I could recall. Mr. Waters's son was too young to join the army when they left the city in 1862. I heard later the South was taking boys as young as fourteen by the end of the war, so I don't know if Grant Waters joined up or not."

"Then who needed you?" Jael's question echoed my own.

Frankie settled back in her chair, rubbing her gnarled fingers as she often did when deep in memories. The clock on the wall ticked several minutes away before she finally answered.

"Someone I never expected to see again."

———

Sam improved a little each day. He had a long way to go to be fully recovered, but every morning brought new victories, like sitting up, feeding himself, and reading from his Bible.

The matron of the hospital, a disagreeable woman with the fitting name of Miz Stoney, never had a kind word to say when I passed her in the hallway. She seemed put out that the men in the beds refused to mend as fast as she desired, and nothing I or any of the volunteers did ever met with her approval.

"That woman shouldn't be working in a hospital," I said to Sam one day after hearing Miz Stoney rail at the young woman I'd seen stargazing. I didn't know what infraction the young volunteer had committed, but she was in tears after

Miz Stoney was finished. "She's too mean. Miz Illa should be the matron."

"Miz Illa doesn't want to be a matron. She's free to go between hospitals and the camps, tending to the needy in ways she couldn't if she was kept at one hospital."

I saw the wisdom in his observations. "Well, if not Illa, then someone else who has a heart that isn't made of stone."

Sam smiled. "You'd make a good matron."

I rolled my eyes heavenward. "As though they'd allow the likes of me to be matron." My gaze swept the room. More beds had been added to accommodate more wounded, and the room now had thirty patients crowded into it. I helped the volunteers tend some of the men, but Sam was my main concern.

"Listen, Frankie," Sam began, but I held up my hand to cut off his words. I knew what he intended to say. He'd already said it a dozen times.

"I told you. I won't go nurse the prisoners, so stop asking."

Hurt filled his eyes, and I regretted the harshness in my voice. My tense shoulders eased. I didn't want to argue with Sam. "Do you want me to read to you?"

He nodded.

I took up the Bible, turning to the book of Psalms, when Sam said, "I'd like to hear Luke, chapter 6."

I eyed him. He'd never asked for a text so specifically before. I flipped pages until I found the passage and began reading. I smirked when I came to verse 24. "'But woe unto you that are rich! for ye have received your consolation.'"

I looked up. "That sounds like he's talking about the Confederates."

"All Confederates aren't rich," Sam said softly, his eyes remaining closed as he listened.

I scowled. He was right, although I didn't like to admit it. I kept reading. "'Woe unto you that are full! for ye shall hunger. Woe unto you that laugh now! for ye shall mourn and weep.'"

I didn't say it aloud, but I thought for sure Jesus must have had the Confederates in mind when he spoke those words. They were sure mourning now that the Yanks had whipped them and sent them on the run with their tails between their legs.

Eagerly I went on to the next verse, wanting to prove to Sam the text was indeed about Southerners, but I stopped halfway through verse 27. I silently read the remaining words, and I knew. This was why Sam chose this passage.

"What's it say, Frankie?" asked Henry from the bed next to Sam's. The young man with a leg missing waited for me to continue.

Sam's eyes were open now. I fumed when I met his steady gaze. "I think I'm done reading for the day."

He ignored my hard tone and gave me a patient look. "Please finish it, Frankie."

I narrowed my gaze. "It don't change anything."

He nodded.

With gritted teeth, I read, "'But I say unto you which hear, Love your enemies, do good to them which hate you. Bless them that curse you, and pray for them which despitefully use you.'"

I felt every eye in the silent room on us. The other patients had heard me argue against tending the prisoners. Their nods of agreement told me I was right. Every one of them had been used by white people. They'd all suffered at the hands of masters and overseers. They lay in this hospital because of men who wanted to keep us in bondage simply because of the color of our skin.

Sam didn't speak, but it didn't matter. I knew what he'd say, and I didn't want to hear it.

Low conversations eventually resumed throughout the room. Henry sent me one last look of sympathy before he closed his eyes. He'd joined the Federal Army mere days before a Confederate cannonball blew off his leg. How would he feel if I up and left him and the others to go tend the very men who'd done that to him?

I closed the book and laid it in my lap, staring at the black leather cover. Since the day I'd made peace with God, I'd fallen into a comfortable belief in him and the words printed in the Bible. I wasn't as passionate about it as Sam was, but it felt good to know there was Someone more powerful than the white people in charge of my world. Why he let them rule over us was still a mystery, but I thought I'd begun to trust him.

Now I wasn't sure I trusted him at all. How could he ask me to love my enemies? The very thought left me with a feeling of betrayal deep in my soul. Betrayed by God and by Sam.

"Give me one good reason why I should step a toe in that prison hospital."

Sam's eyes were closed again, but I knew he'd heard despite me trying to keep my angry voice lowered so the others wouldn't hear.

He turned his head and met my gaze. "Because you ain't like them."

It wasn't the answer I expected. "What do you mean?"

"You ain't like them," he repeated. "You wouldn't treat someone badly because they had white skin. I've seen you care for the officers the last two years, doing their laundry, tidying their rooms. Sure, it was your job, but you didn't have to give so much attention to them as you did."

I thought back to the days before the battle began. In my hearing, General Thomas told one of his colonels that I'd taken such good care of his officers, their wives would be jealous upon their return home. The comment pleased me then, but now I wished he hadn't noticed. I wished Sam hadn't noticed.

Why, I wondered, had I worked so hard for the officers? The gold coins I received might be an obvious answer, yet I knew it wasn't because of them. I'd worked just as hard for Mr. Waters back at the warehouse and never earned a cent.

"You ain't like them, Frankie." Sam's soft voice drew me from my thoughts. His eyes held no condemnation. Only peace.

Suddenly my anger with him ebbed until nothing remained.

This man knew me. He saw me. And he loved me in spite of it all.

"I can't do it, Sam," I whispered, fear rising at the thought of entering the prison hospital. I'd been willing to tend white

Union soldiers, but I could not bear the thought of touching the men in gray. Their kind had wounded me too deeply with their hands, their words, their actions.

"Will you think on it?"

My every instinct screamed to refuse even that small concession, but the earnestness on his face was too much. "I'll think on it."

Over the next three days, we settled into a truce. Sam didn't ask me to help the Confederate prisoners, and I pretended everything was fine. But on the inside, I was a mess. Even my dreams were haunted by men in gray, begging for help.

Illa came to my tent early the fourth morning. I hadn't slept well. Nell hadn't come back to the tent last night, and I worried she'd found another good-for-nothing to spend time with. Between Sam and his confounded plea, and Nell and her confounded naiveté, I wanted to pull the blanket over my head and hide from the world.

"Sam told me of his request for thee to work in the prison hospital," Illa said at my questioning look.

I sat up, shivering in the chilly morning air. I wasn't in the mood to hear another sermon on why I should help those men. "If you're here to tell me you agree with him, I'd rather not hear it."

She sat on the edge of Nell's empty bed. "Then it will surprise thee to hear me say I don't believe thee should do it."

She was right. I was plumb shocked. "I don't believe it. You, the woman who left your home and family back in Pennsylvania to tend slaves and strangers alike, you're telling me *not* to go help in the prison hospital? That isn't what the Good Book says."

"No, it isn't. Thee is correct on that. But it also says, 'Though I speak with the tongues of men and of angels, and have not charity, I am become as sounding brass, or a tinkling cymbal.'"

I frowned.

She continued. "'And though I have the gift of prophecy, and understand all mysteries, and all knowledge; and though I have all faith, so that I could remove mountains, and have not charity, I am nothing.'"

I'd known Illa long enough to know she wasn't a woman who wasted words. There was a lesson here, and she wanted me to discover it.

"Sam says we are to love our enemy."

"Yes, we are," she agreed, "but love cannot be forced or coerced. It has to be freely given. The words I quoted from the apostle Paul tell us we can do great and wonderful things, but without love, without charity of heart, they are meaningless."

Understanding slowly seeped into me.

I was willing to help my fellow man at the hospital. I was even willing to nurse the white Federal soldiers who'd arrived the night of the battle. Those men had given a great sacrifice for me and all the other slaves. Freedom didn't come without a price, and they'd been willing to pay it.

But to offer care and compassion to men who fought against freedom? Who wanted to keep me in bondage? That I couldn't do.

"Sam will be disappointed."

She remained quiet for a long moment. "Sam has learned to love as Christ loves. It doesn't matter to him what the person looks like or what they've done. He simply loves them. That isn't an easy thing to do. I've struggled with it myself at times."

This surprised me. "I woulda never guessed. You've never shown that here."

She smiled. "That's because thee sees me now, filled with God's grace and love. Had thee seen me before I went through the Refiner's fire, thee would know my failures. I overflowed with hatred for people I'd never even met."

"Who?"

"White Southerners who owned slaves."

I stared at her. "You hated your own kind?"

"They were not my kind, at least in my mind. They were evildoers, the lowest of mankind. I had no pity for them and certainly held no love in my heart for someone like that."

My breath caught. Her words exactly described what had lived inside of me since the day I was sold away from Mammy.

Hatred. Darkness, always lurking in the shadows of my soul. Sometimes I could hide it and pretend it wasn't there. Since meeting Sam and Illa, I'd witnessed what love truly looked like, felt like. I wanted that, and yet the darkness wouldn't let it take hold. Not completely, anyway.

"How did you overcome it?"

She stood, a look of peace shining in her eyes. "I didn't, Frankie. Not on my own."

After she left, I mulled over everything she'd said. I knew she wanted me to ask God to help me love the wounded prisoners. Sam wanted the same. But did I? It was easier to hate. Hatred had been my constant companion for so long, I wasn't sure I could love. Not the way they wanted me to.

The next morning, I made my way into the city. With my head down against a cold wind, I nearly ran into a well-dressed young woman standing in the middle of Cherry Street, not far from the prison hospital, silent sobs shaking her slim shoulders. She looked so lost and forlorn I couldn't pass on by.

"Ma'am, can I help you?"

She stared at me, blue eyes brimming with tears. "My husband just died."

I stood with her while she wept. When she quieted, I asked, "Was he a soldier?"

She nodded, her lips trembling.

"I'm sorry for your loss, ma'am. The Federal Army has done a lot of good in these terrible years of war. I hope your husband's death won't be in vain."

She looked aghast. "Whitley was a captain in the Confederate Army. He's been here in this wretched prison hospital for weeks. They refused to let me take him home to Richmond, where he could get proper care, and now he's dead. I hope every one of your Federal soldiers suffers the same fate."

She ran off sobbing, leaving me with a terrible ache in my gut. Illa's words echoed in my mind, like the loud-sounding brass she'd spoken about. *"Without charity of heart, they are meaningless." Meaningless.*

I stared after the woman, although she'd disappeared in the morning crowds. Like my Sam, didn't her Whitley deserve decent care whether he lived or died? Whether he was white or black? No matter which side he'd fought on? Like as not, I wouldn't have been able to save her husband, but did that matter?

I ran the rest of the way to the hospital on College Street, directly to Sam's bedside.

He read the anguish on my face and reached for my hand. "Tell me."

With sobs, I told him about the young woman and her husband, about Illa's visit and my nightmares.

"What should I do, Sam? What should I do?"

A soft smile slowly lifted his lips. "'But I say unto you which hear, Love your enemies.'"

CHAPTER
TWENTY-THREE

My insides tumbled and my knees shook, but I walked into
the prison hospital with my head high two days later. Illa
had secured a volunteer position for me with the matron,
and I was assigned to the second floor. The smell of sickness
lingered in the air when I entered. Illa confided that this hospital was not as well maintained as the others, even the one
for black soldiers. I couldn't blame those in charge for their
neglect. These men were the enemy, after all. Illa and Sam's
encouragement to get past those sentiments was the reason
I was here, but not everyone felt the way they did. I would
have never stepped a toe inside the building if it weren't for
Sam's persistence.

The Federal soldiers standing guard eyed me as I climbed
the stairs, but they didn't prevent me from passing by. With a
deep breath, I opened the door of the room I was to attend. My

task was to shave the men who couldn't do so for themselves, yet the very thought of being so near a white man—especially a Confederate—sent wave after wave of fear coursing through my veins.

Low murmurs of conversation hummed in the big room. Several windows along the far wall revealed the disagreeable weather outside, and the space held a chill despite a stove in the corner.

A nurse with bright-red hair poking from her cap changed the bandage wrapped around the foot of a patient. I'd heard many of the Confederate soldiers didn't have shoes and had resorted to binding their feet in rags. The bitter weather, however, was no match for such inadequate coverings, and frostbite had claimed far too many toes and feet.

The nurse glanced up at me and noted the shaving kit and bowl of water in my hands. "You can start there," she said, indicating a gentleman lying abed near a window. He gazed out to the cloudy sky, and I imagined he wished he were any-where but this prison hospital. He looked older than most of the soldiers I'd seen, his once-dark hair nearly completely gray. A days-old scruffy beard covered hollow cheeks.

I made my way to the man's bedside. "Sir, would you like a shave?"

He turned and frowned when he saw me. His eyes darted to the nurse. "Where's that other lady? The white one. I want her to shave me."

The nurse continued to wind a clean bandage around her patient's foot. "Mrs. Williams transferred to a different hospital. If you wish to be shaved, then Miss . . . ?" She glanced at me.

"Frankie." It was custom for slaves to take the family name of their masters, but I'd never done so. I didn't want to be known by the name of a white person who'd done me wrong, not even Mr. Waters. He might not have ever beat me, but he'd owned me same as he'd owned his horse.

"If you wish to be shaved, Miss Frankie will see to it. Otherwise, you will forfeit the opportunity to have your beard removed."

Despite the tension in the room, I noticed she had a different way of talking. Almost musical. I was certain she wasn't from around here.

The man huffed and seemed to weigh his options. Finally he gave me a curt nod. "Fine. You best not cut me, gal."

I bristled at his demeaning attitude. After nearly three years of relative freedom, I wasn't used to being spoken to as though I were a slave again.

"There are no 'gals' in this hospital, sir." The nurse drew everyone's attention with her stern voice. "You will address her as Miss Frankie, or you will not receive a shave." Her gaze swept the room. "That goes for all of you."

A rumble of assent filled the space before the nurse gave me a nod to proceed.

I set the items on a small table between the beds, my hands shaking. I wished I hadn't listened to Sam. I'd never shaved a man before. Now certainly wasn't the best time to learn either, especially on someone so unwilling.

With a steadying breath, I picked up the brush, dipped it in water, and began creating a lather from the shaving soap. The woman who'd given me the kit said the razor was recently sharpened, and I prayed she was right.

I was nearly ready to commence shaving the man when his eyes landed on my knotted fingers.

"She ain't even got two good hands," he bellowed, panic in his widened eyes. "I won't have a cripple cut my throat."

Although I didn't usually give my hand a second thought, his ugly words made me tuck it between the folds of my skirt.

The nurse walked over. She sent the man a dark scowl before addressing me. "May I see?"

Shame washed over me. No one had ever asked to see my poor hand before. Most people avoided looking at it and pretended it didn't exist. Slowly I raised both hands for her examination. The bent, knobby fingers of my left hand looked so pathetic next to the normal ones on my right. I rarely considered my disfigurement, but now I saw it through the eyes of the soldier and the nurse. It occurred to me I would probably question the ability of someone with a hand like mine had I been in their place.

Several long moments ticked by in the silent room. I felt the stares of the men on me, and I wanted to find a dark corner and hide. The nurse finally met my gaze. In that look I saw compassion and something else. Solidarity, maybe.

"Are you able to shave these men, Miss Frankie?"

The room grew still while they waited for my answer.

My shoulders pulled back on their own, as though to

challenge anyone who didn't agree with me. "Yes, ma'am. I am."

She studied me a long moment. A hint of a smile appeared on her lips. "Very well." She looked at the man. "Sir, do you still wish to be shaved?"

His glare went between us before he shook his head and returned his attention out the window.

"As you wish." She spun around, taking in the other occupants of the room. "This is your only opportunity for a shave today, gentlemen. The nurses are far too busy to attend to your grooming needs, yet our volunteers are happy to do so. Miss Frankie will approach each of you to inquire if you would like her to shave you. You may decline, but you will do so in a respectful manner."

She returned her attention to me. "You may proceed, Miss Frankie."

I wasn't sure what to do. Part of me wanted to flee from the room, never to return. Yet another part wouldn't let me give in to the likes of these men. *"Love your enemies, Frankie,"* Sam said. But weren't they supposed to adhere to that same command?

With my jaw clenched tight, I picked up the shaving cup, the razor, and a towel and walked across the aisle. The sandy-haired soldier lying in that bed met my gaze.

"Would you like a shave, sir?" I spoke through tight lips, expecting him to decline as the other man had done.

His gaze traveled from my hand to my face. Finally, with every eye in the room on us, he gave a slight nod. "I would."

His quiet answer took me by surprise, but I recovered quickly. I set to work spreading the lather on his cheeks and chin. I couldn't help but notice one sleeve of his shirt was empty. His green eyes bored into me, but I avoided looking at them and focused on the job at hand. With a silent prayer, I applied the razor to his face and scraped off lather and whiskers as gently as I could manage. By the time I moved around the bed to do the other side of his face, he'd closed his eyes.

When I finished, I wiped the last remnants of lather from his face. I noticed blood oozing from several nicks, although the man hadn't budged through my ministrations. Before I could clean those cuts, his eyes opened, and my hand stilled. I braced myself for his complaint. It didn't come.

"Thank you." He spoke so softly I barely heard the words.

"You're welcome." I gave a slight nod, then moved on to the next patient.

Some hours later I'd shaved a dozen men's faces. Several soldiers declined, scowling at me before they turned away, while others possessed full beards that didn't require a shave.

As I headed to the door with my supplies, the nurse approached.

"You did very well." She cast a glance into the room. Some of the men were resting while others spoke in low tones. I noticed the fellow with the green eyes watching us. "They don't like me too much either."

"Why not?" In the time I'd been here, she'd seemed capable and pleasant yet had a firm command of the room.

"I'm Irish. Some of them—" she nodded to the wounded men—"don't see a difference between you and I."

I felt my eyes widen. "You fooling me?"

She shook her head. "My name is Cait Fitzgerald. I'm from Dublin by way of Boston."

I'd never heard of that first place, but it didn't matter. "Pleased to meet you, Miss Fitzgerald."

"Me father was among the potato farmers whose crops failed because of the blight. I was just a wee girl when we left Ireland and came to America. We'd hoped for better times, but alas, many folks here say we Irish are a blight ourselves."

"I'm sorry," I said, even though I'd had nothing to do with her family's rejection in their new home. I knew what it felt like to be mistreated simply because of who you were. "But you're a nurse. That's something to be proud of."

She nodded. "'Tis indeed. I wish my father could have seen my achievement, but he died at Gettysburg."

"He fought in the army? Even after being treated so badly?"

A look of pride came to her blue eyes. "He did at that. Papa was honored to be an American. It was important to him to fight for the freedom of others."

"Nurse?"

We both turned to see one of the patients lift his arm.

"We best get back to work, Miss Frankie." She moved away, but not before giving me a nod and a smile.

I spent the remainder of the day emptying slop buckets, helping Miss Fitzgerald change bandages, and feeding the men who couldn't manage the bowl of thin soup. When I sat down to help the soldier with the green eyes with his supper, his expression grew dark. I was mighty tired after a long day, so I was in no mind to suffer through his ugly looks.

"If you'd rather wait for one of the nuns to help you with your meal, I'm happy to be on my way home." I knew as well as he did the Catholic nuns helping in the hospitals throughout the city were all white.

His brows rose, and he met my gaze. "You're very outspoken, aren't you?"

I tempered my anger. "I'm just tired, is all, sir."

After a long moment, he nodded. "If you'll help me sit up, I'm getting fairly good at using the spoon with my left hand."

Together, we managed to get him settled against the pillow and wall. I noticed a circle of fresh blood on his sleeve where his arm should have been.

"I best check your bandage. Looks like you've opened the wound."

A wave of despair washed over his face when he looked down at the spot. "I wish I would've died out there," he hissed and turned away.

The vehemence of his words rendered me silent. I imagined life would be difficult for a one-armed man once the war was over. I didn't know his occupation, but I did know life was full of opportunities, especially for a white man. He would heal eventually, both inside and out, and what he did after that was entirely up to him.

I cleaned what was left of his arm, barely more than a stump, and wrapped it in a fresh bandage. Once his shirt was back in place, I settled down with the bowl of soup. He glanced at it, then at me.

"Why are you doing this?"

The question caught me off guard. "Doing what?"

"This." He motioned to the soup, then to his arm.

I understood then. Sam's words echoed in my mind.

"You ain't like them, Frankie."

I shrugged. "Because it's the right thing to do."

He let me help him with the soup then. I held the bowl while he carefully spooned it to his mouth. Some dribbled on the cloth I spread across his chest, but for the most part he got it all past his lips.

"You did real well," I said when the bottom of the bowl appeared. I hadn't intended to say anything, but a bit of pleasure brightened his eyes when he handed me the spoon.

I left the prison ward and headed over to see Sam. I told him about my day, and he beamed like a proud pappy.

"Best watch out, or they might find out you ain't as mean as you want folks to believe."

Only Sam could say something like that and make me laugh.

I returned to the prison hospital the next day and the next, surprising myself. While none of the men were overly friendly when I tended them, the dark looks I'd endured the first day had diminished.

Miss Fitzgerald approached me when I arrived for work at week's end. "I fear Captain Wallace has taken a turn for the worse," she whispered, a grave look on her face.

I glanced past her to the gray-haired man. He'd refused a shave every morning, and yesterday he hadn't eaten anything.

We went about our duties, but something about the cantankerous man drew me time and time again. I'd offer water; he'd refuse. Broth? A cool cloth? The answer was always a terse *no*. The man grew weaker with each passing day, but he didn't seem to care. It was as though he'd given up on living.

I lay in my cot later that night, troubled by the man's listlessness. Why should I care if a captain in the Confederate Army died? So many thousands of men had perished in the war, one more wouldn't matter. Would it? I tossed and turned, gaining Nell's mumbled complaints from her cot. Finally, long before the sun rose, I knew what I needed to do.

When I arrived at the hospital, Miss Fitzgerald wasn't there yet, and most of the men were still asleep. An older nurse presided over the room, but she gave me little notice. With my coat buttoned tight to ward off the morning chill, I quietly made my way to Captain Wallace's side. His face looked ash-colored in the dim light, and his breathing was labored. He wasn't long for this world, I suspected, and I thought of the woman in the street whose husband died inside these walls.

Did Captain Wallace have a family who would miss him?

I carried a chair over and sat beside him. With a glance around the room to be certain no one was watching, I reached into my pocket and pulled out the Book of Psalms Sam had given me. To quiet my nerves, I took a breath, then opened the book to the first page and began reading, keeping my voice low.

By the time I reached the end of the third psalm, sunlight was streaming through the windows. I glanced at Wallace. He looked exactly the same. I tucked the book back into my pocket and stood. I had work to do.

Captain Wallace succumbed the following afternoon. I'd arrived early once again to read to him from the Psalms before anyone else awakened. I didn't know if the man heard me or not, but I was glad I'd followed my heart.

After his body was removed, a pall fell over the other soldiers. The man in the bed next to the now-empty one looked at me as I cleaned the area. "I heard you reading to Wallace."

I thought my heart might stop beating as everyone turned to stare at me. Would I be punished for having a book in my possession?

Miss Fitzgerald glanced at me from across the room, surprise on her face.

"Would you read to us?" the man continued, his request turning to a plea. Several others chimed in with their concurrence. "I ain't heard the Bible read in a long time."

I stood there in shock.

Cait came over and put her hand on my arm. "Would you, Miss Frankie? It might bring the men some comfort on this sad day."

I looked around the room. Not one of the men appeared angry that not only could I read, but that I had a book hidden in my pocket. Tears sprang to my eyes, and I nodded. "I'll read."

Cait set the chair in the middle of the aisle so everyone could hear. I felt conspicuous at first, and I faltered over several of the words, but no one complained. When I reached the Twenty-third Psalm, some of the men had drifted off to sleep while others continued to listen, the same peace resting on their faces as I'd seen on those of the men in Sam's room.

The noon meal interrupted our reading, but after the men were fed, some wanted to hear more Psalms. Cait thought it a fine idea, so my afternoon was spent reading the beautiful words.

When I told Sam about it later that evening, he offered to let me take his Bible. "They need it more than I do right now."

The man's generosity never ceased to amaze me. "How are you feeling?" I asked, noting he looked better each time I saw him. He still had a long recovery process, but unless infection struck, he seemed to be out of danger.

"Good. Miz Illa says I might leave the hospital in a day or two. She's found a woman who will let me stay in her house. She has some others there who are convalescing."

"That's wonderful news." While the nurses and doctors in the military hospitals did their best, the care Sam would receive in a private home was sure to be more personal. I hoped the house wasn't too far away so I could still see him on a regular basis. I'd ask Illa about its location when I saw her next.

My spirits were high when I entered the ward the following day. Cait hurried over.

"There's a rumor some of the soldiers will be transferred to prison soon."

I glanced at the men in their beds. Most of them weren't healed enough to travel. Although I knew them only by their ranks along with a few surnames, I'd begun to think of them as men rather than Confederate soldiers.

I gathered the shaving kit and began my rounds. When I reached the green-eyed lieutenant, I noted he seemed more somber than usual. He never said much to anyone but was always watching. I found his eyes on me often throughout the days, sometimes staring at my hand. I wondered if the loss of his arm made him notice how I got along with only the use of one good hand.

"Good morning, Lieutenant. Would you like a shave today?"

He nodded but didn't look at me.

I set to work mixing up a lather, then carefully completed the task. When I reached for the towel to wipe the remaining soap from his face, his eyes finally met mine. An intense look filled them.

"Who crippled your hand?"

The low words barely reached my ears. He gripped my arm and tugged me closer. "Who?" he hissed, his grasp tightening.

Startled by his behavior, I couldn't imagine why he wanted to know such a thing, but I feared he'd make a ruckus if I didn't tell him. "The mistress of the plantation where I was born. She struck me with a fireplace poker when I was six years old. It ain't been right ever since."

His face paled. His breath came in hard heaves, and I thought he might strike me for saying such a thing about a white person.

I tugged free from his grip and backed away.

When his eyes met mine again, the hatred I expected to see wasn't there. Instead, I saw something I couldn't quite believe.

Shame.

My thoughts whirled, trying to understand what was happening. Who was this man? I stared into his green eyes a long time before a thought so alarming yet so clear stole my breath away, and I stumbled backward.

"No." I shook my head. It couldn't be.

I wanted to run from the room, to flee what I suddenly knew was true, but I stood where I was, staring at the boy who'd witnessed the attack that left me maimed.

"Who are you?" I whispered as my entire body trembled.

Everything else in the room faded while I waited to hear the name I'd tried a lifetime to forget.

"Burton Hall."

CHAPTER
TWENTY-FOUR

We sat silent in Frankie's tiny living room. Alden's and Jael's stunned expressions surely matched my own at the shocking turn in the story.

"Oh, Mama Fran," Jael breathed, tears flooding her eyes.

Frankie simply nodded, yet she didn't appear as upset as I might have imagined. Surely retelling this portion of her story was as painful as experiencing it that long-ago day.

A dozen questions tumbled through my mind, but I didn't voice them. I glanced at Alden. He must have understood my silence because he tightened his own lips and gave me a small nod.

We waited until Frankie was ready to continue, all the while my heart aching for her then and now. The war had changed her life in so many ways, many for good. Sam, Illa, freedom. The future must have looked far more promising than frightening to the young woman Frankie had become by then. So why did she have to come face-to-face with the son of her worst enemy?

"I never thought I'd hear the name Hall again." Whether she meant to or not, Frankie tucked her deformed hand beneath her good hand, protecting it as she must have done a thousand times over the years.

"He remembered you," Jael said, anger in her words.

"He remembered. I don't think either of us wanted to, though." Her lips pursed. "As soon as he spoke his name, all the memories of that terrible day flooded my mind. Miz Sadie's wild eyes. The pain that shot through me. Burton's indifference while he watched his mother beat me. I'd tried so hard to forget it all, and there he was, bringing it all back up, like vomit."

"What did you do?"

Frankie gave a humorless laugh. "What I'd been doing all my life. I ran. I ran out of the room, down the stairs, and out of that hospital. I had me no idea where I was going. I just ran. When I finally stopped, I stood in front of Sam. He took one look at me and knew something bad had happened. I fell to my knees on that hardwood floor and sobbed. All Sam could do was hold my hand, but I could hear him praying too."

She sighed. "I figured the men in the room thought I was crazy, but when I finally calmed, the looks of sympathy and understanding are ones I'll never forget. No doubt every one of them had times when they faced their greatest fears, but on that day, it was my turn.

"I stayed on the floor next to Sam's bed until the sun had long been tucked behind the hills. Miz Illa came and tried to talk to me, but I wouldn't listen. What does a white woman know of this kind of pain? It was late before I finally dragged myself up, stiff, sore, and completely spent. My stomach was empty, but I couldn't eat a thing. Sam hadn't said a word to me the whole time I lay in a heap on the floor. He just held my hand and prayed."

Prayed for what? I wondered. The damage had already been done. It would have been better if God had prevented her from meeting Burton in the first place.

"When I finally sat up and looked at him, he had tears rolling down his cheeks. 'Frankie,' he said, 'if I could, I'd take this cup from you. But you gotta drink it yourself.'"

"What'd he mean, Mama Fran?" Jael asked.

Frankie gave a sad smile. "He meant I was gonna have to go back and face Burton."

Jael gasped. "No."

But Frankie nodded. "I knew Sam was right, but I'd been fighting it."

"Why would you need to go back? That man didn't deserve the kindness you'd already shown him. He didn't need another chance to hurt you."

Frankie considered Jael's venomous words.

"Maybe not, baby girl, but it wasn't for him that I went back. It was for me."

The ward was dark except for a pitiful circle of light coming from a lantern just inside the door. My heart raced, and I feared it was loud enough to wake the sleeping men. I stood a long time staring into the room. I couldn't see Burton, for it was too dark, but I knew he was there. The same boy who'd stood by while his mother forever damaged my hand and my spirit. I could still picture him as he'd been that day. A sandy-haired boy on the verge of manhood, more curious than concerned at the beating of a six-year-old child.

"I can't do this," I breathed into the chilly hallway.

But then Sam's voice filled my mind. *"Yes, you can, Frankie,"* he seemed to say. *"You ain't going in alone."*

A glance out the window revealed it was still dark outside, but it wouldn't be long before the first signs of morning would color the horizon. What I needed to say to Burton had to be said before everyone else woke.

Squaring my shoulders, I took a step forward, then another, until I was beside his bed. When my eyes adjusted to the dimness of the room, I was surprised to find him awake, looking at me, almost as though he'd expected me to come.

Neither of us spoke. I'd thought of everything I wanted to say to him on the way over here, yet now I couldn't form a coherent sentence.

"You came back," he finally said. Although his voice was barely audible, his words echoed in the still room.

"I did."

He seemed at a loss for something to say. So be it. I was the one with the grievance. I'd speak my piece and leave.

"Your family wronged me," I hissed. "No child should ever be treated the way your mama treated me. No child should ever be taken from their mother the way your pappy took me from mine. Don't matter that I was a slave owned by Master Hall. Don't matter that my skin was dark. What matters is that I is a human being. What kind of person treats another human being the way your mama treated me?" I shook my head, my chin trembling with emotion. "But I ain't here to judge you, Mr. Hall. That day will come soon enough. For you. For me. For your mama and pappy."

I turned to leave.

"Wait."

I had opened my mouth to remind him I wasn't his slave anymore when he added, "Please."

Tears threatened to spill over my lids, but I refused to let them. I wouldn't have this man see me cry.

"I . . ." He stopped. Swallowed hard. Started again. "I . . . it . . ." He heaved a breath and looked at the ceiling. "My mother shouldn't have struck you. My daddy shouldn't have sold you."

His gaze met mine.

I waited.

"Nothing was the same after that day."

I puzzled over this. "What do you mean?"

"Everything changed. Lucindia refused to come to the house after you were taken away. Mama wanted to sell her and your brother and sisters, but Papa refused. He said he'd never sell another slave again, especially a child. He and

Mama argued all the time after that. Charlotte wasn't the same either. She cried a lot and had nightmares."

I stood in stunned silence. It never occurred to me Mammy would refuse to go up to the big house after I was sold or that anyone ever regretted what happened to me. I'd always assumed life on the plantation continued with its usual rhythm, as though I'd never existed at all.

"What happened to Mammy?"

Burton turned away. "Papa put her in the fields. She took sick just before the war began. Papa called the doctor . . . but she passed on."

I clutched at my heart, feeling it shatter into a thousand pieces. A silent sob shook my shoulders, and I closed my eyes against the pain. *Oh, Mammy.*

"My brother and sisters?" A tiny speck of hope ignited, only to be dashed by his slight shrug.

"Papa sent most of our slaves south when Tennessee fell to the Federals. I don't know what's become of them."

In the span of a heartbeat, I'd lost my mother and my siblings all over again. Anger shot to the surface, like a ball fired from a cannon, exploding with red-hot words.

"Your family stole everything from me. Everything. I will never forgive you. Do you hear me? Never." I didn't care that my voice had risen, causing the sleeping men to stir. They were as guilty as Burton Hall in my mind. White men who believed it their right to own me, simply because of the color of my skin.

He wouldn't look at me. I wanted to spit and call him a

coward, but instead I turned and fled the room. Cold air hit my face when I exited the building, but I didn't stop. I wandered the city, grieving over Mammy despite the fact she'd been gone for years. I didn't want to go to Sam. He'd be disappointed in me, but I wouldn't forgive Burton as Sam would want me to do. The Halls had taken everything away from me except my hatred. That I refused to relinquish.

I was near frozen when I came to the river. I stood there shivering while the eastern horizon filled with the colors of dawn. Dark shapes on the water turned into ships and fishing boats. Sailors, workers, and tradesmen appeared on the docks, going about their early morning business.

I remained where I stood, a block of ice carved into a woman. My heart felt hard and frozen. And tired. So very tired of the struggle. I looked down to the dark water. Perhaps I should simply slip into its depths and bring an end to it all. Wouldn't that be for the best? Mammy was gone from this world. Why shouldn't I go? What did I have to live for?

Voices drew my attention.

A group of passengers made their way to a steamship not far from where I stood. Most of the passengers were white, but I noticed a dark-skinned woman near the back. She held the hand of a small girl, and they each were carrying a bundle. I watched their careful progress up the gangplank, unable to look away. Just before they disappeared into the belly of the ship, the little girl turned, smiled, and waved to me, as though she knew I was watching.

I lifted my hand.

The child nodded, and then she was gone.

Tears formed and slid down my cheeks as the ship pulled away from the dock and started north. To a new beginning, I hoped. For the girl and her mother.

What about me? Didn't I deserve a new beginning too?

Sam wouldn't want me to end my life. Not when his life had been spared. Not when we had such hope and dreams for freedom, we could almost taste it. I'd been offered marriage by a good man when the war was over. And despite the horrors I'd witnessed in the hospitals, a small flame flickered somewhere inside me at the thought of becoming one of the first black nurses. If I walked into the river and let it carry me to my death, I would allow fear and hatred to win.

I looked upstream just as the steamer rounded a bend and disappeared, carrying the little girl into her future. I lifted my hand again, but it was to the scared six-year-old who'd existed inside me all these years that I bid farewell.

It was time for me to live. To love. To forgive.

When I arrived at the prison hospital later that morning, the place was in an uproar. Federal soldiers swarmed the hallways, dragging patients from their beds to be loaded into wagons outside.

I hurried upstairs and found Cait in the hallway outside the ward. "What's happening?"

"They're removing prisoners they deem well enough to travel. The men will be marched north to prison."

Although we'd known it would happen eventually, the news was disheartening. Most of the men in our ward were

not well enough for the long journey to Camp Chase in faraway Ohio.

I looked into the room to where Burton Hall waited with
the others. He stared straight ahead, and I wondered if he
was scared.

Two Federal soldiers stood in the aisle between the rows
of beds, conversing in low tones. Finally the senior officer
stepped forward.

"You, you, you, and you." He pointed to four men, including Burton. "Gather your belongings and prepare for immediate departure." They exited the room, brushing past me.

I wanted to run after them and protest. To remind them
Burton had lost an arm and still required help with the most
basic needs. How could he manage a long march north in the
bitter weather?

Cait hurried into the ward and set to work packing one of
the soldiers' meager belongings. I made my way to Burton.
He was trying to button his coat.

"Let me help you," I said.

Surprise registered on his pale face. "Frankie."

I gently moved his hand away and fastened the rows of
brass buttons on his dirty gray coat. There were so many
things I wanted to say, but now that our time was cut short,
only one mattered.

"I was wrong last night to say I wouldn't forgive you."
Tears sprang to my eyes unbidden. "I do, Burton. I forgive
you. You were just a child, like me. You couldn't have stopped
what your mama and pappy done."

His throat convulsed, as though he too fought emotions.

A Federal soldier filled the doorway. "Move out."

Fear, raw and full, came to Burton's eyes, and I knew I couldn't let him go without hope. I grasped his coat by the lapels. "You listen to me, Burton Hall. You're gonna make it. Don't let that missing arm rob you of the life God has for you. When this war is over, you come on home. You hear me?"

Unshed tears glistened as he nodded.

I let go, and he reached for his haversack. He joined the other men, but before he walked through the doorway, he stopped and faced me.

"Charlotte will be mighty glad to know you're doing so well, Frankie. She never forgot you."

And then he was gone.

CHAPTER
TWENTY-FIVE

My sister and her children moved in with us while I was at work the following day. Boxes, suitcases, and toys littered the foyer and spilled into the living room when I opened the door. If I'd been told it was happening, I couldn't remember. It was a shock to come home from interviewing an elderly gentleman who lived down the street from Frankie to find the house in bedlam.

"He took my doll," Holly wailed at the top of her lungs from the middle of the staircase as I stood in the doorway.

"Did not," James screamed over the banister above her. "I don't have your stupid doll."

Somewhere in the house, Buddy was crying and Mary yelled to her older children to stop arguing. They ran back upstairs, bickering loudly before a door slammed, muffling their voices.

My instincts told me to flee. I could escape to Grandma

Lorena's and no one would be the wiser. Besides, I truly did need to talk with Grandma. Frankie's story about Burton Hall sparked more questions that were beginning to demand answers.

"Rena, I'm glad you're home." Mama rounded the corner from the kitchen with Buddy in her arms, trapping me before I could get away. His thumb was tucked in his mouth and his eyes drooped. "I'm going to put the baby down for a nap. Mary's cooking dinner. She could use your help."

She passed by me, cooing to the little boy, and climbed the stairs.

"How was your day, Rena?" I whispered sarcastically after she'd disappeared. I took off my hat and coat and hung them in the hall closet. "Did you meet anyone interesting, Rena?"

I knew I was being as childish as my niece and nephews, but would it kill Mama to show a little interest in me?

Mary stood at the counter snapping green beans when I walked into the kitchen. She glanced up and offered a small smile, but I could tell she'd been crying. Her eyes were puffy and bloodshot.

She sniffled. "The kids are hungry."

I nodded and set to work peeling a pile of potatoes. We stood beside each other in silence. I didn't know what to say to my sister. Her life was a wreck.

"Daddy thinks I should file for divorce."

I looked up, surprised. Not just by her statement, but that our father had actually crawled from his hole to offer his daughter advice.

"Are you going to do it?" Divorce wasn't common in our circle, but it did happen.

She shrugged.

"I'm sorry, Mary." I didn't know what else to say.

Mama returned to the kitchen. "I put him down in my room since the children are playing in yours." She opened the oven door and peeked inside. The aroma of roast beef wafted out before she closed it again, offering me a pleasant surprise. A cut of beef was expensive, so we didn't have it often.

Her gaze landed on me. "Rena, please go down to Mother's and walk back with her. She's joining us for dinner."

I leaped at the opportunity and hurried from the house.

The sun clung to the edge of the horizon and filled the sky with muted shades of orange and blue. I loved autumn in Nashville. Crisp air nipped at my nose, and the hint of woodsmoke told me someone in the neighborhood thought it cold enough for a fire in the fireplace. Winter would be here soon enough, and though we didn't receive too much snow, cold days would keep me inside more often than I wished.

Grandma was in her bedroom sitting at a small dressing table when I arrived.

"How was your day, dear?" she asked as she ran a comb through her short gray curls.

I sat on her bed. "Good. I met an interesting gentleman who went out west after the war. He had all kinds of wild stories to tell."

Grandma chuckled. "No doubt. Your grandfather always

talked about going west, but thankfully we stayed right here in Nashville." Her eyes met mine in the reflection of the mirror. "How is Mary, poor girl? It breaks my heart to see her little family move in with your parents."

I heaved a sigh. "Dad wants her to file for divorce."

Grandma shook her head. "Oh no. I hope it doesn't come to that."

I shrugged. "Homer is a fool and a cheat. I wouldn't blame her if she left him for good."

We walked into the living room. While she went to get a coat, I looked at the black-and-white photographs on the mantel. Some were of her and my grandfather in their younger years. A cute little girl grinned in another, and I wondered when my mother had stopped smiling like that.

"I'm ready." Grandma waited for me by the door.

We linked arms and started for home.

"Grandma, do you know anyone by the name Hall? I feel as though I've heard that last name before."

She smiled. "Why, yes, dear. My grandmother's maiden name was Hall."

A tremor swept through me. "What was her name?"

"Helen. Helen Hall Morris."

I let out a breath full of relief. That must be where I'd heard the name before. As common as it was, I'd felt unsettled ever since Frankie mentioned it. Thankfully, Grandma's answer put those feelings to rest.

"Why do you ask, dear?"

We turned onto the walk leading to the front porch of

my house. A carpet of gold and brown leaves decorated the concrete and lawn. "Frankie mentioned a family named Hall. I knew I'd heard it before, yet I couldn't recall where. But the person Frankie knew was named Charlotte, not Helen."

Grandma turned to face me, surprise in her widened eyes.

"Rena, my grandmother had a younger sister. Her name was Charlotte."

———

The meal dragged on all night, or so it seemed.

Dad made a rare appearance at the table. He sat next to Buddy's high chair and seemed to enjoy the antics of his two-year-old grandson. Holly sat on one side of Grandma Lorena while James sat on the other side, both of them bickering and vying for Grandma's attention. Mama tried to keep Mary engaged in conversation about anything but her sad predicament.

I endured all this while keeping an eye on the clock. Were the hands on its face even moving? I was desperate to get Grandma alone.

One dreadful thought soured my stomach and prevented me from appreciating the fine meal.

Was Grandma's great-aunt Charlotte the same Charlotte Hall whom Frankie had known as a child? Ripples of horror continued to roll through my mind as I considered the implications if that were true.

"Rena, you've barely touched your food," Mama said, pulling me from my dark thoughts. "Do you feel well?"

I offered a weak smile. "I'm fine, Mama. Maybe a little tired."

Her keen eyes narrowed. "You spend too much time *working*." Her emphasis on the word as well as her look of disapproval drew Dad's attention.

"I thought we decided you would quit that job." He reached for his glass of water, looked at it with disgust, and set it back down.

My back stiffened. "It's a perfectly respectable job with decent pay. There isn't any reason to quit." I glanced at Buddy as he swirled mashed potatoes on the tray of his chair. "Especially with four additional mouths to feed."

I'd thought to throw in that last part to remind him of his lack of income, but it was Mary who looked hurt.

"I hope we won't be a burden for long, Lulu." She sniffled.

Mama sent me a glare, then softened as she patted Mary's hand. "You and the children are not a burden, dear. This is your home, and you're welcome here for as long as you need."

Remorse over my careless comment washed away my ire with my father. "I didn't mean you're a burden, Mary. Like Mama said, this is your home."

She offered a small nod, but I could tell I'd wounded her.

The meal finally drew to an end. I volunteered to wash the dishes since I hadn't helped cook. Mary took the children upstairs to give them all baths and ready them for bed. Dad disappeared behind the study door, and Mama and Grandma went into the living room and spoke in hushed tones.

I sped through the kitchen work, anxious to walk

Grandma home so we could talk. Anxiety had hold of my stomach when we were finally able to put on our coats and head outside.

"I enjoyed being with the family," Grandma said, pulling up her fur collar to ward off the chilly night air. Stars twinkled in the black sky above as did lights in the neighbors' windows.

"You should come more often."

She chuckled. "Margaret couldn't tolerate seeing her mother more than once a week."

The comment was sadly true. "Has she always been like that?" I asked, thinking of the picture on Grandma's mantel of Mama as a happy little girl.

"I suppose in some ways, yes. We spoiled her since she was our only child. I probably gave in to her wishes far more than I should have." She pressed her lips into a smile. "But she has a good heart, Rena. Underneath the layers of self-importance and harshness, she loves me. She loves you girls, too."

I knew she was right, but it was difficult to accept some days. Mama cared too much about what other people thought. I wished she cared more about what I thought.

When we reached Grandma's house, she turned to me. "Come inside and tell me more about the woman your Frankie knew. You have me quite curious."

I followed her in. We decided on hot cocoa to take away the chill in our bones, then settled into comfy chairs in the small parlor, each with a mug of the delicious drink.

"Frankie said she was born on a plantation about a day's

ride from Nashville," I began, trying to recall the details of Frankie's early life. In my haste to hustle Grandma out of the house, I'd forgotten to run upstairs to retrieve my notebooks. "It was owned by a family named Hall."

Grandma sipped her cocoa, a look of contemplation in her eyes. "Go on."

"I don't recall the man's name, but his wife's name was Sadie."

"Hmm." Grandma frowned. "That doesn't sound familiar, but then I'm not so good with names these days."

The tightness in my chest eased some with her admission. Maybe the similar name was simply a coincidence. Helen and Charlotte were both fairly common.

"When Frankie was six years old, Sadie beat her with a fireplace poker after Frankie accidentally wet the carpet. It broke her fingers, and she still has a deformed hand."

"Oh, my, how dreadful." Grandma shook her head. "It's hard to imagine a woman treating a child in such a way, but I fear things of that nature happened far more than we would like to admit."

"Not long after the beating, Frankie took a book from Sadie's daughter, Charlotte. She hid it outside, but she was eventually caught. They sold her the next day." Emotion welled in my throat. "She never saw her mother again."

Tears glistened in Grandma's eyes. "Poor child. What an awful thing to happen to one so young."

I leaned forward. "But you don't think Sadie is related to your great-aunt Charlotte?"

"I can't say for certain, dear. Aunt Charlotte married a gentleman from Ohio and moved before I was born. She'd visit Grandmother Helen from time to time, and Mama always took us to see her when Charlotte was in town." Her eyes squinted. "You know, I believe I have a box of old photographs and things that belonged to Grandmother. If I recall, there's a picture of Charlotte among them."

We hurried to her bedroom, where a large, old trunk with a rounded top sat beneath the window. I lifted the heavy lid for her, and she rummaged around, exclaiming over this item or that, until she came to a cloth-covered box that looked like it had once held sewing items.

When we returned to the parlor, we sat side by side on the sofa. Opening the box was like stepping back in time. Dozens of black-and-white photographs filled it, all of people long dead.

"This is Grandmother Helen," she said, taking out a picture of a woman who looked to be in her fifties. Her dress was in the style of the late 1800s, and she held a lacy parasol over her head despite obviously posing inside a studio.

Grandma turned the picture over and nodded when she read the handwriting on the back. "Yes. Helen Hall Morris, taken in 1875 here in Nashville."

She flipped it back over and we studied Helen.

"You look a little like her," I said, noting the similar facial features.

We dug through more pictures, some of people Grandma recognized, some she didn't. Near the bottom, she found one of a pretty young woman with pale curls piled on her head. She sat posed with her bell-shaped skirt spread out around her.

"I believe this is Aunt Charlotte." She turned the picture over and smiled. "Charlotte Hall, 1850."

I reached for the picture, studying my ancestor. "She was very pretty."

"She was, even as an older woman. I remember her smile."

Grandma kept digging in the box while I studied Charlotte's picture. She looked to be in her late teens, with a fresh face and sparkling eyes despite the lack of color to the picture. It made me wonder what I might have been like had I been born in her day. Would I have accepted slavery as most residents of Tennessee had?

A gasp next to me drew my attention back to Grandma. "What is it?"

She held a small picture inside a book-like frame. Her wide eyes met mine before she handed it to me.

I recognized it as an old-fashioned daguerreotype. Although the images behind the slightly clouded glass weren't as clear as some of the paper photographs we'd found in the sewing box, I noted a woman dressed in her finery sitting in a chair while two children, a boy and a girl, stood beside her. None of them smiled, but the woman looked especially sour-faced. I turned it over to read the scrawling on a slip of paper glued to the back.

Sadie Pope Hall and children.

CHAPTER TWENTY-SIX

"It can't be." My whispered words were more plea than statement. I turned to Grandma, her face as pale as I believed my own must be. "How can this be possible?"

She shook her head and bent to retrieve the picture, which had slipped from my fingers and fallen to the floor. We both stared at it, stunned that the image of the very woman who'd abused and sold Frankie was now in our possession.

"I wish I had remembered her name earlier." Grandma sighed. "It might not have been such a shock, I think."

My stomach roiled, and the meager dinner I'd consumed threatened to come forth. I squeezed my eyes closed to block out the horrid woman's face. "This can't be happening."

A thousand questions flooded my mind. *How? Why?*

I looked at Grandma, the edges of anger beginning to take hold. "Is this some sort of terrible joke God is playing on me? Why would Frankie Washington be on the list of former slaves for *me* to interview? Why not Alden or one of the other FWP employees? Why me?"

She placed her wrinkled hand on mine. "God isn't like that, Rena. You have to know there is a reason behind all this."

"What?" I couldn't keep my voice from rising. "What good can possibly come from this?"

She gave a slight shrug. "We'll have to wait and see. Perhaps after you tell Frankie, you'll understand."

I stared at her. Surely she wasn't serious. "I can't tell her this. In fact, I can't ever see her again. How could I face her, knowing my own great-great-great-grandmother was none other than the hateful and vicious Sadie Pope Hall?"

"Rena," she said, surprise and admonishment in her voice, "you have to tell her. She deserves to know the truth."

I shook my head stubbornly. "No. She's trusted me with her life's story. I won't break that trust by telling her I'm . . . I'm . . ."

"You're what?"

"I'm a Hall." I nearly choked on the words.

"You're not a Hall. You're a Leland. Your ancestors were Halls, but you had nothing to do with Sadie injuring Frankie."

I stood, fear and anger swirling through me so fast, I had to get up and move. "My family owned her. My skin is as white as theirs." I pointed an accusing finger to the picture still in her hands. "That woman's blood runs through my veins, just as it does yours."

We were silent for several long ticks from the clock on the

mantel. Finally Grandma raised her eyes. "Be that as it may, I don't believe Frankie will hold it against you. You had no more control over our ancestor's actions than she did."

I paced the small room, anxiety mounting. "What will I say to her?"

"The truth."

Grandma's simple answer brought me to a stop. Tears filled my eyes. Before I knew it, I was sobbing. She stood and wrapped her arms around me, her own sorrow mingling with mine.

When I quieted, she led me back to the sofa. She picked up the picture again and studied it, but I couldn't look at it. It made me sick to my stomach.

"I assume the girl is Charlotte, but I don't recall her brother's name."

"Burton. Burton Hall."

She nodded. "Ah, yes. If I recall correctly, I believe he was a Confederate soldier."

"He was." Curiosity got the better of me, and I glanced at the teenage boy in the picture. Burton had been a handsome fellow. I wondered what life was like for him after the war with only one arm. "Frankie worked in the prison hospital where he was brought after the Battle of Nashville. She didn't know him at first, but he recognized her because of her hand."

"What a shock that must have been." Grandma shook her head. "I'm sure it was quite difficult for her once she discovered the truth. What happened?" Grandma looked up at me.

I gave a shrug. "She forgave him."

A small smile lifted her mouth before she handed the picture to me.

"Then you will rob yourself of the freedom forgiveness brings if you don't tell her the truth."

———

Early the next morning I called Alden at the boarding-house to tell him I didn't need a ride. I simply couldn't face him until I'd spoken to Frankie. He asked the reason, but I wouldn't tell him. Not over the telephone.

"Can we meet for dinner somewhere? I have something to tell you."

We decided on the diner on Main Street at six o'clock.

"Is everything all right?" he asked, the concern in his deep voice nearly bringing me to tears.

"I hope so. I'll see you tonight." I hung up, wondering what Alden's reaction would be to my news.

Mary was already in the kitchen, sipping a cup of coffee, when I arrived.

"Morning." Her greeting held little enthusiasm. I noted dark circles beneath her eyes as she stared into the mug.

"You're up early." I moved to pour myself a cup from the enamel pot on the stovetop. I needed something stronger than orange juice to face this day.

"Buddy didn't sleep well. He misses his crib."

I plunked a cube of sugar into the dark liquid, then carried it to the table and sat across from her. I'd been so preoccupied with discovering who Charlotte Hall was last night after dinner that I'd completely neglected my sister. By the time I came home from Grandma's, everyone was in bed for the night.

"Is there anything I can do to help? Maybe with the kids?"

She glanced up and shrugged. "Now that Homer's parents live in Nashville, his dad volunteered to take James to school. It'll just be Holly and the baby here with me during the day. Besides, you have your all-important job to go to."

I didn't tell Mary I'd stayed up half the night wrestling with whether or not I should continue with the FWP. Finally, after the grandfather clock downstairs sounded four chimes, I'd come to my decision.

"Maybe not for long. I know Mama isn't happy with me going down to Hell's Half Acre for the interviews."

Mary's brows rose. "Did I just hear you say you're giving in to Mama's demands?"

I sent her a disparaging look, just like in the old days. "It's my decision." I paused before adding, "But I'll admit she's worn me down."

We sat in silence for a while, each sipping our drinks.

"You need to follow your dreams, Lulu."

Her quiet words surprised me. She met my gaze, looking older than her twenty-five years. "I made one bad decision and look at me now. I love my kids—don't get me wrong—but this isn't the life I thought I'd have. Don't let anyone, not even Mama, take your dreams away from you."

"Thanks, Sis," I whispered. We hadn't been close in years,

but in that moment, I felt a kindred spirit with my sister. Briefly I considered telling her about Frankie and Sadie but ultimately decided against it. The story was too long and too convoluted. Besides, I didn't want her to tell Mama. There would be time enough to confess the whole sordid tale later.

"May I borrow your car today?" I'd planned to take the streetcar to Frankie's, but now I realized it would be much faster and safer in Mary's old Hudson.

She nodded. "Sure. After helping me pack things up yesterday, Papa Whitby filled the tank with gas and gave me some extra money." She heaved a sigh. "He really is a nice man."

One of the kids called from upstairs, and Mary rose. "The keys are on the table in the foyer," she said before she exited the kitchen.

I finished my coffee, thinking about the life Mary would never have. But she had three kids she was crazy about. Something good had come from her mistake despite everything.

Was that the key to surviving, no matter what life hands you? Find the good among the ashes?

I made a mental note to spend more time with my sister and her children. Which, if I went forward with my plan to quit the FWP, I'd have plenty of opportunities to do.

It had been a while since I'd driven a car, but I managed to make it to Hell's Half Acre without a problem. I pulled up in front of the familiar yellow house, my stomach in knots. Frankie wasn't expecting me this morning, but I wanted to come while Alden was at work and Jael in class. The speech I'd rehearsed on the way over was for Frankie's ears only.

The curtains in her window moved, and I saw her gaze intently at the strange automobile. I didn't want to frighten her, so I hurried to exit the car and wave. She returned the greeting, and a moment later the front door opened.

"Well, lookee who's here in a fancy new car."

I closed the door of the weather-beaten vehicle and forced a smile to my lips. "It belongs to my sister."

She waited for me to gain the porch. "What brings you here so early? Don't you have an interview today?"

I shook my head. My heart hammered so hard I was sure she could hear it. "I need to talk to you about something."

Her keen eyes roamed my face. "You look near done in with whatever it is. Come on inside. You want coffee?"

I declined, ready to get on with my confession. The sooner I spoke the vile truth, the sooner I could leave.

We settled in our normal places. If she noticed I didn't take out my notebooks and pencil, she didn't mention it. I held the handles of my purse in a fierce grip, knowing the two pictures concealed inside would change everything.

I thought my nervousness might seep over onto her, but she sat watching me with a calm, almost-peaceful expression. Oh, that I didn't have to do this. What would she think when she heard the truth?

Finally I took a deep breath. "When I first came to see you, I wasn't sure what to expect. I'd never met anyone who'd been a slave. The things I learned in school about slavery times weren't like the stories you told, and I found myself captivated by them."

She didn't respond but simply let me speak my mind.

"The day you mentioned the name Hall, I knew I'd heard it before."

Her brow furrowed a bit, but she remained silent.

I swallowed hard, the lump of fear in my throat growing with each guilt-ridden word. Tears filled my eyes, and my chin trembled. "My grandma Lorena remembers having a great-aunt named Charlotte Hall."

Confusion washed over her face. I wanted to run out of the house and speed away in Mary's car, but I knew I couldn't. I had to confess my family's sins to this woman. A woman I'd come to care about.

I reached into my purse and pulled out the two pictures. A sob shook me as I handed her the photograph of Charlotte. "This is my grandma's aunt Charlotte." She took it, her eyes widening in recognition. I forced myself to remain seated and extend the second photograph to her. "And this is Charlotte's mother."

Frankie's eyes met mine before her gaze shot to the daguerreotype I held out. "It can't be."

Her words echoed those I'd uttered upon learning the truth.

She shook her head and jerked away from the picture as though it held the stench of death. "Where'd you find that?"

"In a box that belonged to my great-great-grandmother Helen."

"Helen?"

I nodded.

She stared at me a long moment, then glanced at the picture she held. "I remember Charlotte had an elder sister who was already married by the time I went to live in the big house. I believe her name was Helen." She glanced up. "You say she's your great-grandmother?"

My chin trembled as I nodded. She'd left off a *great*, but it didn't matter. I couldn't meet her gaze and instead stared at the floor.

"Lord have mercy," she breathed.

A long silence followed. When I found the courage to peek at her, I found her studying the picture of Charlotte.

"She sure growed into a purty thing, didn't she?"

I didn't respond. Her quiet words weren't for me.

She exhaled a deep breath. I glanced up to find her gaze fixed on the daguerreotype I still held.

"That Miz Sadie?" Her voice hardened.

I nodded, unsure whether to extend the framed picture to her again or not.

Her glare bored into it, as though the woman herself stood in the room. About the time I wondered if I should put it away, she held out her hand. I relinquished the final dagger into the heart of our budding friendship.

I wasn't sure what I expected her to do upon seeing Sadie's face again. If she tossed the photograph into the furnace of her kitchen stove, I wouldn't blame her. If she yelled and cursed, I would hear her out. But her quiet study of the images nearly undid me. I tried to think of something, anything, to say that would lessen the pain I'd brought to her, yet I knew nothing I said could do that.

"Mm-hmm. That's just how I remember her." She lifted the picture up to the morning light streaming in from the window. "This must've been taken after I was sold."

My stomach knotted. Now was the time to offer a long-overdue apology for the sins of my family, yet what could I say?

I stood. "I don't know if you can—"

Her sorrowful eyes met mine, and a sob brought an end to my inadequate speech. Before I knew it, a flood of tears, remorse, and pain came forth, and I was powerless to stop them from consuming me. I stood there and cried as I'd never cried before. Wailing for six-year-old Frankie. For her mammy. For myself.

I sobbed louder when I felt her frail arms go around me, tugging me into a fierce embrace in the same way Grandma Lorena had the previous evening. We wept together there in her tiny living room, a former slave and the white offspring of her worst enemy. I don't know how long we remained there, but even after the heart-wrenching sobs ceased, we stood, arms around each other.

When her grip on me loosened and she pulled back, red-rimmed eyes met mine. "Tears wash the windows of the heart."

I sniffled and nodded.

She settled back in her chair and pulled a handkerchief

from the front of her dress. I had need of my own handkerchief tucked in my purse, but I couldn't move. I had to
know. I had to know what she thought of me.

"You have every right to hate me and my family."

She blew her nose again, wiping it this way, then that.
When she looked up, I recognized the expression in her eyes.
I'd seen it the previous day, when she told of forgiving Burton
Hall.

"Hatred is a powerful thing. It can turn a person into
something they ain't. It don't matter what color your skin is."
She picked up the photograph of Sadie, her eyes narrowed.
"I hated that woman. I hated her with every bone in my
body. For years I let that hatred feed my soul. Every white
person I met felt it. Even after Mr. Waters bought me and
gave me a comfortable life, I hated. I 'spect my life might
not have been so hard had I let go of the hate. Sam and Miz
Illa talked about God and his love, and I learned to read the
Bible myself, but that hatred never really left me. I hid it, I
suppose."

She looked at the picture again, and I noticed she held it
in her gnarled hand. "It wasn't until I saw Burton in that hospital, his arm cut off and looking so pitiful, that forgiveness
finally took hold inside me. Them Federals was planning to
take him away to prison for who knows how long, and there
weren't nothin' he nor his mama coulda done about it. It was
as though I finally saw him as he was—a man who had no
control over his situation, just as I'd been the day Miz Sadie
beat me." She shook her head. "He looked as helpless as a

newborn baby that last time I saw him. I've often wondered what happened to him."

"Grandma could only remember that he served in the army."

Her eyes on the photograph, she said, "When I forgave him—when I actually said the words—all that hatred slipped away. Even the hatred I'd carried so long for Miz Sadie. It was gone. I remember that feeling like it was yesterday. Like I dropped something heavy that had weighed me down for too long. Seeing her face now, all these long years later, don't bring it back up."

She laid the picture in her lap and met my gaze. "God healed the scars inside me, Rena. I could never hate you nor your family."

I fell to my knees at her feet. "They don't deserve your forgiveness. Sadie probably never admitted what she'd done was wrong."

"Maybe not, but that's between her and her Maker. I won't let hatred steal away the peace I have in my heart. You can't let it steal yours either."

I clasped her crippled hand in both of mine. "I'm sorry, Frankie," I whispered, tears falling down my cheeks. "I'm sorry for what a member of my own family did to you. I'm ashamed to know they're responsible for this."

A look of peace settled over her features as she held up her hand. "God will heal these ol' fingers someday."

"How can you believe that? He hasn't done it yet."

"Chile, you remember the day you come to my door the first time?"

I nodded.

"What did I tell you?"

I thought back to that day. I'd been so nervous. Frankie had come to the door and said something I still didn't understand. "You said the Lord wouldn't let you go home until you talked to me."

She smiled. "Nothin' surprises the Lord. He's got a plan and a purpose for everything. We just have to wait on him."

I stared at her. "You believe God brought me here . . . on purpose?"

She chuckled. "It sure couldn't be a coincidence, now could it?"

I knew she was right. "But why?"

Her gnarled fingers grasped mine. "For this. If I'd told my story to anyone else, that's all it would've been to them. A story. But *you* came to my door, and lookee what the Lord done."

I still wasn't sure I understood, but I was grateful she didn't hate me or my family.

"What happens now?"

She put her other hand on my cheek. "Now you and that fella of yours go out and change the world."

It felt good to laugh. "Alden and I aren't dating, you know."

"I know, but you should. He's perfect for you, just as Sam was perfect for me."

"Did you marry him after the war ended?" I asked, still at her knee, like someone who belonged.

"I did. Soon as we heard General Lee surrendered to General Grant. We decided to stay in Nashville and help with the rebuilding. I thought about going to school to become a nurse but in the end chose not to. Sam and I worked as a team. I didn't like the thought of being in a hospital away from him all day, if you can believe it." She chuckled; then her smile faded. "Things weren't easy after the war. We were free, but jobs were scarce. A lot of white folks didn't want to pay us for work that'd been done without wages during slavery. It took many years before the city and the people recovered. 'Bout the time we settled in and started to figure out freedom, the Ku Klux Klan came around, scaring folks and causing trouble."

Her expression grew soft. "Sam wasn't a preacher, but he was close enough for most folks. He'd read from his Bible—the same one he let me take to the prison hospital—and share the gospel with anyone who'd listen. He did lots of other work, too, but sharing God's Word . . . that's what he knew he was supposed to do.

"We were married almost ten years before the Lord blessed us with our son. I'd given up hope of having children. God had given me four babies, but I figured my hatred had killed them all. Sam never stopped praying, though. He told me the Lord would give us a son someday, and he was right."

I glanced at the framed photograph of a young man I'd

seen on the table by my chair the first day I came to see Frankie. "Is that him?"

She nodded. "That's Caleb. He's so much like his pappy. That boy is smart, too. He went to Fisk University and got his teacher certificate. He married a gal whose people were from Georgia, and they settled in Atlanta. He wanted Sam and me to come live with them and get away from the Acres, but we was needed here." She winked. "Caleb give me nine grandchildren, and at one time or another, most all of them has come to live with me and Sam so they could go to school. Now it's my great-grandchildren who's coming to see me. Jael is his granddaughter."

I smiled, wondering why I hadn't guessed Jael's identity before now.

Despite all the hardship, the long years of pain and suffering, Frankie had survived. And then she'd thrived.

"And Sam?" I asked, knowing the story wasn't complete without understanding what happened to her sweetheart.

Sorrow filled her eyes. "He passed on to glory five years ago now. I miss him every day, but I know it won't be long till I'll join him and Mammy."

We spent a lovely afternoon talking, laughing, and baking cookies for the Sunday school children's bake sale. When it was finally time for me to leave, Frankie pulled me into a tight embrace.

"I'm glad you come to me, Rena."

Tears threatened, but I nodded. "So am I."

As I drove away from the yellow house, with Frankie standing on the porch waving, my heart swelled with love. Real, sweet love for a woman who'd been a nameless stranger a short time ago. A woman whose life went beyond the stories she wove. Whose legacy of courage needed to be told to the generations.

I knew I would never be the same.

CHAPTER
TWENTY-SEVEN

Our fried chicken dinners grew cold as Alden gaped at me from across the table in the noisy diner.

"You can't be serious?"

I shushed him when several dinner patrons glanced our way at his exclamation. "I am. Trust me. The shock still hasn't worn off."

His gaze went from me to the picture he held of Sadie Pope Hall and back again. "She's your great-great-grandmother?" His incredulous tone hadn't lowered.

"Great-great-great-grandmother."

He shook his head. "This is the craziest thing I've ever heard." He turned the picture over to reread the hand-written names for the third time. When he finally laid the picture down, he met my gaze. "What are the odds of you and Frankie even meeting, let alone you being assigned to interview her?"

"Frankie and Grandma Lorena don't believe it was a coincidence."

His eyes narrowed. "Let me guess. They think some all-powerful, all-knowing deity worked it out."

I stirred the mashed potatoes on my plate. His skepticism echoed my own, and yet what other explanation could there be?

"What do you think?" he asked when I didn't respond.

I shrugged. "It does seem . . . orchestrated, don't you think?"

He glanced at the picture again and sighed. "I admit it's a wild twist of fate."

I wasn't sure what to believe, but I knew one thing. Meeting Frankie had changed me. Hearing her stories had opened my eyes to a world I never knew existed. To people I had cared little about. It amazed me now to realize I might have gone my entire life without knowing the truth about slavery—about my own family—had it not been for Frankie.

"I don't think I'll have a job with the FWP after Mr. Carlson hears about this."

Alden leaned back against the booth. "I hadn't considered that. It certainly is a unique situation."

"I'm not sure I can continue with the interviews anyway." I shrugged again. My emotions felt raw, my mind confused and heavy with the truth. "I know it's unlikely any of the other former slaves were owned by my relatives, yet I can't help but wonder who they were and what their lives are like now. It would be too painful to uncover more dark secrets. Does that make sense?"

He reached across the table and put his hand over mine, the first intimate contact he'd ever initiated with me. "It does. And honestly, I wouldn't blame you. I can only imagine the . . . responsibility and guilt, I suppose . . . that you must be feeling."

I nodded, grateful he understood. "Frankie doesn't hold it against me or my family, but my ancestor maimed Frankie for life. They sold her when she was just a child. She may have forgiven them, but I can't. I won't."

Alden squeezed my hand. "Let's take a drive. There's something I'd like to show you."

We took his car, leaving Mary's at the diner. I was surprised when he parked at the bottom of a hill. The sun hung low on the horizon, a big orange ball coloring the city in shades of autumn.

"Where are we?" I asked. It looked like a construction site of some sort.

"Fort Negley."

I gasped. "Truly?"

He smiled. "Frankie's stories about the place made me curious. Tom Ellison, the foreman of the project, was in the WPA office when I stopped by. He invited me out to visit. I thought you might like to see the progress they've made reconstructing the old fort."

We carefully made our way up the hill, deserted now

that the workday had ended. Alden explained the rebuilding process.

"The original limestone blocks that were used to construct the walls surrounding the fort were carried off after the war. People used them to build or repair homes and businesses damaged in the battle. Like Frankie said, the walls were laid out in a multipoint star, with these—" he indicated a triangular-shaped wall jutting out in front of us—"as a perfect place for a cannon."

I gazed at the stone walls, trying to envision the fort as Frankie had seen it. To know she'd walked here, frightened and preparing for the impending battle, felt surreal. "It's as though I've gone back in time. I almost expect a Union soldier to come traipsing down the hill or to hear cannon fire in the distance."

"I know what you mean." His gaze took in the tools, stacks of stone blocks, wooden posts, and other construction items scattered throughout the area. "I've always enjoyed visiting historical sites, but this is different somehow. Frankie's stories made this place come alive. She lived right down there—" he pointed to an area below us—"in the contraband camp for more than three years."

We hiked to the top of the hill, keeping to the path that circled the fort. To the north lay downtown Nashville and the Cumberland, and I couldn't help but remember Frankie's description of seeing dozens of warships on the river before the battle began. Buildings obstructed the view now, but I could well imagine the sight Frankie witnessed that day.

"I wonder if this was where Frankie and Nell hid when the fighting started." I turned to study the reconstructed fortification again. The wooden stockade in the center of the fort wasn't quite finished, but it helped me envision what the original might have looked like.

"Probably somewhere near here." Alden pointed to a grassy area between two of the wall's points. "The Confederates attacked from the south, so this side of the fort would offer the most protection."

We stood silent, taking in the view. A train blew its whistle in the distance.

"I've lived in Nashville my entire life, and yet I knew nothing about Fort Negley."

"You can thank President Roosevelt and his New Deal programs for breathing life into the old fort."

I chuckled. "It appears we have much to thank the president for, since we both work for the FWP."

With a last look at the city below, we headed down the hill. The sun slid over the horizon just as we reached Alden's car.

"Thank you for bringing me here." I wouldn't forget this place anytime soon.

After we returned to the diner, where I'd left Mary's car, Alden offered to escort me home, but I declined. It wasn't far. We said good night and I drove away. I pulled into the driveway a short time later, hoping no one would hear me arrive. The need to be alone ran deep, and I simply couldn't face Mama or Mary just now. I didn't even want to see Grandma, although I knew she was anxious to hear how Frankie took the news.

I entered the house through the back door. Voices came from the front of the house, so I tiptoed down the hallway and hurried upstairs without being seen. Exhaustion swept over me. Ever since I learned Sadie Hall was my ancestor, my entire world had felt upside-down.

Stretching out on my bed in the dark, I stared at the ceiling. Mama and Mary's muffled conversation carried up the stairs, but their words didn't interest me. My imagination conjured images from Frankie's story. I saw a little dark-skinned girl, joyful and smiling, wearing a pretty new dress. She twirled and giggled and ran outside with a book held against her chest. She settled under a tree with her treasure, happily looking at the pictures, until a large white hand snatched her up. Sadie's face crowded my mind then, her eyes blazing with fury, her lips lifted in a snarl. She reached for the fireplace poker, but I screamed for her to stop.

"Frankie, run!" I yelled, but it was too late. The poker came down on the little girl with a horrific crash.

"Rena?"

I woke, startled to find Mama's face looming above me. Light came from the hallway and illuminated her worried expression.

"We didn't realize you were home until I heard you yell. Are you all right?"

I sat up, shaken by the nightmare. "I guess I fell asleep."

She turned on the lamp on my desk. "Have you eaten? There's leftover meat loaf in the refrigerator."

I nodded. "Alden and I stopped at the diner."

Surprise registered on her face. "Was this a date?"

"No, Mama. We needed to talk about work."

Her eyes narrowed as she settled on the edge of the bed. "Mary says you told her you might quit your job."

I refrained from emitting a growl. My sister had never been able to keep a secret. "I might. I haven't decided yet."

Mama studied me. "Did something happen?"

I would tell her about Sadie Pope Hall someday, but I wasn't ready yet. She'd have too many questions and strong opinions, and I simply couldn't manage them right now.

"I finished Frankie's interview today. As much as I enjoyed meeting her, I'm not sure I want to continue with more interviews."

"Well." Mama's satisfied smile irked me. "I'm sure it's for the best. You know I didn't approve of you going down to that . . . *neighborhood*. I'm sure you can find another job that suits you better."

I glanced at the notebook on my desk. "I still need to type up my notes and turn them in to the FWP office."

She frowned as she eyed me. "You look tired. Those notes will be there in the morning." She stood and walked to the door but turned to face me before leaving. "I think it best if we keep your involvement with the FWP quiet. You're quitting, so there's no need for anyone to know where you've been or what you've been doing."

"I'm not ashamed of it, Mama. And I'm not ashamed of the time I spent with Frankie. I still believe the interviews are important. Maybe more so now than when I first started."

Her lips pinched, as they usually did when she was unhappy with me. "Be that as it may, there's no reason to give the gossips something else to hold over us. I expect you to abide by my wishes."

She turned and left the room. Her bedroom door closed a moment later.

I lay back down, frustration keeping my muscles tense. Would telling Mama about Sadie change her mind? Doubtful. She'd probably side with our ancestor. At the very least, she would argue that Sadie lived so long ago, her actions had nothing to do with us.

I rolled onto my side and stared out the window into the night sky. Stars twinkled on a black canvas, the same stars visible to everyone, no matter the color of their skin.

What I'd said to Mama was true. I wasn't ashamed of my work with the FWP. The interviews I'd conducted in Hell's Half Acre showed me another side of the story. The world as I'd always known it now looked different. Felt different. I was different. Would Frankie's story affect others the same way?

I got out of bed and sat at my desk. With light from the lamp, I opened the notebook and read through a page of notes about the day six-year-old Frankie was sold. A terrible ache settled in my heart reading her word-for-word description, especially when I reached the part involving my very own great-great-great-grandfather. I couldn't fathom how a man, a father, could stand by and watch a child dragged away, screaming for her mammy.

The very image brought tears to my eyes. Tears of sadness . . . and shame.

With the house quiet for the night, I rolled a clean sheet of paper onto the cylinder of my Underwood. I stared at the blank page, thinking of Frankie. Because of her, I'd come to understand that everyone has a story to tell. It wasn't always pretty or happy, and, like my own family's tale of woes, it could be a bit messy at times. But our stories mattered.

Frankie's story mattered.

I smiled, and my fingers began their dance across the keys.

───

It was ten o'clock the next morning when I woke to the sound of the telephone ringing downstairs. I'd stayed up through the night typing, refusing to let my eyes close each time they drooped in exhaustion. When I finally fell into bed just before the sky began to lighten, a neat stack of typed sheets of paper sat on the desk.

"Rena?" Mary knocked on my door, then opened it slowly. "Good. You're awake." A sly grin creased her face. "Mr. Norwood is on the telephone."

I sat up, rubbing sleep from my eyes. Why was Alden calling? He'd volunteered to go to Mr. Carlson's office with me this afternoon. I hoped he hadn't changed his mind. The thought of facing the stern head of the Federal Writers' Project alone left a knot in my stomach.

With my bathrobe and slippers on, I descended the stairs to the nook in the hallway where the telephone receiver lay on a small table.

"Hello? Alden?"

"Hi, Rena."

Something in his voice sent a chill racing up my spine. "What's wrong?"

"I need to tell you something, but I'd rather do it in person. Can I come over?"

I swallowed hard. Had Mr. Carlson already learned of my family ties to Frankie? "Tell me now."

A heavy sigh came over the line. "Jael called the boardinghouse this morning."

My heart seemed to stop beating. "Why? Is Frankie ill?"

But in the next moment I knew. I knew before Alden said the dreaded words.

"She passed away in her sleep last night, Rena. She's gone."

The crack in his voice was my undoing.

I closed my eyes against the pain gripping my soul. "Nooo." The wail brought my sister running, but I couldn't speak. I just fell to the floor, sobbing.

Mary took the receiver from my hand. I don't know what she said to Alden, but a moment later I was cradled in her arms.

I cried until there was nothing left inside me. Mary smoothed my hair and rubbed my back, like I was one of her children. When my sobs and hiccups quieted, I heaved a shuddering breath.

"Thanks," I croaked when she handed me a handkerchief. I dried my tears and blew my nose but remained on the hardwood floor.

"I'm sorry, Lulu. I know she was special to you."

I nodded without looking at Mary.

"Mr. Norwood said he'd call on you this afternoon."

I nodded again. With great effort, I rose to my feet.

Mary rose too. "You should eat something. Do you want some coffee?"

I shook my head. "I just want to be alone right now." I turned toward the stairs but stopped and faced her again. "Thank you, Mary."

When I entered my room, my eyes immediately went to the stack of papers on the desk. Tears came again as I lifted the top sheet. The words blurred, but it didn't matter. I knew them by heart.

I was born on the Halls' plantation. Don't know exactly where their place was, but it were about a day's ride to Nashville, I 'spect. Mammy always said I was born in 1835 when the leaves started changin' color.

With the story in hand, I crawled back into bed and cried myself to sleep. When I woke, it was nearly two o'clock. Mary must have come in at some point because a tray with a sandwich and a cup of now-cold tea sat on my bedside table. My stomach rebelled at the sight of food, but I gratefully sipped the tea. Alden would be here soon, so I needed to clean myself up.

I was pulling on a dark-navy dress when Mary poked her head through the doorway.

"How are you?"

I shrugged. "It hurts."

Sympathy shone in my sister's eyes. "I'm really sorry, Lulu." She came over and fastened the clasp at the back of my dress. "I don't know what I can do, but if you need anything or just want to talk . . ."

"Thank you." I noticed the house was quiet despite three rambunctious children in residence. "Where are the kids?"

She busied herself straightening the covers of my bed. "James is still at school, but Holly and Buddy are playing checkers with Dad."

I looked at her in disbelief.

She chuckled. "Buddy has really taken to him. James and Holly finally wore him down last night with their pestering to teach them how to play the game, but I don't think he minds."

"What about his drinking? You don't want the kids around that."

"I told him I wouldn't let the children see him if he was drunk. He's actually stayed sober since we moved in."

I kept my thoughts to myself. Finding fault with our father wasn't something I wished to dwell on just now.

"I don't know when I'll be home." I picked up the stack of papers that held Frankie's story. With utmost care, I tucked them into my notebook and placed it all in my school book bag.

"I'll let Mama know." She hugged me then, long and tight. I fought to keep my tears at bay.

Alden arrived a short time later. Instead of waiting for me in the car as usual, he came to the door. My resolve crumbled at the sight of him, so handsome and solemn in his dark suit. I fell into his arms and shook with silent sobs. The kids came to investigate, but Mary thankfully shooed them into the kitchen and left us alone on the porch.

When I finally quieted, we sat on the steps.

"Jael invited us to come to the house this afternoon. She said there would be people coming and going all day. The funeral is tomorrow."

I sniffled. "I'd like to go. To both, if you wouldn't mind coming with me."

"Of course. Frankie was a special person. I'm glad you introduced me to her."

We drove to Hell's Half Acre under cloudy skies. It seemed fitting that the sun wasn't shining on this day. The number of cars parked along the street in front of the yellow house surprised me. People gathered on the porch and on the path leading to the house, chatting. The door stood open and I could see more guests inside. Every face I saw, however, was a different color from mine.

"Maybe we shouldn't go in." Uncertainty swirled through me. It was one thing to meet with Frankie and her great-granddaughter in the privacy of her home. Mingling as one of only two white people in a crowd was quite another. They belonged here. I didn't.

Alden studied the group on the porch. He had far more experience with people from different walks of life than I did. I waited to hear his opinion.

"Frankie was our friend. We might not know all of these people, but I believe the majority will be as welcoming as Frankie and Jael. Think of all Frankie endured throughout her life. I don't think she'd want fear to prevent you from honoring her."

I looked back to the crowd. I might not have known Frankie as long as they had, but she'd become dear to me in our short time together. It was only right that I join with those who mourned her passing.

"You're right. Let's go inside."

Alden came around and opened the car door for me. In an unexpected move, he took my hand in his and we made our way up the path. A hush came over those on the porch as they watched us approach. A man stepped out to block our progress, and I recognized him as the one who'd chased me—or so I'd thought—when I came to visit Frankie alone.

Alden's hand tightened on mine. "We've come to pay our respects. Jael invited us."

The man's stare bored into Alden a long moment before his eyes met mine. My knees trembled beneath my skirt, but I didn't look away.

Finally he nodded and stepped aside. "Anyone who was a friend of Mama Fran's is welcome here."

We climbed the remaining steps, with all eyes on us. Thankfully, Jael met us at the door.

"I'm glad you came." She took me by the hand and led us into the room. Conversations slowed until everyone grew quiet.

"This is Rena, Mama Fran's friend I was telling you about." She turned her smile to me, her eyes red-rimmed. "Mama Fran never talked to anyone about her life as a slave. Not even my grandpa." She indicated a gray-haired man nearby, and I recognized Frankie's son from his picture. "Mama Fran always said the past was best left in the past, but you changed all that. She told me after you left that first day that if anyone else had shown up at her door asking to hear her tales, she would have sent them packing."

Several people in the crowd chuckled.

Jael squeezed my hand, and tears slipped from her eyes. "But the Lord sent you. Last night before she went to bed, she said she was glad she'd shared her story with you. Said if change is gonna come, it has to start somewhere."

Murmurs of agreement swept the room.

Jael let go of my hand and reached into her pocket. She pulled out a small book with a worn leather cover. It looked quite old.

"This is the Book of Psalms Papa Sam gave Mama Fran when she was in the contraband camp." She offered it to me. "Mama Fran wanted you to have it. She wrote a note for you. It's inside the cover."

I gasped. "Oh, Jael, I can't take this. It's a family treasure. You keep it."

She smiled. "Mama Fran left each of us a keepsake. She had it all planned." She put the book in my hands. "Just last night she added this to the list. It already has your name inside."

I opened the book with trembling hands. When I saw my name scrawled in shaky handwriting beneath Frankie's own, I could no longer contain the tears.

For Lorena Ann Leland. May these words become more important to you than silver or gold.

"Isn't that what Sam told her the day he gave her that book?" Alden asked from his place next to me.

I nodded, rendered speechless by Frankie's generosity.

Jael hugged me, her own tears wetting my shoulder. When we separated, she whispered, "I have something wonderful to show you."

Alden and I followed the young woman down the hall to the bedroom where I'd helped Frankie with her earrings only a few days ago. I clutched the book to my chest before crossing the threshold, needing strength from the words inside.

Frankie was laid out on her bed, her eyes closed as though she were simply asleep. Wrinkles on her face had smoothed, and her lips rested in an eternal smile.

"She looks so peaceful," I said softly, missing her already.

Alden came up beside me and put his arm around my shoulders. I leaned into him.

"Look closer," Jael said.

I studied Frankie. She wore a simple dress, with a blanket pulled up to her waist. Her arms were folded across her chest, with her hands resting one on top of the other. The thin gold band I'd seen the day Alden took her picture shone in the lamplight.

I was about to turn away when I stilled.

Something about her hands seemed different. I stared, not understanding what my eyes were seeing. The ring, I realized, was on her left hand, not her right as it had been. A hand that should have been bent and knotted with deformity . . . but wasn't.

Jael reached out to touch Frankie's hands, tears streaming down her cheeks. "I found her like this." She met my gaze, smiling. "God healed her, Rena. Just like she said he would."

CHAPTER
TWENTY-EIGHT

After we left Frankie's, Alden dropped me off at Grandma's house while he took my typed notes to Mr. Carlson. Now was not the time to meet with the man, but I knew I would need to confess the truth about my family connection to Frankie someday soon. In the meantime, I wanted to be sure her story was included in the FWP collection.

When I told Grandma about Frankie's forgiveness, her death, and her healed hand, Grandma cried.

"I would have liked to have met her in life and offered my apologies for the things our family did to her," she said, wiping tears off her translucent cheeks. "To honor her in death would be a privilege. If it's all right with you, I'd like to attend her funeral."

I smiled. Nothing could make me happier.

At home, Mama and Mary offered their sympathies,

although I wasn't convinced Mama was entirely genuine. I felt drained and excused myself to my room. Fresh tears wet my face when I saw the notebooks on my desk. While it might have been comforting to read through them, the pain of losing Frankie left my heart too raw. I picked up the book on the life of Harriet Beecher Stowe instead.

As I thumbed through the pages, a quote from a letter she wrote to the editor of an antislavery magazine captured my attention.

> I feel now that the time is come when even a woman or a child who can speak a word for freedom and humanity is bound to speak. . . . I hope every woman who can write will not be silent.

Words written more than eighty years prior, yet they resonated within me with profound clarity. Mrs. Stowe's courage to face the problem of slavery in her day sent a wave of inspiration crashing through me. I wasn't sure if my participation with the Federal Writers' Project counted when compared to works like *Uncle Tom's Cabin* and her other writings against human bondage, but I couldn't help but think she would be pleased at the progress I'd made over the past weeks of getting to know Frankie.

When Alden arrived to pick us up the next morning, he seemed unusually quiet. With the somberness of the day, it made sense, yet something told me his frown went beyond Frankie's passing. Grandma insisted we take her sedan and went to retrieve the key. While she stepped out of the room, I pulled him aside.

"Are you all right?"

He nodded but avoided eye contact. "We need to talk, but later."

We arrived at the church on the outskirts of Hell's Half Acre and joined an even larger crowd than had formed at Frankie's home the previous day.

"She was well loved," Grandma said.

Alden assisted her from the car and we made our way inside. I was pleasantly surprised to find we were not the only white people in attendance. Although I guessed Illa Crandle was long dead, I wondered if any of her descendants had heard the tales of Frankie and Sam and come to pay their respects.

The service was like nothing I'd ever experienced. Spirited music and singing filled the rafters. When the singers grew quiet, Pastor Silas gave a beautiful eulogy. Then one person after another stood to speak about Frankie. How she and Sam had helped them in their time of need. How she'd taught them to read. How she'd changed their lives. Like Grandma, hearing the stories made me wish I'd known Frankie longer than the short time I was granted.

When the service was over, we followed the long procession to an old graveyard near the ruins of Fort Negley. There, not far from where she'd lived in the contraband camp, Frankie was laid to rest in the shade of a tulip tree, Sam beside her.

We dropped Grandma at her home after she treated us to lunch. Despite the sadness of the day, I enjoyed introducing Alden to Grandma Lorena and letting them get to know one another. She winked at me when I walked her to her door. "I hope you'll bring Alden around again. He seems like a fine young man."

We took Alden's car to Centennial Park. The rebuilt Parthenon and several small lakes were all that remained from the grand Tennessee exposition held in celebration of Tennessee's one-hundredth birthday in 1897. Only a few other people milled about, no doubt due to the clouds above us growing darker and threatening rain, so we practically had the place to ourselves.

Settling on the steps of the huge replica of the Greek building, we sat quietly. Birds trilled and fountains gurgled nearby, but the lack of human voices allowed my mind and body to relax. I needed this moment of respite to prepare for whatever Alden had to tell me.

"I know this sounds crazy, but I've often wondered who will attend my funeral."

I turned to him. His statement was not what I expected. "I don't think I've ever once considered such a thing."

He chuckled and gazed out at the natural beauty of the park. Fading lawns dotted with leaves of various colors spread out beyond us. Autumn was in the air, and soon the trees would be completely bare.

"I suppose it's a strange thing to ponder, especially for someone my age. But—" he paused and looked heavenward—"everyone dies eventually. And after what I witnessed yesterday . . . with Frankie's hand, I mean . . . I'm not entirely sure what I believe about life and death anymore."

I considered this. "Maybe that's the whole point. What we believe and what we think are not static. Experiences and people leave a mark on us and change us. Meeting Frankie and hearing her stories opened my eyes, almost like a blind person having their sight restored and seeing the world for the first time."

I spread my hands in front of me. "Witnessing the transformation of her hand . . ." I still found it nearly impossible to believe. "Well, I don't see how we could remain the same people after that."

"Her story needs to be told."

Alden's quiet words drew my gaze. "Yes, it does. You took my pages to Mr. Carlson, didn't you?"

"I did." He heaved a sigh.

"What? What aren't you telling me?"

He reached for my hand. "Mr. Carlson looked over your submission. He said it was too long. He also suggested that some of the more graphic details will need to be removed."

I stared at him. I couldn't believe what I was hearing. "He himself told me to take down the former slaves' stories word for word. That's what I did. Frankie's story is told in her words, her way."

"I know. I said as much to him, but he has his own ideas about what should and shouldn't be included in the narratives."

I sat in stunned silence.

"He wants you to turn in an edited version next week."

A spark of rebellion ignited somewhere inside me, reminding me of Frankie. "And if I don't?"

"He won't include Frankie's story with the other narratives."

I gaped at Alden. "He can't be serious." I stood and stared down at him.

Alden rose. His expression revealed the truth. "He was perfectly serious, Rena. I feel exactly the same way you do. We should take down the stories word for word, just the way the interviewee describes their life, with the exception of clarity now and then. But Mr. Carlson doesn't agree. He feels they should be more uniform in length and similar in content."

My fists clenched. "To do that would forfeit the truth. Their lives weren't neat and orderly. They were messy and ugly, and yes, sometimes the details were graphic. How can he—we—edit someone's life story when we weren't the ones who lived it?"

"I don't know." He seemed resigned to Mr. Carlson's demands, but I was not.

"I'll speak to him myself tomorrow. Make him see that I can't—I won't edit Frankie's story."

He shoved his hands into his coat pockets. "I don't believe it will do any good, Rena. His instructions were very clear. Edit the story or he won't use it."

Tears of anger spilled over, but I stepped out of his reach

when he tried to comfort me. "She deserves better, Alden. She deserves to have her life story told exactly as she lived it."

"Yes, she does, but how? Carlson won't use it unless you alter it. What other choice do you have?"

A light rain began to fall, but I didn't care. There had to be another way. My mind whirled.

"What other choice is there, Rena?" he asked again, softening his voice this time, as though encouraging me to find a solution.

The words of Harriet Beecher Stowe came back to me.

"I hope every woman who can write will not be silent."

Suddenly I knew.

An idea so preposterous, so ridiculously improbable took root in my spirit, I nearly laughed at the absurdity of it. Yet something about it felt completely right.

For the first time that day, a smile inched up my wet cheeks.

———

I parked Mary's Hudson in the shade of the two-story building on Printers Alley. It had only been six weeks since the last time I'd come down to the *Banner*'s offices, yet so much had happened since. After Mr. Armistead let me go, I thought I couldn't survive if I didn't work at the newspaper. Funny that I didn't realize until just this moment I hadn't missed it at all.

Typewriters hummed as I entered the office. The familiar smells of ink, cigarette smoke, and coffee hung in the air, but they didn't beckon to me as they had in the past. Several reporters glanced my way. I smiled and kept walking. By the time I reached the door to Mr. A.'s office, I'd gained the attention of most of the men in the newsroom.

"Gentlemen," I said before turning to find Mr. A. standing at his desk, a look of surprise on his face. "Hello, Mr. Armistead. It's good to see you."

"Leland." He glanced through the window that separated his office from the newsroom. A number of men continued to stare at me. "What are you gawking at? Get to work," he bellowed. When the noise of typing resumed, he returned to his seat and eyed me over the rim of his glasses for a long minute. "Something's different."

I hid a smile. "Oh?"

He motioned to the chair in front of his desk. I settled in it, keeping my purse on my lap.

"How are things with the Federal Writers' Project?"

"I interviewed seven former slaves for the FWP. Their stories will be included in those being gathered and sent to Washington."

He nodded, but his narrowed eyes remained on me. "And now you're out of a job and you're here to beg me to hire you."

I chuckled. "Not exactly, but I would appreciate you hearing me out. I have an idea I'd like to discuss with you."

"An idea?"

I settled back against the chair. "It's actually a story about an incredible woman I recently met."

Never one to miss a thing, he said, "A former slave, I take it."

"Yes. Her name is . . . was Frankie Washington, and hearing her story changed me."

He crossed his arms over his ample belly. "How so?"

I'd rehearsed this speech a dozen times over the last few days, but now the practiced words fled me. Instead, I spoke from my heart. "Frankie lived a life I never knew existed. In school we learned about slavery, but not like this. Not the real, raw, and sometimes-horrifying truth of their lives in bondage."

A look of doubt clouded his face. "The war ended seventy years ago. No one wants to hear about slavery these days."

"That's the point, Mr. Armistead. No one wants to talk about it, yet that doesn't mean it didn't exist. People who are still alive today endured it. They were forced into labor, never given a choice. They had no say about their lives, their destiny. They were *owned*." I let that word sink in. "They were property, bought and sold at the whim of their master. Our generation—my generation—can't begin to understand how such a thing was possible or what it felt like. The people who lived it are the only ones who can tell their story. They'll be gone soon—" my voice cracked with still-raw grief at the thought of Frankie—"so we mustn't let this opportunity slip past us."

"Isn't that what the FWP is doing? Collecting stories from these people so they'll be on record?"

"It is, but I have reason to believe not all the stories will be told in the way they should be." I didn't want to accuse Mr. Carlson of any large-scale wrongdoing based on the situation with Frankie's interview, but I also knew I couldn't allow her story to be edited in order to fit his idea of a slave narrative.

His eyes narrowed again, but in a familiar way. I knew he was considering my words. "What do you propose?"

I took a deep breath. My time had come. "I'd like to write an article about her. About the other slaves too. To tell their stories in their own words, holding nothing back. Frankie's story would only be the beginning. There are hundreds of former slaves living in Tennessee. But it wouldn't always be about slavery. I want to interview former soldiers who fought in the Civil War, nurses who tended the wounded, riverboat captains, and even plantation owners. All sorts of voices from the past, telling their stories in their words. The possibilities are endless."

My passionate speech came to an end. I feared he would laugh me out of the room, but he didn't. He tapped his pencil on the desk, deep in thought. "It's an interesting idea, Leland. I'll give you that. But we don't run this type of human-interest story. With the economy the way it stands, folks want to read about jobs and what's being done to help those in need now, not what happened in the past."

"I realize times are still hard for a lot of people," I said, thinking of my own family. "But if they knew that others had suffered and survived, it could be encouraging. Life-changing, even."

He chuckled. "You're putting a lot of stock in your writing abilities, Leland. Even the best newspapermen have a hard time getting their message across."

"My confidence isn't in my ability, sir, but in the people whose stories I'll write." I thought of Frankie's courage and smiled. "It's their lives that will offer hope. Not all of them have a happy ending, I imagine, but they still deserve to be told."

The clock on the wall ticked off time as Mr. Armistead's gaze bored into me, his face giving away nothing. Finally his chair squealed as he leaned back against it. "Tell me about this Frankie of yours."

I couldn't keep from grinning. "I'll do one better." I opened my purse and pulled out the story I'd been working on since the day after Frankie's funeral. I handed the typed sheets to Mr. A.

He glanced at the title page. "'Their Stories, Their Words.' You've already written the article?"

"Yes, sir. I knew I'd have to prove myself."

A look of appreciation crossed his features before he continued reading. I watched his face for the slightest reaction, but not a wrinkle moved. I tried not to let disappointment creep in while he shuffled the pages.

Finally, after he'd gone over it a second time, he tossed the whole bundle onto his desk. My hopes plummeted.

"The thing is, Leland," he began, shaking his head. He picked up the first page, glanced over it, then returned it to the pile.

I steeled myself against the imminent rejection and the disappointment it would bring.

"The thing is, I wish I'd come up with this idea myself."

I held my breath.

He indicated the papers on his desk. "This is good stuff, kid. Your Frankie sounds like quite a lady."

My entire body trembled with excitement. "Are you saying—?"

He held up his hand before I could finish my hope-filled question. "Unfortunately, it's not a good fit for the paper. Like I said, people want to read about the economy and what the folks in Washington are doing about it. Things like that."

I swallowed hard. I knew it had been a long shot, but still, I'd hoped Mr. A. would see the potential. It hurt down deep that Frankie's story might go untold. I felt as though I'd failed her.

He glanced over the article again, his chin jutted out in thought. "However, I've got a friend in New York who might be interested." He glanced up at me, a glint in his eye. "He's the editor of a little rag called *Collier's*. Ever heard of it?" He laughed at his own joke.

My mouth fell open. "*Collier's*, sir?"

"Bill and I go way back to our university days. I've sent him some writers over the years." He waited for me to focus on his intense gaze, although my mind was spinning. "Listen to me, Leland. This article is good. Good enough for a national magazine."

I stared at Mr. A., unsure whether to bawl like a baby or dance like a fool. There was no guarantee his college buddy would print the article, but it meant the world to me that

Mr. Armistead truly did see the potential in Frankie's story. That he liked my writing was icing on the cake.

"Thank you, Mr. A.," I said, my voice shaky with emotion.

"You're welcome." He grew contemplative. "You're different, Leland. More sure of yourself. I like it. Now get out of here and let me get back to work."

His gruff compliment followed me through the newsroom and out the door into glorious sunshine. I couldn't wait to share my news with Alden and Grandma Lorena, but first there was someone else I had to tell.

I drove to the cemetery. Frankie's grave stood out among the others. A simple wooden cross bore her name, but I knew a granite headstone had been ordered. The residents of Hell's Half Acre had taken up a collection to pay for it.

Seeing the mound of fresh dirt covered in wilted flowers brought tears to my eyes. How had this woman become so dear to me in such a short amount of time? She would forever be part of my life. Her story was connected to mine. Despite the shame and pain of the past, together we'd overcome it. I'd sought forgiveness for my family's transgressions, and she'd willingly given it.

There, under the tulip tree, peace—real, tangible peace—settled in my soul.

"I'm going to tell your story, Frankie," I whispered. "Thank you for entrusting me with it."

CHAPTER
TWENTY-NINE

The aroma of roasting turkey filled the house. Children's voices echoed down the hallway to my bedroom, where I sat at my desk, fingers hovering over the keys of my Underwood typewriter. How was I supposed to write my article with such pleasant distractions?

"'Precilla Gray was born in Williamson County before the Civil War began.'" I reread aloud the opening line for the fourth time. "'At 107 years of age, she attributes her good health to taking care of herself and wearing yarn petticoats.'"

Mary's soft laughter sounded behind me, and I turned to find my sister standing in the doorway. "Yarn petticoats?"

I chuckled. "That's what she says. Maybe we should try it."

She grinned, and I realized how much I enjoyed having my sister in the house again, noisy children and all. She still looked sad and worn from time to time, but the stress lines in her face had eased since she'd moved back home. After Mrs. Watkins retired and made Mama the manager of the sewing shop last month, Mary had stepped in and taken over the household responsibilities. I had to admit she was a much better cook than either Mama or me.

"Alden just arrived. He's downstairs with Grandma Lorena."

I glanced out the window to the street, surprised to see his car parked at the curb. "I didn't hear him knock." I stood and stretched, working the knots in my shoulders that tended to form when I sat at the typewriter too long.

"I'm glad you invited him to join us for Thanksgiving, Lulu. He seems like a really good guy." The wistful tone in her voice brought an ache to my heart. Homer filed for divorce last week despite threats from his father to cut him off financially. He had a new girlfriend and had no desire to see his children.

I hurried downstairs and found Alden sitting next to Grandma on the sofa. She laughed at something he said, his grin revealing his pleasure at her response. When his gaze shifted to me, he stood. I'd taken more care with my appearance today, and the look of admiration in his eyes made all the effort worthwhile.

"Don't you look pretty, Rena," Grandma said. She started to rise, and Alden offered his hand. "Margaret told me she didn't need help putting the finishing touches on the meal, but I think I'll go pester her anyway." She winked at me before disappearing into the kitchen, where Holly's high-pitched voice ordered James to "stop sneakin' licks of the punkin pie."

Alden and I settled on the sofa. "Your grandmother's right. You look beautiful."

I felt my face flush under his intense study, but I relished the compliment. "You look quite dashing yourself." My gaze traveled his length, noting the charcoal-gray suit he'd purchased for his new job with the Works Progress Administration.

He reached into his pocket and took out something bulky. "I was going to wait and give this to you at Christmas, but it seemed appropriate to give it to you today."

My curiosity piqued, I reached for the gift, thinking the size and shape revealed it as a book. Tearing off the tissue paper, I gasped.

It was a framed picture of Frankie.

"I'd forgotten you took her picture that day."

She sat in a chair on her front porch, her deformed hand resting in her lap while her other hand hid her mouth. I remembered wondering what she was thinking about.

"She'd be proud of you, Rena."

Alden's soft voice caused my eyes to fill with tears as I gazed at her precious face. "I hope so. I'm glad Mr. Carlson changed his mind about including her story in the collection of narratives. He didn't even ask for one edit."

Alden laughed. "I'm sure reading Mr. Armistead's editorial in the newspaper about you and the FWP helped change his mind. Not to mention the fact that *Collier's* is set to publish your series of articles on the lives of former slaves. Everyone assumes slavery died with the war, so I doubt many people have heard of the turpentine camps in Florida. Your interview with the man who escaped from one will open a lot of eyes and hopefully bring some change."

I smiled and wiped the wetness from my cheeks. "I still can't believe I'm writing for *Collier's*. I can never thank Mr. A. enough for submitting my article to his friend."

He stole a quick glance toward the kitchen, where happy voices rose and fell, then took my hand in his. "Some of the WPA employees were talking about you the other day. They say your articles will make people stop and think. About how we need to learn from the past and make the future a better place for everyone."

I squeezed his hand. "Mr. Armistead received several letters to the editor from readers saying as much. Of course, he's received some nasty letters too from people who say we need to go back to the days of slavery. He won't let me read those, but I can imagine what's in them."

He let go of my hand and put his arm around my shoulders, drawing me to his side. We'd gone on our first official date a week after Frankie's funeral, and I smiled every time I thought about her insisting Alden was perfect for me. She was right, of course.

"There are always going to be people who oppose change, but I think they're in the minority. Most people desire to live in harmony with others, no matter their differences."

I hoped he was right. It would take more than a few articles in a magazine to bring about the changes necessary to accomplish such a feat. I felt honored to be a small pebble on the path to the peaceful existence among people of different races and socioeconomic status, beginning with my own family. Mama had been shocked to learn about Sadie Pope Hall and her treatment of Frankie. When I told her my article about my experience with Frankie would appear in a national magazine, I thought she'd be furious. Instead, she asked to read it before I turned it in to my new editor. She found me on the back porch a little later.

"This isn't what I expected." She handed the pages to me.

I waited for the lecture about the embarrassment I would bring to our family if I allowed the article to go to print, but it never came.

"I think I see now why you admired Mrs. Washington." A sheen of tears filled her eyes as she met my gaze. "I'm proud of you, Rena."

Before I could respond, she turned and disappeared into the house.

I'd sat there, stunned. For the first time in my life, my mother said she was proud of me. The day after Mr. Armistead's editorial about me and the FWP ran in the paper, Peggy Denny had called Mama and let her know everyone at the women's club was talking about it.

"We can't imagine our little Lorena Ann has turned into such a fine reporter. Why, the whole country will read her articles when they appear in *Collier's*," she'd oozed. "Even the governor's wife said we need to help those poor, unfortunate people down in the Acres. We'll be discussing an initiative at our next meeting. We'd love to have you join us."

Mama and I shared a grin when she hung up the phone.

Nothing more was said about me going down to Hell's Half Acre to interview the residents.

Holly and James escorted me and Alden to the table, where a feast awaited. Mama, Mary, and I had worked all morning preparing the food, laughing and enjoying each other's company while Dad entertained the kids and kept them out of the way. It still amazed me to find my father sober these days. Having his grandchildren around worked some kind of miracle and helped him climb out of the dark pit he'd lived in for seven years. He still had a long way to go, but for the first time in a long time I saw hope in his eyes.

We gathered around the table, Alden on my right and Grandma Lorena on my left. Mama asked Grandma to offer the blessing, and as we all joined hands, my thoughts turned to Frankie. I would always be grateful God brought me to her doorstep. She'd taught me about life, about pain and sorrow, and about courage in the face of it all.

As Grandma prayed, thanking the Lord for his goodness to our family despite the hardships each of us faced, I silently said my own thanks for the events that led me to this place in life. Seven years ago, my hopes and dreams for the future had shattered in the wake of the stock market crash. I couldn't see a way through it to the other side. Meeting Frankie and hearing her story changed that. Her courage to overcome the pain and suffering she endured taught me what it meant to be a survivor.

"Thank you for Frances Washington," I whispered.

After the blessing, Dad carved the turkey while Mama

bemoaned the lumps in her gravy. Mary tried in vain to keep Buddy from throwing peas on the floor while James and Holly fought over the basket of rolls. Grandma simply sat and watched it all with a small smile on her wrinkled face, enjoying the antics of our imperfect family.

I glanced at Alden and found his dancing eyes on me. I gave a shrug. *This is my family, like it or not,* it said.

He winked, then reached for the bowl of mashed potatoes, exclaiming over how delicious everything looked. Mama beamed from her place at the end of the table.

My satisfied sigh went unnoticed amid the commotion, but it didn't matter. Life might not be exactly as I'd envisioned it seven years ago, but I wouldn't change a thing.

A Note from the Author

———

I first learned of the slave narratives, as they're called, while researching slavery in Texas. Drawn to the word-for-word and often heart-wrenching telling of life in bondage, I wanted to learn more about the narratives and how they came about.

In 1935, well into the Great Depression, President Franklin Delano Roosevelt established the Federal Writers' Project as part of the Works Progress Administration, a New Deal program that put out-of-work writers, librarians, teachers, and others to work. The FWP produced thousands of publications, including the more well-known American Guide series and the Life History and Folklore project. An estimated ten thousand people were employed by the FWP in the years leading up to World War II.

Beginning in 1936, employees of the FWP were sent across the South to interview people who were once enslaved prior to the Civil War. More than seventy years had passed since the war ended and these former slaves were aging. Their stories would soon be lost forever if measures were not taken to preserve them for future generations. The result was over 2,300 first-person accounts of slavery as well as 500 black-and-white photographs, all archived in the Library of Congress today. A handful of unforgettable recordings also exist, leaving the listener awed that the person speaking not only endured but survived one of the most shameful practices in history.

It was during this time of research that the story of Frankie and Rena began to emerge in my imagination. I wondered what it would've been like to sit at the feet of a former slave and hear their story unfold in their own words. As a lifelong student of history, I've come to appreciate a simple truth: Everyone has a story to tell, and no one should be silenced. The stories included in the FWP narratives are worthy of being told despite the sometimes-graphic details that are difficult to read and imagine.

Although *Under the Tulip Tree* is a work of fiction, bits and pieces of the lives of many former enslaved people, as well as FWP writers, are incorporated into the characters of Frankie and Rena. My hope is that their story of friendship, love, and forgiveness honors those whose lives now fill the pages of history.

Acknowledgments

Without courageous people willing to share the stories of their lives, the slave narratives would not exist. Reading their own words about life in bondage changed me, and for that I'm grateful. I'm also thankful for the many FWP writers who simply needed a job yet ended up creating a body of work that brings a deeper understanding of slavery that will last for generations.

Thank you to Brian, my wonderfully supportive husband, best friend, field trip buddy, and so much more. I'm blessed to call you mine.

To my amazing sons, beautiful family, and dear friends: Thank you for your love, prayers, and support through the years. Each of you holds a special place in my heart.

To Jan Stob, Erin Smith, and all the fabulous team members at Tyndale who worked on this book in various capacities: There aren't enough words to express my deep gratitude for your hard work and your warm embrace of this story. I'm honored to be part of the Tyndale family.

To Bob Hostetler, my agent: Your advice, knowledge, and crazy sense of humor are greatly appreciated.

To Paula Scott Bicknell, my prayer and critique partner: Your love and prayers are part of every book I write. Thank you, my friend.

Much appreciation goes to the Battle of Nashville Preservation Society, the Fort Negley Visitors Center and Park, and all those who tirelessly work to preserve historical sites in and around Nashville.

Above all, I'm eternally grateful for a heavenly Father who loves me unconditionally and for the Son who set me free. *Soli Deo gloria.*

About the Author

Michelle Shocklee is the author of several historical novels. Her work has been included in numerous Chicken Soup for the Soul books, magazines, and blogs. Married to her college sweetheart and the mother of two grown sons, she makes her home in Tennessee, not far from the historical sites she writes about. Visit her online at michelleshocklee.com.

Discussion Questions

————

1. Rena Leland's life is turned upside down when the stock market crashes. What changes occur in her family after October 29, 1929? Why do you think Rena believes her father blames her for the financial crisis? Think about a time in your life when your family experienced a devastating loss. How did you cope? What, if anything, gave you hope?

2. When Rena is presented with an opportunity to become part of the Federal Writers' Project, she wonders why the government felt it was important to preserve the stories of former slaves. How would you answer that question? What can we learn when we take the time to ask for and listen to each other's stories? What do we gain when we share our own stories?

3. Rena's grandmother encourages Rena, who admits to feeling "stuck," to step out in faith and take the FWP job. But Rena still wonders, "How could interviewing

people who'd lived in bondage decades earlier help me
see my future more clearly?" What does Rena learn
as she begins her new job? How does she change as a
result of seeing the world with a different perspective?
When have you been able to step into someone else's
shoes and view things in a new light?

4. As Frances Washington begins to tell her story, what
   surprises you about her life? What makes you sad? How
   realistic does her account seem?

5. Frankie's mother has no choice but to send Frankie
   back into the Hall home the day after a traumatic
   event. Later, Frankie tells Rena that while society has
   improved since her childhood, "times is still hard" for
   Frankie, her family, and many others. In what ways has
   our culture grown in race relations since the Civil War?
   Since 1936? Where do we still fall short and what can
   we do to continue improving?

6. What is Frankie's secret to survival after she is sold away
   from her family? What does it cost her? How would
   you answer the questions she and Alden have about
   God, including "What kind of love was it to enslave
   people simply because of the color of their skin?" and
   "What's the point of putting one's faith in something
   or someone who allows slavery and evil to exist?"

7. Frankie remembers her mother encouraging her, "Ain't
   nothin' you can't do if you set your mind to it." What

was Lucindia hoping to instill in her children? What does Frankie eventually take away from her mother's words? When has someone spoken into your life and given you the confidence you needed to take the next step?

8. A trip to the library to pick up *Uncle Tom's Cabin* leaves Rena meeting a sour-faced librarian who grumbles, "Literature like this only stirs up things best left in the past." Yet this was a book that President Lincoln credited with starting the Civil War. What does that say about the power of story? Consider the parables Jesus used with his disciples. Why is story valuable?

9. Frankie initially resists getting to know Sam. Why is she so hesitant? When he tries to give her a Christmas gift, why does she run away? What is she afraid of? What changes her mind about him?

10. While he is recovering, what does Sam ask Frankie to do that she is adamant she will not do? Why is he so insistent she help? What does Luke 6:27 say? How does Frankie respond to that biblical instruction initially? Put yourself in her shoes. How would you feel? Have you ever had an opportunity to serve your enemies in a tangible way?

11. Jael describes an incident on a streetcar. Why do you think the conductor denies a passenger's ticket book? Why doesn't the would-be passenger accept the help

of another? How do you react when you see similar instances of injustice happening today or when they happen to you? Are there times when it's more appropriate to stand up and fight or to sit back?

12. As Frankie considers Sam's request to help in the prison hospital, what counsel does Illa give her? What transformation does Frankie need to undergo to overcome her fear and hatred?

13. Why does Rena worry about a connection between her family and Frankie's? What does she fear? What does she learn about forgiveness? When life doesn't make sense, how do you trust in God's promise that in all things, he is working for our good?

14. What does Frankie say about hatred? Do her thoughts line up with what you believe hatred can do to a person? Does she ever receive an apology from the people who wronged her? What does Frankie need to do to get rid of the hidden hate she is holding on to?

15. At different points when both Rena and Frankie are confronted with difficult revelations, their initial response is to run. In what other ways do people react in the heat of the moment? How do you typically handle unpleasant news?

16. Rena finds inspiration in the charge Harriet Beecher Stowe gives: "The time is come when even a woman

or a child who can speak a word for freedom and humanity is bound to speak. . . . I hope every woman who can write will not be silent." Rena knows her articles for the FWP are "a small pebble on the path to the peaceful existence among people of different races and socioeconomic status." What pebble can you contribute?

TYNDALE HOUSE PUBLISHERS IS CRAZY4FICTION!

Fiction that entertains and inspires

Get to know us! Become a member of the Crazy4Fiction community. Whether you read our blog, like us on Facebook, follow us on Twitter, or receive our e-newsletter, you're sure to get the latest news on the best in Christian fiction. You might even win something along the way!

JOIN IN THE FUN TODAY.

 crazy4fiction.com

 Crazy4Fiction

 @Crazy4Fiction